AN EMMA WINBERRY MYSTERY

THE ELUSIVE RELATION

HELEN MACIE OSTERMAN

WHEELER PUBLISHING
A part of Gale, Cengage Learning

GALE
CENGAGE Learning·

Detroit • New York • San Francisco • New Haven, Conn • Waterville, Maine • London

GALE
CENGAGE Learning·

LIBRARY OF CONGRESS CATALOGING-IN-PUBLICATION DATA

Osterman, Helen Macie.
    The elusive relation : an Emma Winberry mystery / by Helen Macie Osterman.
        p. cm. — (Wheeler Publishing large print cozy mystery)
      ISBN-13: 978-1-4104-4314-4 (softcover)
      ISBN-10: 1-4104-4314-0 (softcover)
      1. Older women—Fiction. 2. Americans—England—Fiction.
    3. Kidnapping—Fiction. 4. Large type books. I. Title.
    PS3565.S8235E58 2011b
    813'.54—dc22   2011033297

Published in 2011 by arrangement with Tekno Books and Ed Gorman.

Printed in the United States of America
1 2 3 4 5   15 14 13 12 11

FD343

To the historic village of Roydon
and all the folks who live there.

ACKNOWLEDGMENTS

I would like to thank Five Star Publishing for again giving me the opportunity to bring back Emma Winberry in her third adventure. Also to my editor, Brittiany Koren, for her astute observations. Thanks to my writer's group, the Southland Scribes, for their valuable critique.

I want to thank Melanie and Jeremy Hackwell, of London, England, for reading the manuscript and assisting with the British idiom.

Special thanks to Karen and Simon Paxton of Roydon for allowing me to share their home and its history as background for this story.

My appreciation to the Essex County Police Department for answering my many questions; to Danny Bruin of the Essex Fire Department for his invaluable information; and to Kevin Hemlold, Chicago firefighter.

My gratitude to Zoe Harvey-Ellis, Investigator, for her information on Essex police procedures.

And many thanks to Lynn Schoorl and John Morton, as my first readers, for their valuable input.

CHAPTER 1

Emma Winberry thrashed and turned, her sleep disturbed by bizarre dreams. She moaned as she woke with a start. Was someone calling? She sat up and shook her head. No one, just a dream.

Her skin felt cold and clammy. Oh dear, I'm not well at all. A wave of nausea gripped her as she swung her thin legs over the side of the bed and sat for a moment. Light-headedness seized her. She gripped the mattress. When it passed, she cautiously made her way to the bathroom, switched on the light and studied her reflection in the mirror. Her thin face appeared pale, heavy eyes surrounded by dark circles.

Suddenly dots danced before her eyes. She clutched the sink, swaying from side to side.

"What's the matter with me?" she muttered, overcome with weakness. She sat down on the toilet hoping it would pass, then everything went black.

The next thing Emma knew she was hanging over the bathtub, half in and half out. She couldn't muster the strength to pull herself up.

"Nate, Nate. Help . . ." she called. No response. She took a deep breath and called louder. "Nate!"

"Emma, what's the matter?" He stumbled into the bathroom, rubbing the sleep from his eyes. "What's wrong?"

"Help," she whispered as she felt his arms pulling her out of the tub and sitting her down on the floor. "I . . . I guess I passed out — I'm so weak — feel sick to my stomach."

"All right, let me wipe your face," Nate's voice was filled with concern.

Emma heard running water then felt a cool cloth across her face.

"You're burning up," he said, feeling her head and her cheeks. "Let me get you back to bed."

He pulled her slight frame to a standing position as she grabbed the sink for balance.

"Do you think you can walk?" he asked, a worried tone to his voice.

"I, I think so." Leaning heavily on him, Emma managed to get back to the bed and flopped down.

"Maybe I'd better get you to the hospital,"

he said, fussing with the covers and feeling her face and forehead.

"No, no," she protested. "It's probably that virus that's going around. Just let me sleep . . . so tired."

He lay down beside her and cradled her in his arms until she fell into a disturbed sleep.

A woman is walking through a mist. She's calling, "Dad, Dad, where are you? I need you."

"Who are you?" Emma calls to her. "Where are you?" She sees a woman dressed in a black coat and hat but the fog obscures her face. The vague outline of a large house looms in the distance.

"Dad, Dad, I need you . . ." The voice trails off.

"Who are you?" Emma calls again. But there is no answer. The woman walks into the mist and is gone.

When Emma woke, her nightgown was soaked with perspiration. She breathed a sigh as she remembered passing out the night before.

"Oh Guardian Angel, what a mess I am and what a peculiar dream. Was it the fever, or something else?"

"Are you talking to yourself?" Nate asked, walking out of the bathroom. He rubbed his sparse hair vigorously with a bath towel, another wrapped around his no longer trim waist.

"No, I was talking to my Guardian Angel." This was something she had done all her life.

He shook his head and raised his eyebrows. "How do you feel this morning, my Sparrow?"

"Yucky. I'm sweaty and smelly and badly in need of a shower."

He ran his hands over her face and neck, then nodded. "You feel cool now. The fever must have broken. Last night you were burning up. Had me worried."

Emma looked up into his concerned face, a face she dearly loved. "You are sweet to fret about me so." She ran her hand over her unruly hair.

He smiled. "You must admit, in the two years we've lived together you've done some unusual things, but this is the first time I've found you hanging over the bathtub."

Emma started to laugh. "I must have looked pretty strange with my backside sticking up in the air."

She sat up carefully on the side of the bed. Nate grasped her trim waist and helped her to a standing position. "I'm all right this morning, I think." She stumbled, then grabbed his arm.

"No, you're not. I'll wash you and change the linens, then you will spend the rest of the day in bed, my dear. After all, you're not a young woman anymore. Have to take better care of yourself."

"Are you insinuating that I'm old?"

"No, but the years are passing, for both of us." He gave her a hug as she nestled in his arms. "You do smell a little rank," he said, leading her into the bathroom.

Emma relished being loved and pampered after twelve years of widowhood. She had met Nate Sandler at the Midwest Opera Company where they were both supernumeraries. When he bought this condo on Chicago's Lake Shore Drive, Emma gave up her old house in the suburbs and moved in with him. She had never regretted that decision. Their grown children approved of the arrangement. Every morning, when Emma looked out over magnificent Lake Michigan, she pinched herself to make sure it wasn't all a dream.

After she was resettled in a freshly made bed with a tray of tea and toast on her lap, Emma thought about the previous night.

13

"I had the strangest dream."

"So what's new about that? You're always having bizarre dreams."

"But this one was different. I actually heard a woman in the distance calling for her father, saying she needed help. One minute she was shrouded in mist, then she was gone." Emma felt a familiar chill as she recalled the dream. Someone was in trouble, she knew it. This "sixth sense" she was born with had given her premonitions all of her life.

"It was probably the fever," he said. "Just forget it."

"You're right," Emma said, sipping her tea.

But she wouldn't forget it. It meant something. Her dreams always did.

CHAPTER 2

Emma tried to concentrate on the approaching visit with her family to celebrate the birthdays of two of the grandchildren, but she couldn't clear the dreams from her mind. She had a similar one two nights in a row, always a woman searching for her father. But Emma was never able to identify her. Each dream was more detailed than the last. She actually saw a vine of some sort growing on the sides of the house, which became more distinct each time. An aura of mystery surrounded the house as well as the woman.

Who was she? Did she have something to do with Emma? The thought disturbed her. She didn't like things unexplained.

She switched on the radio, went out onto the roof garden of their sixth-floor condo, took a deep breath of the warm spring air, and stared out at the lake. This is a great place to live, Emma thought again and again. I'm so lucky that Nate came into my life. He gave it new meaning. She smiled, turned to the huge pots lining the deck and began planning. Trays of seedlings and young plants sat in the large atrium facing the roof, ready for transplanting when the weather permitted. Spring was late this year and Emma was restless. Perhaps she would transplant the hardy herbs, after all it was late March.

"Emma," Nate called, walking toward her. "Gladys is on the phone." He handed her the instrument and smiled.

"Thank you," she said, wrinkling up her nose, then turned her attention to the phone, anticipating a long talk with her lifelong friend. "Hi Gladys, how are things on the East Coast?" She settled in a comfy deck chair and put her feet up.

"It's been raining here," Gladys said, "for days. How's your weather?"

"Lovely," Emma answered. "Take heart, it's coming your way."

"I hope so. I'm tired of cloudy skies. So, what's new in your life?"

They talked about their children and grandchildren, then Emma frowned. Should she tell Gladys about her illness and her dreams? Why not? She shared just about everything with her friend. "I passed out in the bathroom the other night."

"What? You're never sick. Whatever happened?" Her voice became serious and concerned.

"I think I had a virus, but I'm okay now. Still kind of weak, though."

"Did you go to the doctor?"

"No, the symptoms were gone the next day, so I just stayed in bed. Nate fussed like a mother hen."

"He *is* sweet. You didn't hit your head, did you?"

Emma smiled. "Not to my knowledge, but ever since that night I've been having strange dreams."

"So what's new about that? You're always dreaming about someone in trouble. Who is it now, the Pope?"

Emma screwed up her face. "You're going to think I'm crazy." She ignored her friend's throaty laugh and went on to describe the dreams.

After a pause from the other end, Gladys said, "So, you've dreamed of some strange woman looking for her father and you don't know what she looks like. Right?"

"Right, and it's driving me nuts. I consulted my dream dictionary but nothing in it pertained to this particular situation."

"You always told me that dreams

shouldn't be taken literally," Gladys said in a matter-of-fact tone. "So maybe it means something else."

Emma sighed. "I discussed it with my Guardian Angel, but she was no help either."

"My advice to you, my friend, is to get busy with something and take your mind off the unknown. It has gotten you into trouble in the past, you know."

"I suppose," Emma said with a sigh. "I'll try and take that advice." But, deep down, she knew better.

"Get plenty of rest and keep me posted," Gladys said.

As Emma broke the connection she stared out to the south at the huge Ferris wheel on Navy Pier, mesmerized by its slow, continuous motion. The comforting sounds of a Chopin etude issued from the living room.

Put the dreams away, her inner voice told her. *There will be time for them.*

A few days later Nate came in with the mail, a scowl on his face. "Emma, here's a letter addressed to Frank, your late husband."

Startled, Emma felt a sudden weakness, almost dropping the watering can she carried. She placed it on the atrium floor and turned to Nate. "Let me see that." Her hands trembled as she took the letter. "This went to the business firm where he worked and was forwarded to our old house in Brookfield," she mumbled aloud. The envelope was stained as if it had been handled by many hands. No return address appeared in the left-hand corner.

Nate looked over her shoulder. "The stamp is from the U.K.," he said. "How did it get here?"

"Well," Emma said, "the period for forwarding is long passed but the postmaster in Brookfield knew us well. It looks as though he wrote the new address and sent it on. See?" Emma stared at it for a long while.

"Are you going to open it?" Nate asked.

She rubbed her hand across her forehead, recalling her dreams. "I can't. You open it."

He took the letter out of her shaking hand then led her to the sofa. "You'd better sit down, you look pale. You're not well yet."

He went into the study and returned with the letter opener, slit the envelope carefully so as not to damage the contents, then pulled out one thin sheet of paper.

"What does it say?" Emma asked, her brow furrowed, her hands still trembling.

Nate scanned the sheet. "It's from a Lindsey Bellingham, dated two months ago.

Do you know anyone by that name?"

Emma shook her head.

Nate blew out a breath and began to read.

Dear Mr. Winberry,

You probably don't even remember me, but I am your niece. My father was Andrew Winberry. He left when I was very young so I don't really remember him. It wasn't a proper marriage between him and my mother.

Mum told me that she met you once when you were on a business trip to London and you seemed like a very nice man. I was just a slip of a girl and Dad was still with us. Mum said you and Dad hadn't communicated in a long time. Before you left you told Mum that if she ever needed help, to contact you. Dad left shortly after that and we never heard from him again.

Mum told me all this six months ago when she was dying and she gave me your business card. I hesitated to contact you until now. I live with my cousin, Isabel, who has a severe physical condition that keeps her confined to the house. I fear for her safety as well as my own. Someone is threatening me and I have no one to turn to. The authorities investigated but found nothing tangible. Do you know where my father is? I need him now, desperately.

Sincerely,
Lindsey Bellingham

"There's an address here, someplace called Roydon."

Emma and Nate exchanged glances. "Did your husband have a younger brother?" he asked.

She frowned as she vaguely remembered. "I seem to recall Frank mentioning a younger brother who went abroad and was never heard from again. No one in the family talked about him, so I guess I forgot he ever existed."

"Do you think it's true?" he asked.

Emma shrugged. "I don't know. Perhaps I should call Frank's cousin, Alphonse. He might know something about all this."

"Well," Nate said. "Maybe you shouldn't take it too seriously. It could be a scam, someone looking for money."

Emma didn't answer as she felt the familiar goose bumps crawl up her arms. Was this the woman in her dreams?

CHAPTER 3

The following morning Emma was still ruminating about calling Alphonse. Was she being foolish? She tried to remember if Frank ever went to London on one of his business trips. She was sure he went to Brussels and Switzerland, but she had not been well during her first pregnancy; the entire nine months were a blur.

"What are you puzzling about?" Nate asked as they sat at the breakfast table. "You're making faces."

She shrugged. "Nothing in particular. Just wondering what to buy for the grandkids."

"Why don't I believe you?"

"All right," she pursed her lips and stared at him. "I'm trying to remember if Frank ever went to London. He did travel a lot, but I don't seem to recall where."

"It was a long time ago. Would someone else remember?" he asked.

"Maria might know. She came over to take

care of me while Frank was gone." Maria — her neighbor and dear friend for so many years. "I think I'll call her." Emma took the address book from the end table drawer and walked into the study.

She sat for a moment thinking of her friend, Maria Russo. They had lived next door to one another in that Brookfield neighborhood, watching their children grow up, supporting each other through widow-hood, always there for one another. Now Maria lived with her daughter, Carmela, on Chicago's north side. That loving family had even taken in the troubled teenager who lived in the condo next door when Emma and Nate moved in. She took a deep breath, punched in the number and waited.

"Hallo." A voice answered on the first ring.

"Maria, it's Emma."

"Ah, I was thinking about you. We no see each other for too long. How are you and Nate and all the little ones?"

"We're all fine," Emma said. "And little Robin, the youngest grandchild, is a year old already."

"*Mama Mia,* we getting old, Emma."

"Not old, my friend, just seasoned, like fine wine."

"Eh, I don't know what that means, but it sounds good." She laughed.

They talked about family and friends for a while, then Emma got around to the real reason for the call. "Do you remember when I was pregnant with Stephen? How sick I was?"

"*Madonna Mia,* I was sure somebody put the *malocchio* on you. I bring you chicken soup and still you throw up. You was skinny like a stick."

Emma could visualize the plump motherly woman repeatedly making the sign of the cross over her and worrying about the evil eye, the so called *malocchio.* "Do you remember if Frank went on a business trip at that time? My mind is kind of foggy."

"Hmm." Maria hesitated for a moment. "I think I remember he called me and said he had to go away a couple of days. I was mad at him, leaving you. He ask me to take care of you."

Emma's mind began to retrieve the old memory: Frank telling her his co-worker couldn't make the trip for some reason and Frank would have to go in his place. He had promised her that would be the last time and had kept his word. Yes, she did remember. But where did he go?

"Maria, do you remember where he went?" Emma bit down on her lip and frowned. The destination, along with the co-worker's name, remained out of reach.

"Eh, I don't know. Someplace far away. Why you asking now?"

She heard the question in her friend's voice. What to tell her? "I got a letter from somebody in England who knew Frank, that's all. I don't know if he went to England."

"I think there's something else, something you not telling me. Your voice sounds funny," Maria said. "Are you okay?"

"I'm fine, really. It's nothing important. When can we go out to lunch together?" I have to change the subject, she thought. Can't put anything over on that crafty Italian.

After Emma finished the call, she knew little more than she had before. I must call Alphonse, soon. He may be able to give me some answers. But did she really want to know? Would it be wiser to simply ignore the letter? But she couldn't do that. And she knew it.

CHAPTER 4

"And where are we to meet for this gala celebration?" Nate asked as they discussed the birthday party.

Emma didn't seem to hear him, her thoughts were a jumble of possibilities.

"A meteor is going to impact the earth in a half hour," he said casually.

"That's nice, dear." She turned to him. "What did you just say?"

"You haven't been paying one bit of attention to me. I asked if the party is to be at Sylvia and James's house in Wicker Park? They have the most room for your brood."

"Yes, it makes sense, with five grandchildren whose birthdays are close together, to combine some of these into one big party." She tried to sound enthusiastic, but she dreaded seeing everyone. Her daughter, Sylvia, was the most perceptive; she would know something was wrong. Emma could always fool her sons, Stephen and Martin, but not Sylvia. And what about this Lindsey Bellingham? Did her children actually have a first cousin in the U.K.? She would be a few years older than Stephen, putting her in her mid-forties. As fantastic as it sounded, could it be true? And did she have a responsibility to this woman?

"Are you sure you're all right?" Nate asked as he pulled the car up to a parking spot. The old tree-lined street was coming to life, young leaves sprouting out everywhere.

Emma heaved a sigh and turned to him. "Yes. I'm going to put everything out of my mind and have a wonderful day."

"Good." He squeezed her hand as he helped her out of the car and loaded his arms with gifts.

And Emma did just that. Her grandchildren kept her busy with questions, new toys, tricks, all the things important to the young.

But Emma noticed Robin, only thirteen months old, staring at her with eyes much too wise for one so young. She was certain she had passed on her "sixth sense" to this little one. She had felt the connection as soon as the child was born. It had gone from Emma's grandmother Lizzie, to Emma, and now to Robin. Each had the strange fish-shaped birthmark on the inner right thigh and each had been born on the thirteenth of the month.

Emma sighed. "I'm sorry, baby," she whispered, hugging the child. Robin giggled and kissed her as if she were saying "It's all right." Then she tottered on unsteady legs toward her cousins.

As they drove home after a pleasant afternoon, Emma sat quietly, from time to time letting out a small sigh.

"You put on a good act," Nate said, "but you didn't fool Sylvia. She asked what was bothering you. Said you looked preoccupied." He glanced at her momentarily.

"I never could put anything over on that one. What did you say?"

Nate shrugged. "I just told her you had a virus last week and hadn't gotten your strength back yet."

"Did she buy that?"

"I don't think so. She thinks you're worried about something, so don't be surprised if you get a call from her. You know how she is."

Emma let out a half laugh. "It's funny, as we get older there seems to be a role reversal. My daughter has taken on the mothering role."

"You must admit that in the past few years you have given all of us plenty of occasions to worry about you," Nate said as he pulled into their parking garage. "You don't seem to be able to let other people sort out their own problems."

"I suppose. But this time, I've decided to take your advice and forget all about this elusive Lindsey Bellingham." *Guardian Angel, please help me to do just that.*

CHAPTER 5

For the next few days Emma kept busy helping to plan a fundraiser for the Midwest Opera where she and Nate were supernumeraries. It was challenging and kept her mind occupied. But, at night, the dreams persisted. She couldn't dispel the nagging fear that the mysterious woman might be Frank's niece. She stared at a picture of her three children. Suddenly a hazy figure appeared behind them. She squeezed her eyes shut and, when she opened them, the figure was gone. Her imagination? Or was it a sign that she must pursue this mystery?

Finally, she decided to bite the bullet. She searched through her drawers for her old address book. After she recopied a new one she always kept the old one for a number of years. This time she was glad she had. She looked up Alphonse Winberry, a distant cousin of Frank's. She hadn't seen him since Frank died, hoped he still lived at that address.

Since Nate had gone out to the hardware store, this was as good a time as any. She reached for the phone, then pulled her hand back. What would she say? She had received a strange letter from the U.K.? The man might think she was mad, but everyone else did, so what difference did it make.

Emma grabbed the phone and punched in the numbers. It rang five, six, seven times. She was just about to disconnect when a shaky voice said, "Hello?"

"Is this Alphonse?" she asked.

"At your service, ma'am."

He always did have a quirky sense of humor. "This is Emma, Frank's wife." I hope he remembers me, she thought.

"Little Emma — my dear, I haven't talked to you in years. I do hope you've put on some weight." A coarse laugh from his end of the line.

For a while Emma told him of the changes in her life: her role as a supernumerary, her meeting Nate, and the arrival of the grand-children.

"That's fantastic," he said. "My life is rather dull compared with yours."

How do I approach this? Emma thought. She decided the best way was to be honest. "Alphonse, do you remember Frank's

31

brother, Andrew?"

"Huh, that one. He was the black sheep of the family, never amounted to anything. Started stealing and fooling around with the girls when he was in high school. Ran off and no one ever heard from him again."

He hesitated for so long that Emma thought he had disconnected. But, after a time, she heard his voice again.

"Now that I think about it, Frank did mention hearing from him once. As usual, he asked for money. I think he was somewhere abroad. Why do you ask?"

Tell him everything, her inner voice said.

"I received a letter from a woman in the U.K." She picked up the letter and read it to him.

"That's very strange. I find it hard to believe. I can't imagine Andrew ever assuming responsibility for a child. It could be some sort of scam, you know."

"Yes, I considered that. I know Frank went to Zurich when we were newly married, but I don't recall any trips to London or anywhere else in England." The more Emma thought about it, the more she, too, believed this might be a scam.

"Thank you, Alphonse. I'll probably just forget all about it."

"I think that's wise, Emma. Let me know

if anything of any interest results from all of this. And, we must get together some time. It's been too long."

"Yes, definitely." She gave him her phone number and ended the call, then put the phone back on the charger. She walked into the atrium, her favorite room to contemplate. *Frank would have told me if he had a niece anywhere in England,* she thought, plopping down in her favorite chair.

She looked out over the lake at a few sailboats gliding by, a definite sign of spring.

Perhaps he didn't tell you for a reason, her inner voice said.

Nonsense, we kept no secrets from each other, Emma frowned.

Oh no? What about that fling with Sam?

I was young and inexperienced. There was no reason to tell him about that. She was annoyed with her Guardian Angel for reminding her of a silly romance that happened long before she met Frank. No, she hadn't told him about it.

Had he kept some secrets from her? After all, it wasn't wise to dredge up the past. So, it was feasible that he didn't want to talk about a brother who had brought shame on the family name. Frank's parents had been very traditional. Perhaps the entire family had disowned Andrew Winberry.

But, if this Lindsey Bellingham was really Frank's niece and in need of help, wasn't she obliged to, at least, investigate the matter? I'll call Gladys and run it by her.

With a deep sigh Emma made herself a cup of tea, picked up the phone, returned to her chair, and punched in the numbers. She didn't expect Nate back for at least another hour, so she felt safe from his admonishing comments.

"Hi Emma, what's up?" came Gladys's cheery greeting. "I hope you're fully recovered and free of those dreams."

"Yes, thank you, I'm feeling fine, but I need to run something by you."

"I'm all ears. Knowing you, it's probably something outrageous."

Emma read the letter and waited for a response.

"Did you know Frank had a renegade brother?" Gladys asked.

"I did, but nothing more." She recounted her conversation with Alphonse. "What do you think?"

"Hmmm. You're the only one I know who gets into such interesting situations. I think you should write back and see what she wants. If she asks for money, write her off."

"Those were my thoughts exactly."

"What does Nate say?"

"You know pragmatic Nate. He thinks she's a scam artist and I should shred the letter."

"But you can't."

"No, of course not."

They spent the next few minutes talking about family. When Emma finally said goodbye, she had made up her mind. She went into the study, took out pen and paper, and began to write a letter.

Dear Ms. Bellingham,

I am the wife of the late Frank Winberry. He died twelve years ago. I do not know the whereabouts of his brother, Andrew. In fact, I know nothing at all about him.

This is rather an awkward situation. I don't know what your problem is nor what I could do to help you from this distance. Please let me know what type of assistance you expect. If it's financial, I am in no position to do anything for you.

Sincerely,

Emma Winberry

She read it twice then realized it sounded a bit harsh. She tore it up and started again, only this time she ended on a more compassionate note. She addressed the envelope, absently omitting the return. But when she went to the post office, the clerk suggested that, since it was going overseas, it should have a return address. Reluctantly Emma scribbled it in the corner. How could the woman answer if there was no return address? Perhaps her subconscious mind had done it on purpose.

CHAPTER 6

Emma kept herself very busy for the next few weeks: cleaning out closets, packing up clothes she no longer wore, baking and freezing three different kinds of muffins.

"What is this frenzy all about?" Nate asked, walking into the kitchen as Emma removed three loaves of bread from the oven.

"I'm just stocking up, that's all."

"Is there a wheat blight I haven't heard about?"

She met the smirk on his face with a frown. "When a woman is in the mood to bake, she must bake. That's one of the laws of womankind." She fussed with the hot pans, a little too vehemently.

"Hmm, I'd like to know where that's written. Never heard it before." He stood immobile, his hands behind his back.

"Why are you standing there?" Emma asked. "And what do you have behind your back?"

As he pulled his hands forward, Emma saw the envelope he held. "I presume this may have something to do with your mood."

She reached for the letter, but he held it tightly. "You wrote to that woman, didn't you? I thought you were going to drop the whole thing." A deep furrow formed between his eyes.

"Oh, dear." Emma sat in a chair, her chin dropping to her chest.

Tell him, her inner voice said.

"All right." She looked up into his eyes and told him about her call to Alphonse Winberry. Then she confessed writing to the woman. "I never expected her to answer."

Nate gave a grunt and placed the letter on the table. "Well, it appears she did."

Emma sat for a long time, looking at the envelope, willing it to disappear.

"Are you going to open it?" Nate asked. "Or do you want me to put it in the shredder?"

"I have to open it. If she is Frank's niece, I need to hear her out. After all, we may be related."

"Not by blood, my dear, only by marriage," he said.

"I still think I owe her some consideration," she said, slowly reaching her hand toward the envelope. She looked closely at it. The handwriting appeared jerky, not smooth and fine as on the first one.

This was written under stress, her inner voice said.

Emma looked at the stamp for a moment then turned the missive over and slid her finger under the flap. It came up easily, the glue barely holding. Emma took a deep breath, unfolded the sheet, and began to read.

Dear Mrs. Winberry,

Thank you so much for answering my letter. I apologize for causing you distress, but I desperately need help — from someone.

If my uncle is deceased, who can help me find my father? I have no other relatives and my situation is becoming more dire every day. I can't explain in a letter. If you can find it in your heart to call me, perhaps I can tell you more.

Sincerely,
Lindsey Bellingham

The phone number was written under the signature.

Emma read the letter a second time then

slid it across the table to Nate. She watched the expression on his face change from surprise to anger, the furrow between his eyes deepening.

He looked at her. "This is certainly melo-dramatic. Either the woman is an actress or she's certifiable. What in the world does she expect you to do for her? I'll bet she'll give you a sob story then ask for money. It's a scam. She's obviously a con artist."

Emma took the letter in her hand again and shook her head. "This woman, whoever she is, is in trouble. I can feel it. The question is, how can I help her from 3,000 miles away?" She looked up at his scowling face.

"If you take my advice, and you never do, you'll shred that letter and forget all about this nutcase." He turned and stomped out of the room.

Oh Guardian Angel, what shall I do?

You've never before ignored a plea for help. Do you want to start now?

Emma sat in her favorite chair in the atrium staring out over Lake Michigan. The movement of the waves was hypnotic, but it failed to quiet her thoughts. They were in a jumble — a woman was in trouble — she might be Frank's niece — could Emma help her?

The ringing of the phone startled her. She

decided not to answer it, didn't feel like talking to anyone.

"Emma," Nate called, "Maria's on the phone." He walked up behind her, planted a kiss on her neck, and handed her the instrument.

Emma gave him a half smile and looked at the phone for a moment before answering. "Hi, Maria, *come stai?*"

"Eh, you no forget your Italian. I'm okay, how are you, my friend?" Maria's full musical voice picked up Emma's spirits immediately.

"I'm fine," she lied. "How's your family?" For the next few minutes they discussed their children.

"Tracie is doing so good in school," Maria said. "When you see her, you gonna be proud."

"I'm delighted to hear that. I'll be over soon, very soon," Emma promised.

Good-hearted Maria had taken in Tracie Adams, the abused, anorexic girl who had lived next door to Emma and Nate the previous year. Under the care of Maria's daughter, Carmela, and her granddaughter, Connie, the girl had grown to be a healthy, self-assured young lady.

There was a lull in the conversation for a moment, then Maria said, "Remember when you call me a couple weeks ago and ask about Frank?"

Emma leaned forward in her chair. "Did you remember something?"

"Well, I was so mad at Frank for leaving you when you so sick that he brought me something when he came home."

"What was it?"

"I was looking in a drawer yesterday for my thimble. I'm always losing it. In a corner I found a pin, like one you put on your coat. Then I remember Frank gave it to me when he got home. I don't know what it's supposed to mean."

Emma wanted to pull the words out of Maria. "What does it look like?"

"A funny little man with a black hat, a red coat, red stockings and black shoes. He's got some kind of big axe in his hand. I ask Connie and she say it's an old battleaxe. You know where he got that?"

Emma squeezed her eyes shut and pursed her lips. Maria had just described a "Beefeater," a guard at the Tower of London.

CHAPTER 7

Emma was grateful that Nate was spending more time at the gym. It gave her time to think.

I'll discuss this new letter with Gladys, she thought as she settled in her favorite chair in the atrium. She knew Nate would be gone for most of the morning so she wouldn't be interrupted.

"Hello, Emma," Gladys answered.

That darn caller ID, Emma thought. No one has any privacy anymore. "Hi Gladys, how are things in the East?"

"Fine. You'll be glad to hear that Cornell and I are keeping off the weight we lost — going to the gym every day and eating a sensible diet."

"That's great! You have to feel better," Emma said without too much enthusiasm.

"We do, but we're getting absolutely boring. No more fabulous dinners and very few parties. One of these days I'm going to have to splurge to get it out of my system. Now what's on your mind? Any new developments?"

Emma hesitated for a moment, then told Gladys about the recent letter she had received. "The woman's in trouble, Gladys, and I feel that I'm morally bound to help her. She could be my children's first cousin."

"You have no proof of that," Gladys said. "But I know you so well and you'll never let it go. I suggest you call her and find out what her problem is. If she asks for money, cross her off. There may be something you can do, but not from here. Are you thinking of going to England?"

Emma hesitated for a moment. "The thought has crossed my mind. Oh, what will Nate say?"

Gladys laughed. "He'll probably fuss and fume for a while but, in the end, he'll go along. He always does, doesn't he?"

"You're right. I must settle this once and for all."

"And," Gladys said, "if you ever decide to write a book . . ."

"I know," Emma interrupted her. "Cornell will publish it in a heartbeat."

Emma kept busy for the next few days waiting for the right time to tell Nate about her decision. As she scrubbed out the refrigerator, she felt him staring at her. She turned to see him leaning against the doorjamb, his arms folded across his chest.

"First it was baking, now it's cleaning. Are you going to tell me what's brewing in that mind of yours?"

She sighed, got up from her stooped position, threw the sponges in the sink and slumped into a kitchen chair. "All right. I've made a decision. I'm going to call Lindsey Bellingham."

Nate grunted, then sat next to her. "Can't you leave it alone? Things have been nice and quiet around here with no problems. The opera season has just ended and we have the entire summer free. Is that too dull for you?"

She winced at the sarcasm in his voice then turned to him. "I can't let it go and you know it. This woman is in trouble. I can feel it. At least I have to talk to her. Maybe I can help with just a phone call."

Nate shook his head. "You don't really believe that, do you?"

"No, I suppose not. But if she sounds like a scam artist, I'll tell her never to bother me again." She gave her head a vigorous nod.

"And, exactly how does a scam artist

sound? Most of them are pretty smooth or they wouldn't get to first base."

"Nate," she covered his hand with hers, "please don't argue with me about this. If there is even a remote possibility that she's Frank's niece, I must try to help."

He slid his arm around her and gave her a gentle squeeze. "Go ahead, but don't promise her any money." He thought for a moment. "Just to be on the safe side, you'd better block the caller ID."

Emma gave him a blank look. "How do I do that?"

"Punch in *67, then the number. That blocks the identity of the caller."

She sighed. "You're so technologically savvy. Stay around, will you?" She gave him a smirk.

"You just try and get rid of me. And, be careful what you say to this woman."

"I will."

Although his tone was stern, Emma knew that he would be sympathetic if she uncovered a real problem.

Emma waited until Nate went to the gym for his morning routine, then decided to make the call. For a moment she looked at the phone as if it were a living thing. She reached out her hand, then drew it back.

Oh Guardian Angel, what am I going to say to this woman?

You simply ask her what she wants, the inner voice said.

Just like that?

Yes, just like that.

With a modicum of determination, Emma's hand hovered over the phone; she grasped it, lifted it off the charger, then looked at the letter. Carefully she punched in the country code followed by the ten digits. There was a pause, then two rings, a pause and another two rings. This pattern continued until she thought there might not be anyone there. She was about to disconnect when a somewhat breathless voice said, "Hello."

Emma hesitated a little too long.

"Hello?" the voice said again, rising an octave.

"I'm looking for Lindsey Bellingham, Emma Winberry calling."

"Oh, thank God," the woman said, her voice flooded with relief. "I was afraid you wouldn't call, would think I was unhinged."

Emma didn't want to say that was exactly what she did think. She decided to be direct and business-like. "What exactly do you want from me?"

"I'm not sure, but I'm in dire need of your

help," the woman pleaded.

Emma noted the tension in her voice. *She is* in trouble, I can feel it. *This is no scam.* But she decided to push her a little. "I really have no way of knowing if you are Andrew Winberry's daughter, but if you're in need of money, I can't help you."

Easy, her inner voice said. *Just let her talk.*

"Please," the woman said, "I'm not looking for currency. That's not the problem. I'm — afraid."

That response surprised Emma. "Afraid of what?"

"I'm being threatened," she whispered.

"Well, why don't you go to the police?" Emma asked. It seemed like the logical thing to do.

"Oh, I have," the woman replied. "You see, I have nothing concrete to show them, no letters, no phone calls. But someone is following me. There were a few attempts to enter my home uninvited, but the constable who came out found nothing." The woman uttered a deep sigh. "After I called them a few too many times, they dismissed me as you Americans would call, 'a nut case.' " She finished with a bitter laugh.

Emma didn't know what to say. She could feel real fear from the woman, but what could she do? Was she being paranoid?

"I don't dismiss your concern. I can tell by your voice that you're frightened and upset, but there is nothing I can do from 3,000 miles away. Even if I were there, I'm no detective. I'm at a loss for any way to help you."

"I suppose this is just a feather in the wind, but I'm desperate. I thought that if I could find my father, he might . . . oh, I don't know . . . it's hopeless!"

Emma heard a sniffle over the wire. She sighed. What to say? "I'm willing to listen if you wish to tell my anything more, but I don't know what to advise you."

"It's a rather complex situation — difficult to discuss over the phone. Let me think a bit and thank you for your concern."

Emma heard the disconnect from the other end. She sat for a moment rethinking the conversation. There was a lot left unsaid. Well, she reasoned, I called, determined that I can't help the woman and now I can put the whole affair out of my mind.

But you can't, the inner voice said.

Emma became annoyed with her celestial guardian. *And just what am I supposed to do?*

She's hiding something. Find out the real reason.

Emma let out a "Humph!" *I'll sleep on it, but that's all.*

CHAPTER 8

The following week Emma received another letter from the U.K. Nate was out at the time so she settled in her favorite chair in the atrium and looked out over the lake. A few waves marred the deep blue reflecting a cloudless sky. I should be walking along the lakeshore, she thought, not worrying about some strange woman across the ocean. With a deep sigh, she pulled the flap on the envelope. The letter consisted of two pages of tight script, some words darker than others as if the writer had used more pressure. I wonder what a writing analyst would say about this, she thought.

She closed her eyes for a moment and said a prayer to her Guardian Angel. *Please keep me on track.* Then she began to read.

Dear Mrs. Winberry,
Thank you for calling. I have decided to be completely honest and tell you the

whole story. I live with my cousin Isabel in a large old house in Roydon, a village just outside of London. My cousin is a sweet girl but she has a severe disability that keeps her housebound. Our only visitors are Professor Wilkins, an old family friend, and Doctor Lunetti, Isabel's music teacher. She has a beautiful soprano voice and her teacher is convinced she can make recordings even though she will never be able to appear in public.

As I told you, Mum said she had met Uncle Frank and he offered to help, so, in desperation, I wrote to him at his place of business. I know it was a daft thing to do, but then you answered.

As long as I'm telling you this, let me present my dilemma. Then, if you can't think of any way you can help me, please try to forget this intrusion into your life.

According to an old legend there is supposed to be a treasure hidden somewhere in this house. My Mum never put any credence to this story, but Grandfather was convinced it was true. He and I looked everywhere through the years but never found anything.

For the past few months I've had the feeling that someone is following me, and recently I have been receiving threatening *phone calls. The caller wants a large sum of money. The threats are not toward me but aimed at Isabel. Any disruption into her life would be devastating.*

I know I am being followed but I never see anyone, only shadows. I've told all this to Uncle Avery, that's what we call Professor Wilkins, but he thinks I'm imagining it. The authorities do not believe me either.

Last week I caught a glimpse of a man's face peeking in one of the windows. He had a port wine birthmark running down the right side of his face. When I ran to look out, he was gone. We have a large property with many bushes and trees behind the house, and vines climbing up the walls, all excellent hiding places. I called the police but they found nothing suspicious. In desperation I thought if I could find my father, he might be able to help me.

As I write this, it sounds like a case in which Conan Doyle would ask Sherlock Holmes for assistance.

I'm sorry to bother you with my troubles, but I do feel a bit better just writing them down. Please let me know if there's any way you can help.

Sincerely,
Lindsey Bellingham

Emma shook her head as if she had just awakened from a dream. Was this woman making up this bizarre tale or could it be true? And should she be writing all this in a letter? Emma felt an overwhelming fear for Lindsey and her disabled cousin.

Well, I'm no Sherlock Holmes. He could leave his Baker Street home and travel to the site of the mystery, unraveling it on the way. She sighed. *Okay, Guardian Angel, I guess that gets me off the hook.*

Does it? her inner voice asked.

Emma frowned. *You certainly don't expect me to drop everything and fly off to London.*

You might consider it. Weren't you and Nate planning a holiday?

"Hmm," Emma said.

Emma left the letter on the kitchen table and began preparing dinner. When she heard the door, she clutched the knife tightly in her hand and began chopping vegetables to a staccato rhythm.

Nate walked into the kitchen and gave her a peck on the cheek. "Stir fry?" he asked.

"Uh huh."

She waited for him to say something as she heard the rustle of pages.

"I presume you left this here for me to read."

"If you wish." She tried to sound matter-of-fact, but even she could hear the edge to her voice.

Finally, Emma turned to see Nate staring at her. "What do you think?" she asked.

"Do you really want to know?"

"I wouldn't ask if I didn't."

He gave a sigh, got up from the chair and poured two glasses of Merlot. He handed one to Emma and took a swallow from the other. "Either she's been reading too many Victorian novels or she's a neurotic. Hidden treasure? Someone threatening her? A disabled cousin? You really don't buy all this, do you?"

Emma turned off the burner under the pan and sat down. "When you put it that way, I guess not."

"You still can't be sure that Frank was her uncle. As for all this other nonsense, there's absolutely nothing you can do about it. Okay?"

Emma raised her eyebrows and gave him an innocent look. "We were talking about a holiday."

Nate's eyebrows almost met in a deep frown. "We had no definite destination in mind, if you recall. The exchange rate to the U.K. is not exactly in our favor at the present time."

Emma sighed deeply and shook her head. "All right. Subject closed. Dinner will be ready in ten minutes." She drained her glass of wine, stuffed the letter back in the envelope and put it in the pocket of her slacks.

CHAPTER 9

Emma tried to put all thoughts of Lindsey Bellingham out of her mind, but bizarre dreams kept invading her sleep, figures in a mist, strange moaning sounds, and the house, always the same house half hidden in the background. She knew quite well from past experience that these dreams were not to be taken lightly. Emma believed the woman was truly in trouble, but she was powerless to help.

A few weeks later Nate burst into the condo. "Emma," he shouted, "you'll never guess what happened." He was as excited as a child finding a shiny quarter on the sidewalk.

She smiled. "Did you win the lottery?" She knew that he was not a gambling man and never, to her knowledge, had even bought a ticket.

"I just came from a meeting of the investment group where I used to work, the one whose bulletin I've been writing all those articles for. I'm going to speak at the International Conference — are you ready for this?" His eyes gleamed and he puffed out his chest. "In Paris!"

Emma's eyes widened. "Paris?" She stood still, her mouth agape, unable to say another word.

He nodded and held out an expensive-looking brochure advertising the conference with his name as one of the speakers.

She looked at it, a quizzical expression on her face. "This has already been printed. How did they know you would accept?"

"Well," he said with a smirk on his face. "They did ask me a few months ago if I might be interested and I said yes. Then I just put it on the back burner and forgot about it."

"Fibber," she said. "I'll bet you have the speech already written."

"Hmm, I did make a few notes." He held out a folder with ten pages of neatly printed type.

"Why didn't you tell me?"

"I wanted it to be a surprise."

She threw her arms around his neck and gave him a resounding kiss. "I'm so proud of you."

He hugged her, lifted her slight body in

his arms and took a few dance steps.

"Watch it," she warned. "You know you've been having trouble with your lower back lately."

"Umm." He put her down and rubbed the small of his back with both hands.

"Sit down, and I'll make us a cup of tea while you tell me all about it."

As they sipped English Breakfast tea and munched on oatmeal cookies, Emma studied the brochure. "This is a full week," she said.

"Uh huh. All expenses paid for both of us in a five-star hotel. There'll be plenty of free time to explore the Louvre, the Sorbonne, and whatever else you like. Pack your bags, we're headed for France." The grin hadn't faded from his lips as he took the brochure and fingered the expensive paper.

Emma sat back thinking. Paris was not far from the U.K.

The Chunnel takes you directly to London, her inner voice said.

This may be a sign, Emma thought, that I may be able to contact Lindsey Bellingham.

"What are you thinking about?" Nate asked, a slight frown crossing his face.

"Oh, just wondering what clothes to pack, that's all." She gave him a disarming smile but knew she hadn't fooled him for a minute. Nate knew her too well.

The next week went by in a frenzy of activity: new clothes to purchase, reading material for the plane ride, notifying children and friends. And then there were Emma's beloved plants. Her next door neighbor, Claude, had graciously agreed to care for them as if they were his own. Claude and his partner, Thomas, had become good friends as well as good neighbors, ever since their adventure at the Performing Arts Center the previous spring. Emma trusted them with a key to their condo and the care of her treasures.

A week before their scheduled departure Nate got a phone call from James, Emma's son-in-law. "Hi James, what's up?" he asked, his curiosity piqued.

"I just talked with Bruce Hamilton, the director of the Center, and told him you were going to France. He said there's an amazing concert scheduled at Covent Garden in London just about the time you two will be overseas."

Nate wondered what that had to do with him. "And?"

"He has some contacts and, if you're

interested, may be able to get you two tickets."

"Hmm," Nate said. "I'm sure Emma will want to go."

"And," James continued, "the ride from Paris to London through the Chunnel is shorter than driving through Chicago, especially in rush hour."

"You're right about that," Nate said with a laugh. "Tell Bruce to go ahead and make the contact. I'll surprise Emma."

After Nate disconnected the call he thought about the situation. Knowing Emma as well as he did, she would surely want to contact that Bellingham woman. Well, what harm could it do? She might even have her problem solved by now, if there actually was one. He put the thought out of his mind and went on the Internet to check out hotels in London.

CHAPTER 10

"What are you reading?" Emma asked. Nate's head was bent over a number of computer pages. "Nate?"

"Oh, just some interesting information on the Eurostar. That's how we'll be traveling from Paris to London."

"Really. I thought we had to cross the English Channel." She looked perplexed.

"We do, my dear. The Eurostar is a modern train that travels through the Chunnel, underneath the English Channel. It's the longest undersea tunnel in the world."

Emma cringed. "Did you say undersea tunnel? I thought we would take a ferry boat."

"That's the way they used to travel. Now the train goes under the channel."

"I don't like the idea of being trapped under all that water." She felt claustrophobic already.

"Emma," he said, standing up and putting

his arms around her. "It takes a little over two hours for the entire journey from France to England and only twenty minutes to travel the twenty-three miles under the sea."

She snuggled in his arms. "Under the sea is what bothers me."

"You can ask the doctor for some tranquilizers if that will make you feel better, or we can forget about London altogether."

She knew he was baiting her. She had to get to London and contact Lindsey Bellingham and, when Nate had told her about the concert, she felt certain it was a sign. Gritting her teeth she said with a melodramatic flair, "Millions of people travel on that train and so will I."

Nate grinned. "I knew you'd agree. Now why don't we finish packing."

When the plane landed at Charles DeGaulle airport in Paris, Emma looked around at all their fellow travelers. There was nothing distinctive about the surroundings except the signs were all in French. She heard so many different languages that she felt a little disoriented. After the arduous wait through customs, they retrieved their baggage and looked around at the crowd of people welcoming friends and family.

"Nate, look over there." Emma pointed to a man in a chauffeur's uniform holding a sign — N. SANDLER.

"Well," Nate said. "That's us." He smiled as he waved to the man.

This is traveling in style, Emma thought as they piled into the limo and headed for their hotel. Before long, Emma's excitement was replaced by a feeling of lassitude. After the long journey she wanted nothing more than a hot shower and a nap.

Emma examined the room, similar to those in the States. There was nothing that shouted, *You're in Paris!*

After unpacking and taking a short rest, Emma dressed in a burgundy silk sheath she had bought for the trip. Pearl earrings and necklace set it off perfectly. As she looked at her reflection in the mirror, Nate snaked his arms around her and planted a kiss on her neck, admiring her appearance.

"You look delicious."

"No sampling now," she warned. "Dinner is in a half hour and you don't want to be late, do you?" She gave him a mischievous look and in turn received a pat on the backside.

"And you look mighty handsome, Mr. Sandler, in that new Italian silk suit."

"You're just saying that because it's true."

He fastened a diamond tie tack through a striped tie in muted shades of blue.

After an elegant sit-down dinner, the guests milled around in small groups. Nate talked shop with some of the executives from the investment firm while Emma made small talk with their wives. Her mind began to wander with thoughts of Lindsey Bellingham. She felt a pull toward the woman, knew her problems were not over but most likely escalating.

"Mrs. Winberry, what is your opinion of this situation?" a stout woman with a prune face asked. She seemed irritated that Emma hadn't answered her.

"I'm sorry," Emma said. "I think jet lag is setting in. My mind wandered just a bit." She tried to smile but was met with raised eyebrows and a look of disdain.

"Hmm, I suppose it really doesn't matter," the woman said.

Emma wanted nothing more than to get away from this dull bunch when she caught Nate waving to her. "Excuse me," she said, hurrying over to him.

"I'm ready to go," he said. "How about you?"

"Absolutely."

They plastered artificial smiles on their faces as they made their way out of the crowded room and toward the elevators.

When they reached their room, Emma collapsed on the bed with a sigh of relief. If this was what business travel was like, she wanted no part of it.

For the next few days Nate was busy attending lectures and interactive sessions so Emma decided to take a guided tour of the city. She knew if she set out on her own, she would become hopelessly lost. The bus took her to the Eiffel Tour, past the Arc de Triomphe, through the Latin Quarter and to the Notre Dame Cathedral.

Emma gaped at the architectural wonder with its flying buttresses and magnificent Rose Window. They passed the Louvre but it was so huge that Emma decided it would take another trip just to see that building alone. The tour stopped in Montemarte where Emma and her fellow travelers strolled through the stalls and watched the street artists.

The last evening they spent in Paris, Nate and Emma strolled along the Seine, the Eiffel Tower lit up in the distance. "It's just like in the movies," she said. "So romantic."

"Yep," Nate agreed. "Can you hear the music coming from those tour boats?"

They watched the boats drifting along the

water, people on deck looking at the sights, the muted sounds of their voices, soft romantic music trailing along in the wake. They stood for a long time with their arms around each other, stealing a kiss and feeling like a pair of young lovers. Finally, a chill in the air sent them back to their hotel.

"Are you packed?" Nate asked as Emma held the phone to her ear. She shook her head in frustration.

"I asked if you're packed."

"Oh, yes, I'm ready, but I still get no answer at Lindsey Bellingham's number. I hope she's all right."

"Maybe she moved." Nate shrugged as he locked the suitcase. "Look at it this way, if you can't contact her, you'll have to let it go. At least you tried."

"I suppose," Emma said with a sigh.

You can't give up, her inner voice said.

Sometimes Emma's Guardian Angel made near impossible demands on her and this was one of them.

"Why are you making faces?" Nate asked.

"Because my Guardian Angel expects me to storm the castle and rescue the princess."

He shook his head, blew out a breath and said nothing. "Come on, the train leaves in an hour."

The cab took them to the Gare du Nord station where they would catch the Eurostar that would take them to St. Pancras station in London. Before boarding the train, they passed through British customs.

"Isn't this rather unusual?" Emma asked.

Nate shrugged. "I read that the British and French governments decided to handle customs this way. Those going to France pass through French customs on the British side and vice versa. It seems to work for them."

Once Emma was settled on the modern train, she barely thought about the fact that they would be traveling under thousands of tons of water. The seats were extremely comfortable. There was even a lounge and a buffet car for those traveling long distances.

Just pretend you're on a subway, Emma told herself as she settled back and, before she knew it, saw daylight. The train sped on above ground until it stopped at their destination.

She looked at Nate and smiled. "It's a marvel."

St. Pancras station was huge, newly remodeled to accommodate the thousands of tourists and businessmen and women who used the facility. Large steel girders supported panes of glass composing an arched ceiling flooding the area with light. They took the escalator up to the station proper.

"Look at that bronze statue of lovers in an embrace," Nate said. "It's at least eight feet tall."

"And look at the one of the man holding his hat and briefcase," Emma said reading the engraving surrounding the statue. "He was a poet."

Nate looked around. "Come on, these signs lead to the underground. I guess we go that way to get outside. We should be able to get a taxi."

They lugged their baggage through the crowded station, shops of all kinds lining the periphery.

More crowds assaulted them as they exited the building. Emma was over-whelmed by the cacophony of sound, so many languages clashing with one another. At that moment she wanted nothing more than to be home sitting in her atrium. I must be getting old, she thought, all I want is peace and quiet. Fortunately, Nate was able to hail a taxi before they were engulfed by more tourists.

"Welcome to London, my dear," he said, helping her into the vehicle.

Emma felt a shiver, London, Lindsey Bellingham. Her "sixth sense" told her their adventure was just about to begin.

CHAPTER 11

Nate had booked a hotel in central London easily accessible to any sights they might want to see. As soon as they were settled in the room, Emma pulled Lindsey Bellingham's number from her purse and punched it into the phone. Again she heard the double ring, pause, double ring, pause . . . until she gave up. As she put the phone down, she sat in a chair and sighed. She was overwhelmed by a feeling of helplessness. The woman was in trouble, of that she was certain, but why wasn't she answering the phone?

"You weren't by any chance calling your children, were you?" Nate asked, a sarcastic tone in his voice.

She gave him a look that said, don't be daft, without verbalizing it. She found herself picking up the local idiom already.

"Give it up, Emma," was all he said.

"I can't and you know it. I'll keep trying

as long as we're here, then I'll have no choice."

"There's a lot to see here in Covent Garden," Nate said, picking up a flyer that had been left in the room. "What do you say we walk out to the piazza for lunch? It's only a couple of blocks."

"Okay." Might as well take in the sights, she thought.

"Now be careful," Nate cautioned as they stepped off the curb. "Look to the right. The traffic goes the opposite way here."

"Why do people have to complicate things," she said. "Everyone should drive in the same direction and speak the same language. It would make life much simpler."

"Watch!" He pulled her back as a car came barreling toward them. "Pedestrians don't have the right of way in this country."

Emma saw the signs painted on the street: PEDESTRIANS LOOK RIGHT.

"Humph," she grumbled as they climbed aboard one of London's famous double-decker buses that would take them to Covent Garden.

"How come you're so knowledgeable about the transportation system here?" Emma asked, looking quizzically at Nate.

"I studied it before we came. I don't intend to get lost in this old city of winding streets."

She was glad he had such a great sense of direction. She often got confused going around the block at home.

When they alighted at their destination, they walked into a piazza that reminded them of one they would find in Rome.

"Look, Nate, there's a street singer." Emma smiled at the lovely girl performing to an appreciative audience while another woman came through the crowd asking for donations. Nate dropped a pound coin into the plate to a gracious, "Thank you, sir."

They sat in a café enjoying an al fresco lunch and watched the people walk around. Afterwards they browsed the shops and Emma bought a few trinkets for the grand-children.

For an entire afternoon Emma was able to detach her mind from Lindsey Belling-ham, but, from time to time, she felt the almost imperceptible nagging of her Guard-ian Angel.

That evening they sat in the lounge of the hotel sipping a nightcap, tired but satisfied with their day. Emma gave a stifled yawn. She hadn't adjusted to the time change even after an entire week. She felt homesick, wondered if Claude was taking good care of her plants, if the children were all right and if Susan had recovered from her cold. Maybe she was getting too old for all this gadding about.

As they were about to leave the lounge, a man got off the elevator and began making his way slowly through the lobby.

Emma's eyes widened. "Nate, that man . . ." He walked slowly, his eyes wide and staring, and — he was stark naked!

"Don't look," he said.

"Nonsense, I'm not a child. I've seen naked men before."

At that moment the hotel staff ran up to the man, covered him with towels, and led him back to the elevators.

"I apologize," the concierge said to the startled gaping people in the lobby. "This happens occasionally when he comes here on business — sleepwalking you know."

Nate and Emma turned to each other and dissolved in peals of laughter.

The following evening, dressed in the same finery they had worn at the banquet, Emma and Nate attended the gala concert at the opera house. People occupying the boxes dressed formally: women wore long gowns, men were in evening wear.

"Isn't this exciting?" Emma asked.

They followed the usher into the huge

horseshoe-shaped auditorium, seats and carpeting in bright red.

Emma looked around in awe. "Fantastic! You could put two of the Midwest's auditoriums in here with room to spare. I wonder if there's a royal box?" She looked around at the tiers of boxes surrounding the main floor.

"I'll bet it's up there." Nate pointed. "The one with the coat of arms above it."

Emma grabbed his arm. "Do you think the Queen will be here?"

"I have no idea."

They found their seats and continued to gaze at their fellow patrons.

The audience broke out in rousing applause as the orchestra entered the pit followed by the conductor. Then a hush fell over the auditorium and the concert began. The audience sat mesmerized by the performance of the dramatic soprano, Rosa Finelli. Emma was disappointed that the royal box remained empty, but she was soon lost in the music and Finelli's glorious voice. The singer had disappeared from the operatic stage for a number of years under a cloud of mystery. Now she was back in full voice, singing more splendidly than ever.

After the concert they stopped in the bar of the hotel for a glass of champagne, then headed to their room.

Emma stretched out on the bed. "What an unforgettable evening. We must do something to thank Bruce Hamilton for getting us those tickets."

"I'd say those opera glasses you bought in the gift shop for an astronomical number of pounds are sufficient," Nate said, taking off his dress shoes with a sigh of relief.

"They are nice, aren't they?" She fingered the compact glasses with Royal Opera House printed in gold along the side. The music and Finelli's voice were still ringing in her ears.

"Come back to earth, my dear," Nate said whispering in her ear. "Our plane leaves from Heathrow the day after tomorrow. So decide by morning how you want to spend our last day in London."

Emma frowned. The thought of Lindsey Bellingham broke through her reverie. On a whim she reached for the phone.

"Who are you calling at this hour of the night?" Nate asked.

Emma didn't answer him. She punched in the numbers that, by now, she had memorized. The double ring, the pause, the double ring — then a soft voice answered, "Hello?"

"Lindsey? This is Emma Winberry. I've

been trying to reach you."

A hesitation from the other end of the line. "Oh, Mrs. Winberry, you have no idea how glad I am to hear from you. Something was wrong with the phone. The repairman said it must have been an animal chewing on the line, but I think someone tampered with it." There was a suspicious note in her voice.

"I'm here in London," Emma said.

"You are? Where?"

"In a hotel in the central part of the city. We attended the gala concert tonight at the Royal Opera House and are scheduled to leave the day after tomorrow."

"Oh, is there any way I can see you before you leave? Please."

"Just a minute." Emma turned to her scowling partner. "Nate, can we see this woman tomorrow?"

He heaved a sigh. "I suppose we have to. Otherwise you'll never get her out of your system."

"Yes, Lindsey. Perhaps we can meet somewhere and you can tell me the entire story."

"I'll be in the last row in St. Paul's Cathedral. We can meet there at ten o'clock. Will that be agreeable?"

"Yes," Emma said.

"I'll be wearing a black coat and hat. And

thank you ever so much."

After Emma hung up she sat pondering the situation. She could hear Nate puttering around in the bathroom.

Oh Guardian Angel, now what? I was almost hoping that I wouldn't be able to contact her and could forget the entire matter.

But you know you couldn't do that, the inner voice said.

Emma lay awake for a long time that night wondering what tomorrow would bring. The beautiful evening, the music, the singing, had already receded from her mind.

CHAPTER 12

The following day the taxi stopped at Saint Paul's Cathedral behind a tour bus that disgorged a group of school children.

"Lots of kids come here with their school teachers," the driver explained as Nate paid the fare.

Emma looked at the towering structure. It took her breath away. The sheer size of the stone building with its massive dome stretched the imagination. How had the architects of old been able to construct buildings such as this one without modern technology?

The rain that had started early that morning had stopped and, briefly, the sun shone through the clouds. "I wish we had time to wander around," Emma said as she looked at a fountain with water spouting from four lion heads.

"Be careful," Nate said, taking her arm as they climbed the steps to the massive doors.

"There's so much to see in this city," he said, "that two weeks wouldn't do it justice. We'll have to come back another time when the exchange rate is better." He gave her a smile and a wink.

Emma was glad his mood had improved as they joined a short queue at the entrance.

"Can you believe it?" Nate grumbled, taking out his wallet. "We have to pay to get in here."

"Well, all that scaffolding outside means there are repairs going on. Upkeep must be astronomical."

"But in churches it's usually on a donation basis," he muttered as he handed a twenty-pound note to a woman behind a desk. She smiled, gave him two tickets, two brochures and two pound coins in return. "Come on, we may as well look around. I want to see what I paid all this money for."

"This place is huge," Emma said as they walked around the periphery. "I want to look at the dome."

They continued around the nave until they reached the dome, walked to the center of the marble floor and gazed up. Emma sat on one of the chairs to steady herself. It was dizzying. Colorful mosaics of intricate geometric patterns surrounded the interior of the structure.

"It's magnificent," she whispered.

"Look." Nate pointed to a flight of stairs. "According to this brochure those lead to the whispering gallery. If you stand on one side and I stand on the other, we can hear each other whisper."

Emma frowned. "I'll take your word for it. I don't intend to trudge up an unending flight of stairs to hear you speak. I do that every day."

Nate just gave Emma a look that needed no words.

Her eyes swept the Quire leading to the altar. This is what a Cathedral *should* look like, she thought, not those modern structures they build today without a single painting nor stained glass window.

They wandered down the other side peeking into the side chapels, one dedicated to All Souls, one to St. Dunstan and one to St. Michael and St. George.

A man stood behind one of the pillars. Emma noticed him because he appeared to be looking for someone. "Nate, look at that man. Does he have a mark of some kind on his face?"

"What man?" Nate asked.

As Emma searched again, the man was gone. Now *I'm* imagining things.

Then Emma spotted the lone figure in

black sitting in the last row of chairs in front of the massive baptismal font. Even as Emma studied her from a distance she noted the striking resemblance to Frank's mother — dark hair pulled back from a forehead a little too high, a small nose, and a mouth too large for the oval face. Her ears protruded from her head just like Emma's son Martin. She wore a small hat with a feather sprouting from the left side. Her face could have been attractive but it was too pale with a slightly bluish tinge, reminding Emma of books she had read of Victorian women using arsenic to give them a delicate appearance.

Emma could see her eyes darting back and forth, like a frightened animal eluding its prey. She hunkered down into the overly large coat, pulling up the collar.

"Nate," Emma whispered, "there she is. You stay here and let me approach her alone."

"All right, but I'm not letting you out of my sight."

She planted a kiss on his chin and walking quietly up to the woman in black, slid into the chair next to her. "Lindsey, it's Emma Winberry."

The woman jumped, then turned to Emma and grasped her hand.

Emma stared into the lovely gray-green eyes of Frank's mother.

"Oh, thank God you're here." Lindsey said. "Did you see him?"

"Who?" Emma asked.

"The man with the birthmark down his face."

"I saw someone, but couldn't make out his features. He's gone now." Emma looked around but saw only schoolchildren and groups of tourists strolling around the church.

"There." She pointed. "He just ducked into the Chapel of St. Michael and St. George. You *did* see him?" She seemed to be at the point of tears.

"Try to relax. You're safe. No one's going to hurt you." Emma turned to Nate and beckoned him over.

Lindsey drew back at his approach.

Emma held onto her hand. "This is Nate Sandler. He and I are traveling together." We're doing a lot more than that, she thought, but Lindsey doesn't need to know that now.

Nate gave Emma a quizzical look, then nodded to Lindsey.

"Please see if anyone is in that chapel over there. Lindsey saw the man who's been following her run in there." She pointed to the one Lindsey had indicated.

Nate frowned but responded to Emma's slight tilt of her head and eye movements.

"Don't worry. If anyone is in there, Nate will find him."

And what is he supposed to do if he does? asked her inner voice.

Emma didn't answer. She was quite sure no one was in there now, but she had seen someone. Was it the same man? The church was filled with tourists. There was no way she could be sure. They both watched as Nate walked into the chapel, only to reappear a moment later shaking his head.

When he returned to them he shrugged. "No one in there now."

"But I saw him. And so did Mrs. Winberry." Lindsey looked from one to the other, her eyes begging them to believe her.

"Perhaps he left by another exit," Emma said, trying to sound convincing.

Lindsey put her hands over her face. "Maybe I *am* losing my mind, like Uncle Avery seems to think." Her body shuddered in silent sobs.

Emma met Nate's eyes and noted the slight shake of his head.

"Let's go outside into the sunshine," Emma said. "I think you need some fresh air."

Without answering Lindsey tried to stand, but fell back into the chair, her head lolling to one side.

Nate immediately knelt down beside her and carefully bent her body forward while Emma grasped her head. She groaned.

"Are you all right?" Emma asked. "Shall we call someone?"

"No, no, just a spell of weakness. I'm quite all right now."

With Emma on one side and Nate on the other, they helped her into a standing position. A hint of color had returned to her white face.

"When was the last time you had anything to eat?" Emma asked, always the mother.

"I don't remember. Sometime yesterday, I believe."

I wish I had some of my muffins, Emma thought. They're so full of nourishment.

She needs more than muffins, the inner voice said.

"I believe there's a café downstairs," Nate said. "I saw the sign."

"Yes, the Crypt Café," Lindsey answered, giving him a weak smile.

"Let's get some hot tea and some food into you," Emma said. She looked at the slim figure just visible from the open front of the coat. "You're nothing but skin and bone."

Slowly the trio made their way out of the Cathedral and down the steps toward the crypt. Lindsey leaned heavily on Nate's arm. When they entered the crowded café, Emma led Lindsey to one of the few vacant tables while Nate went up to the counter and bought three beef sandwiches and three cups of tea. When he set the tray on the table, Emma took one cup of tea, put two packets of sugar and a liberal amount of milk in it and set it in front of Lindsey.

"Drink," she said.

Without a word, the woman picked up the cup and sipped the hot liquid. She sat back in the chair, closed her eyes for a moment, and took a deep breath. After a few more swallows, she picked up the sandwich and took a bite, then another. "I didn't realize how hungry I was."

Emma nodded. "Your color is much better now. Finish the sandwich and perhaps we'll get some dessert."

Emma and Nate ate quietly, each glancing from time to time at the other woman. When they had finished, Emma looked over at the counter displaying pies and cakes. "How about something sweet?"

"Perhaps I'm ready for pudding," Lindsey

said, following Emma's gaze. "I really haven't been eating much lately."

"I don't see any pudding," Emma said, "only pies and cakes."

Nate smiled. "In this country, my dear, the dessert is referred to as 'the pudding' no matter what type of sweet it is."

"How very odd," Emma said. "How did you know that?"

He didn't answer, just gave her a wink.

"Yes," Lindsey said, "I'm sure it does sound strange to Americans. I don't really know how that began, perhaps some old tradition that no one remembers." She shrugged. "I believe I would like a slice of pie." She began to open her purse, but Nate stopped her.

"I'll take care of it. Emma?"

"Pie, please, any kind."

When Nate had gone up to the counter to join the queue that had formed, Emma turned to Lindsey. "Do you feel better now?"

"Much. I've been so upset that I suppose I even forgot to eat anything." She pulled on her left earlobe and gave Emma a weak smile.

Emma remembered that Frank's mother used to do the same thing when she was concentrating. Her left earlobe had stretched until it was noticeably longer than her right.

"You do bear a striking resemblance to my late mother-in-law, even your mannerisms," Emma said. "It's very possible that you are Andrew Winberry's daughter."

Lindsey breathed a sigh of relief. "You do believe me then. I was afraid you would simply write me off."

Emma held up her hand. "I said I believe you are conceivably my —" she hesitated for a moment "— niece by marriage. As for your fears and apprehensions, I can't say." She took the younger woman's hand and gave it a squeeze.

"Yes, I understand." Lindsey looked down and nodded absently.

"Would you like to tell me about your problem now?" Emma asked.

Lindsey's eyes darted around the room. "Not here. It's too crowded. We might be overheard."

"Perhaps after lunch we can find a bench outside where we can talk privately," Emma suggested.

"Oh, yes. That would be better." Again the woman's eyes darted around the café as if she were searching for someone.

What can I tell this woman to cheer her up? Emma pondered.

Tell her about your children. They are her family too, the inner voice said.

Right. "Do you know you have three first cousins in America, my children: Stephen, Sylvia, and Martin? And they all have children. So you have a large extended family overseas."

Lindsey looked up into Emma's smiling face. "That seems so strange. All my life I thought that poor Isabel was my only relation."

"Do you want to tell me about her now?" Emma asked.

Lindsey opened her mouth as if ready to speak just as Nate returned carrying a tray with three pieces of rhubarb pie.

"The pies are disappearing fast," he said. "I snatched these, the last ones." He refilled the teacups and they enjoyed their dessert in a more relaxed atmosphere. Whatever Lindsey was about to say would have to wait.

Emma spent the next fifteen minutes telling Lindsey about her grandchildren. She seemed to enjoy hearing about the antics of the little ones.

This woman is starved for affection, the inner voice said.

I know. The expression on her face is one of regret.

"I hate to break up this pleasant interlude," Nate said, "but we're getting glares from folks waiting for our table."

The women agreed. They deposited their trays at the designated area and walked up the steep flight of stairs leading from the crypt to the street level. Bright sunshine made them all squint. Nate kept a firm grip on Lindsey's shaky arm.

"There's a bench over there where we can sit and talk without being overheard," Emma said.

Lindsey glanced at her watch. "Oh dear. I didn't realize how late it is. I must get back to Isabel."

If we don't find out what her problem is now, Emma thought, we'll have missed the only opportunity we're going to have.

Go with her, the inner voice said.

"How long will it take you to get home?" Emma asked.

"Less than an hour if I make the train on time. I must take the tube to the train station and then the train to Roydon, only a twenty-minute ride."

"Are you steady enough for such a trip?" Emma asked with concern.

Lindsey smiled. "As steady as I ever am these days." She was still holding tightly to the stair railing.

Emma looked at Nate with pleading eyes, trying to send him a message. "I would like to see your village, wouldn't you Nate?"

"Oh, would you?" Lindsey said, her eyes brightening. "Then we can talk on the train."

Nate let out a breath and gave a little shake of his head. "Why not?" He hailed a taxi and they were soon on their way to the train station.

CHAPTER 13

They alighted from the taxi and entered a bustling cavernous station: signs led to the underground, the railroad terminals and eateries along the periphery offered quick meals and snacks that travelers could consume on their journey.

Emma felt disoriented as she always did in crowds. Where are all these people going? She noticed Lindsey scanning the station and clutching her hands together.

"He's not here," Emma said. "You're safe with us."

"Where do we buy the tickets?" Nate asked.

"Over there." Lindsey pointed to the ticket office at the far side of the station. "I have mine. You need two tickets to Roydon with return. Please, let me purchase them." She started to walk forward but wavered as Nate caught her arm.

"Nonsense. I'll take care of it." He looked

around. No place to seat the women, so he took each one by the arm and led them along.

"You are such a gentleman," Lindsey said. "One doesn't see too many of them these days."

He glanced at her and simply grunted. After purchasing the tickets, Nate looked at the schedule on a large lighted sign. It indicated the proper track. "Come on, the train leaves in ten minutes."

They quickly boarded the comfortable coach, Nate and Emma sitting across from Lindsey. No one spoke in the awkward silence.

Soon they were leaving the buildings of London, and the council houses, British-subsidized housing, behind traveling through the countryside.

Lindsey began to relax. She leaned her head back, closed her eyes for a moment and took a deep breath.

"Feeling better?" Emma asked.

"A little, thank you."

"You know the landscape looks very much like ours in the Midwest," Emma said. "This is exactly how our spring greenery looks. When do the roses bloom?"

"They're budding now, should be in full flower in a week or two," Lindsey said.

"I would love to see them. English roses are supposed to be the most beautiful."

You may get a chance to do just that, her inner voice said.

Nate cleared his throat and said gently, "Do you want to tell us more about your problem or would you rather we just see you home and not interfere."

"Oh no!" She looked at them both with genuine fear in her eyes. "I must talk this out — with someone and since you two have been so kind — if you're willing to listen —"

Emma and Nate both nodded.

"Roydon dates back to around 1100. It's a small village with about three hundred people living in the area. We don't even have our own police. I had to ring the constable in Harlow with my suspicions. That's about five miles away." She shook her head and sighed.

"I'm afraid we are rather rural, but it's peaceful and quiet, a lovely place to live, until . . ." She left the sentence unfinished and again leaned her head back, as if it were too heavy to hold up.

After a few moments Emma asked, "How old is your house?"

"It was built around 1534 and, for a time, was used as a free school for the children.

94

My maternal grandfather purchased it in the late nineteenth century and our family has lived there ever since." She stared out the window as if organizing her thoughts.

"I never put much credence to the tales of witches and ghosts that circulated around the village. But now, I don't know what to think. Sometimes I believe that the house is alive and trying to tell me something." Her eyes grew wild. "Does that sound daft?"

"I never judge anything," Emma said. "I talk to my Guardian Angel all the time and she answers me."

"Really?"

Emma nodded, ignoring the prodding in the ribs she got from Nate.

"As I told you over the phone," Lindsey continued, "someone wants a large sum of money. I know it doesn't make sense, but they are threatening to harm Isabel. I certainly don't have that much available cash. I do have a trust fund, which Uncle Avery manages. My grandfather left it to me. That's essentially what we live on. But Uncle says the investments haven't been doing well and the fund's worth is diminishing. Unless I sell the house, there's no way I can raise a quarter of a million pounds." She shook her head.

"Of course there is that old tale about

something of value hidden in the house, but that's all it is. There are some old vases and trunks but they have no intrinsic value. Old volumes fill the library but nothing one would consider a treasure. I think there are some first editions, but nothing that valuable. I'm at a total loss." She rubbed her hands together and stared out the window.

"Well, you certainly wouldn't hand over a large sum of money to total strangers on a threat," Nate said.

"Of course not," Lindsey answered. "But I must be prepared for anything that might happen." Verbalizing her problem seemed to revive Lindsey. She sat up straight and looked from Emma to Nate as if seeking an answer.

"How have you received these — threats?" Nate asked.

"By phone. Someone with a muffled voice calls late at night and says that if I don't agree to leave 250,000 pounds in a designated spot at a certain time, harm will come to Isabel. Before I can say anything, the caller disconnects."

"Have the police tried to trace the calls?" Nate asked.

"Yes, but all they can determine is that the caller uses one of those disposable mobiles. They come from somewhere in

Cambridge and they can't determine the exact location."

Nate frowned, rubbed his chin, and glanced at Emma. Then he turned his attention back to Lindsey. "Has the caller ever given you a chance to respond?"

She shook her head. "Not yet."

"How about a tracer on the phone, can't the police do that?" Nate asked.

Lindsey shook her head. "As I told you, there is nothing concrete to go on. I don't think they believe me." She whispered the last few words.

"Well, we believe you," Emma said. "Could it possibly be a prank?"

"If it is, someone has a sick sense of humor," Nate said. "What does your uncle say about it?"

Lindsey again shook her head. "He thinks it's all in my imagination. You see, I'm the only one who has heard the threats and been followed. I believe he really thinks I'm losing my mind." She pulled at her ear and bit down on her lip.

"What about your cousin?" Emma asked. "Has she received any of these threats?"

Lindsey looked startled. "Isabel? Heavens, no. She's an innocent lamb. I haven't said a thing to her. She would be terrified."

Guardian Angel, she still hasn't told us what

exactly is wrong with Isabel.

She'll tell you when she's ready.

She'd better be ready soon. Tomorrow we leave.

Lindsey continued. "I really should tell you about Amelia Perkins and her son. They also live with us. She is a relative of one of Mum's close friends. When her husband died suddenly, he left her destitute with nowhere to go. So Mum took her in. She acts as a sort of housekeeper in return for room and board. Her son, Davey, does some of the yardwork." Lindsey stopped talking, as if she had said all she could for now.

CHAPTER 14

When they got off the train the ambiance of the village enchanted Emma. She felt as though she had stepped back in time, almost expected to see horse-drawn carriages making their way down the street. "This is lovely. Isn't it, Nate?"

"Uh huh."

Emma knew he really didn't want to be here, was simply humoring her.

They walked along quiet streets with neat houses on either side of the road. The houses were modest in size, most covered with a stucco-like material. They all had well-kept gardens, roses budding everywhere.

Suddenly Emma stopped. A feeling of dread clutched at her. Off to one side stood a large house with peeling paint. Thick vines climbed up the sides like snakes seeking their prey. It was set back from the road with an old rusting iron fence surrounding the entire property.

It was the exact house in her dreams!

"What is it?" Lindsey asked. "You seem upset."

"Who lives here?" Emma asked.

"No one. The house has been for sale ever so long. It's fallen into disrepair."

Nate grabbed Emma's arm. "Come on." He pulled her away from the area.

She gave Lindsey a weak smile. "It's nothing. Sometimes I get — strange feelings, that's all."

"I can understand that," Lindsey said. "Superstition surrounds that house. Some say it's haunted."

Emma felt goose bumps climb up her arms as she glanced back at the house one more time. She began to relax as they walked along toward an old stone church on their right.

"That's an interesting church," Nate said. "It looks very old."

"Our parish church," Lindsey said, with pride in her voice. "The original building dates back to the thirteenth century. It was built by the Lord of the Manor, a member of the Knights Templar."

Nate nodded and rubbed his hand over his chin. "Impressive. But it's been renovated since then. Look at the condition of the stone exterior and the beautifully arched windows."

"Many additions and renovations," Lindsey said. "Lots of history surrounds it as well as many of the old structures in this village."

Before them stood a tall post with a sign atop depicting Henry VIII and Ann Boleyn. It said:

ROYDON
Domesday book
1086

"That's an interesting sign," Nate remarked.

"Yes, it's been there as long as I can remember," Lindsey said.

They turned left, walked another half-block, then Lindsey pointed. "That's our home."

Emma's eyes opened wide. It looked like something out of a novel by one of the Brontë sisters. The property was larger than most of the others. She heard Nate let out a low whistle.

Before them stood a large tan-colored building with a pebbled exterior and a tiled roof. Three chimneys sprouted from various areas. The vegetation surrounding it had grown out of control: bushes badly in need of trimming, grass growing between paving stones in the walkway. A large vine of some sort grew along the front of the house and clutched its way almost to the roof and wound around the side. It lent an ominous air to the place.

"I'm afraid the grounds have been neglected," Lindsey said. "Ever since the gardener left, it's been hit and miss. Amelia's son does what he can, but he's not quite right."

She didn't elaborate on why the gardener left so much work undone. *There's something she's not telling us.*

"I believe Uncle Avery is here," Lindsey said, indicating a red Jaguar sitting along the road.

Emma felt a nudge from Nate, turned and nodded.

Lindsey hurried to the front door, opened it and called softly, "Uncle Avery?"

"I'm here, Lindsey, and where have you been?"

His voice had an abrasive quality that made Emma pull back.

"Do come in," Lindsey said, turning to them. "We have guests, Uncle."

They were greeted with a frown rather than a welcoming smile from a small man with penetrating eyes and a shock of gray hair. A goatee sprang from his chin at a peculiar angle. "These people helped me, Uncle," Lindsey said. "Let's have tea and I'll explain everything."

"Excuse my bad manners," the man said, holding out his hand. "Avery Wilkins." The goatee bounced with every word.

Nate took the proffered hand and shook it. "Nate Sandler, and this is Emma Winberry." Avery Wilkins then shook Emma's hand and let them in to a small parlor to the right of the main foyer.

"Do sit down for a bit and I'll get some tea," Lindsey said.

Before Emma or Nate had a chance to decline, Avery walked out of the room pulling Lindsey after him.

"I think we should leave right now," Nate said. "After that bizarre story she told us on the train, I don't know what we can do. Are you listening to me, Emma?"

Emma turned frightened eyes to him. "Something is terribly wrong in this house. I sense it. And that white house down the road; it's the one in my dreams." She rubbed her arms, feeling the familiar goose bumps again climbing up them.

Watch, said her inner voice.

"All the more reason we should leave."

Nate got up from his chair and was about to walk out of the room when their hosts returned followed by a thin, middle-aged woman carrying a tray. She wore a plain black dress that reached almost to her ankles. Salt and pepper hair was pulled back in a bun from a face with no redeeming features. Emma recognized the squinting eyes as a sign of a very near-sighted woman. Without her contact lenses, Emma did the same thing.

"Set it here on the table, Amelia, please. I'll serve," Lindsey said.

The woman squinted at Emma and Nate through eyes set too far apart, then nodded to Lindsey and left the room.

Emma noticed a few strands of reddish hair clinging to the sofa and picked them up. "Do you have a dog?" she asked.

"Yes, we do," Lindsey answered, "a golden retriever. She's Isabel's dog, a lovely animal. Why do you ask?"

"I just found some reddish hairs here on the sofa, that's all," Emma answered. They didn't appear to be dog hairs, she thought, but possibly human. She noticed a sudden change in Lindsey's demeanor. Her hands visibly shook as she poured the tea.

"The dog is not supposed to be on the furniture but sometimes she does break the rules. Oh, I am clumsy today." She fussed as she wiped up some spilled tea. "I'm afraid I'm still a bit upset by this afternoon."

"Let me do that," Avery said, taking the cup from Lindsey's hand and handing it to Emma. Then he poured one for Nate. "My niece has a very vivid imagination. Sometimes she sees things that aren't really there. Isn't that so, my dear?" He turned to Lindsey and stared until she dropped her gaze.

Emma didn't like his bullying tactics. "I believe her," she said, feeling compelled to defend the woman. "I saw a man hurrying away, just as Lindsey said."

Nate stared at her with a slight shake to his head.

Avery shrugged. "So she's been telling those fantastic tales again." He gave Lindsey a withering look. "Without proof, we can do nothing." With those words he indicated the conversation was closed.

Emma sipped her tea to be polite but noticed that Nate left his untouched.

"You may be right, Mr. Wilkins. There doesn't seem to be anything we can do about it." He turned to Emma. "I think we'll be on our way. How often do the trains run?"

"I believe there is one heading for London

in a half hour," Lindsey said.

"Good. That will give us time to look at the cemetery of the church across the way. I'll bet there are some interesting grave-stones. Come on, Emma."

But she wasn't listening, she was looking at Lindsey and saw despair, or was it uncertainty? No, it was fear. Something was very wrong.

Guardian Angel, what is it? How can I help? You can't leave her. She needs you.

As they walked toward the door, a clear soprano voice filled the house.

"Is that Isabel?" Emma asked.

"Yes, she does have a lovely voice, doesn't she?" Lindsey gave a slight shake of her head.

Suddenly Emma blurted out. "I'd like to meet her." She ignored Nate's glowering look.

"Oh," was all Lindsey said.

"I'm afraid that won't be possible," Avery Wilkens said, heading for the door. "Isabel sees no one."

"Emma, it's time for us to leave now." Nate took her arm and ushered her out the door.

"Thank you both so much for your help and — goodbye." Lindsey called after them. Her voice was dismissing them, but, when

Emma looked back, her eyes sent a message pleading with her to stay.

As they walked out of the house and down the road, Emma hesitated.

"What is it?" Nate asked.

"Someone just darted behind that tree."

He looked around. "I don't see anyone. Your imagination is running away with you."

"No, I feel eyes watching us. Do you think it could be the man who's been following Lindsey?"

Nate grabbed her arm and hurried her along. "I have no idea, but that's all the more reason to get out of here."

"Well, I'm glad that's over," Nate said, putting the last item in his suitcase. He closed it with a forceful click. "I'm sure you're as eager to get home as I am." He turned to see her staring out the window at gray skies and the promise of rain. "Emma?"

"Huh?"

He snaked his arms around her and planted a kiss on her neck.

"I can't get Lindsey out of my mind. She's genuinely frightened. Whether it's real or only in her imagination makes no difference. And these hairs." She pulled them out of her pocket. "Do they feel like dog hair to you?" She looked up at him, worry lines crossing her forehead.

"You actually took hairs from that house?" Nate asked, shaking his head in disbelief.

"Well, they were there on the sofa."

He looked at them. "They can be from any kind of animal or from someone's head for that matter. I agree that it does appear to be a peculiar situation, but there is nothing we can do about it." He emphasized the last words.

Later that afternoon in the hotel room the phone rang. Nate answered it and handed it to Emma. "It's that Bellingham woman. Obviously you gave her this number."

Emma gazed at him innocently as she took the phone. "Hello."

"Oh, Mrs. Winberry, I told Isabel all about you and she was so excited to hear that we have relations, distant ones, I know. She wants to meet you."

"I don't see how that's possible," Emma said. "We're leaving tomorrow."

"Could you perhaps come to dinner tonight? I know it's short notice, but it would mean so much to Isabel. The trains do run quite regularly."

Emma looked at Nate's frowning face. "Just a moment."

She turned to him. "Do we have any plans

for tonight?"

"You know we don't."

"Lindsey wants us to come over for dinner. She told Isabel about us and the girl is eager to meet us. Please Nate, just for the evening."

He let out a noisy breath. "I suppose, but tell her to make it early. I don't want to get stuck out there with no transportation back."

"Yes, Lindsey, we can come, but make it early, will you? We want to be back before it gets too late."

"Don't worry about that. If you take the train at half-seven, we'll plan dinner at eight. Uncle Avery can drive you back. And thanks, ever so much."

As they sat quietly on the train heading for Roydon, Emma could feel Nate's annoyance. She knew he was humoring her and loved him for it. She took his hand and gave it a squeeze. "Thank you," she whispered.

"Emma, Emma, you know just how to get around me, woman. Okay, so I'm a little curious about this elusive cousin, too." He held her hand for the rest of the trip.

When they reached Roydon, Lindsey was waiting. She wore a tweed skirt and sensible brown walking shoes. A light blue jacket accentuated the color of her eyes. Just enough makeup gave her a pleasing appearance. A smile lit up her face when she saw them. "I'm so glad you came back. Now, I must tell you about Isabel before you meet her."

I knew it, Emma thought. Something is seriously wrong with her.

Lindsey slowed her walk to a leisurely stroll and began her narrative. "You see, Isabel was born with a severe case of hypertrichosis, an excess of body hair. I don't know what the statistics are, but it's quite rare. Her father was a wanderer, working in various carnival sideshows. He also suffered from the disease; it's genetic, you see. His case was bad enough for him to be considered an oddity, but Isabel's is much worse." She stopped and took a deep breath. "I don't know if you are familiar with this condition. It's sometimes referred to as 'werewolf's syndrome.'

"Isabel is covered with long red hair, everywhere, except her sweet heart-shaped face, the palms of her hands and soles of her feet."

Emma's eyes widened as she listened to this outlandish tale.

Lindsey's voice faltered as she stopped walking for a moment. "When she was born, she looked like a little monkey.

"Her mother was a rebellious sort of a girl and when she saw her newborn infant, she bolted. Said she could never love a freak and left the country. Since she and Mum were sisters, the family felt responsible. So the girl has lived with me and Mum all of her nineteen years. We've kept her isolated in this house to protect her from ridicule and staring eyes." Lindsey's face contorted in an expression of extreme sadness.

"Oh my dear," Emma said. "I don't know what to say."

Lindsey shook her head and let out a breath. "At first Mum invited other children to play with Isabel, but that didn't work out. They made fun of her and called her all kinds of hurtful names. It was disastrous." As if a dam had broken, she continued in a rush of words. "One year my mum asked her what she wanted Father Christmas to bring her. You know what she answered?" She looked at them, her face a mask of pain.

"A little girl just like me to play with." Tears streamed down Lindsey's face as she continued. "That's when we bought her the first Duchess. The current dog is the second of the breed. But it wasn't enough. She made up an invisible playmate, called her Annabelle. Talked to her all the time. The doctor said it was her way to cope with her

111

loneliness and isolation."

Emma took the woman's hand and gave it a compassionate squeeze. Nate looked away and said nothing.

Lindsey stopped talking for a moment, took a few deep breaths, then continued.

"The problem is that now she's an adult, Annabelle is still very real to her. She actually sees this hallucination, describes her as looking exactly like herself. She even claims that the house talks to her, sometimes even threatens her. She's become completely withdrawn into her own world of fantasy." She stopped again, then continued.

"Her life revolves around me, Uncle Avery, her dog, her fantasies, and her music. You heard her lovely voice; she takes music lessons on a regular basis. Her dream is to make recordings since, obviously, she could never appear in public."

"Is there no treatment for this condition?" Emma asked.

Lindsey shook her head. "We've taken her to many doctors over the years. They've tried various modalities, electrolysis for one, but she is covered with so much hair that it isn't feasible. Medications did nothing but make her ill. Finally, we decided to simply leave her alone. So you can see how devastating any change in her life would be."

"I'm out of my element here," Emma said. "I don't know what to advise you." She turned to Nate but he simply shook his head.

As they walked, Emma was desperate to change the subject. She marveled again at the quaint cottages and the many rose bushes ready to burst forth. "This is such a lovely area," she said. "Isn't it, Nate?"

"It is. Nice place for a restful holiday."

"I love living here," Lindsey continued. "We have a simple life and Isabel has been content. I don't want anything to disrupt it. You can understand that, can't you?"

"Of course," Emma said.

As they approached the house they saw two cars, Avery's Jaguar and a flashy green car parked along the road.

Nate whispered to Emma, "That's a Rolls Royce, top of the line if I'm not mistaken."

Lindsey's face took on an expression of anger, her lips pursed, her brow furrowed. She balled her hands into fists. "Oh, that insufferable American is here again. How many times do I have to tell him the house is not for sale."

As Lindsey walked up to the two men, Emma stared at the American. "There's something familiar about that man. Do you recognize him, Nate?"

"Now that you mention it." Nate looked closely at the man's demeanor. Then turned to Emma and gave her a mischievous grin. "We have seen him before, but this time he has clothes on."

"The man from the hotel, yes, that's him. How strange."

Guardian Angel, is there some meaning to this or just coincidence?

There are no coincidences, her inner voice said.

Suddenly they heard raised voices. "But Lindsey, be reasonable," Avery was saying. "The man simply wants to make you an offer."

"No!" she shouted. "I'm not interested in your offer, Mr. Duncan. Now please vacate my property."

The man smiled, but there was no warmth in it. "You may regret this, Miss Bellingham. I urge you to reconsider."

"That sounded like a threat," Nate said, looking closely at the man and making note of the license number of the car. He took out a small notebook from his pocket and a pen and wrote it down along with the make and color.

"What are you doing?" Emma asked.

"I don't like that man."

"Neither do I."

When Lindsey returned to her guests, she had regained her composure. "Please forgive my outburst, but my nerves are on edge and I can't bear that man. Come in and we'll try to forget this unpleasant incident."

Avery came over to Nate and Emma. "Why are you two here?" he asked, his demeanor decidedly unwelcoming.

"I invited them to meet Isabel. Now everyone, please come into the house."

Avery's frown turned into a forced smile. "Of course, sorry to be so rude."

The sun had disappeared behind a bank of dark clouds. Emma stopped for a moment, felt something menacing, then tried to disregard it as her overactive imagination, but the feeling persisted.

As they entered the foyer, the tantalizing aroma of roast beef assailed them. Emma took off the light jacket she wore and draped it over a chair. Then she saw a face peeking around the doorframe. It was a lovely childlike face: heart shaped with huge blue eyes wide with wonder.

"Come Isabel," Lindsey called softly. "Meet our guests."

A small figure slowly emerged. She wore a high-necked, long-sleeved blue sweater over a pair of jeans. The lovely face was surrounded by a corona of wavy red hair that covered not only her head, but her neck and ears, making its way down into the folds of her sweater. The tops of her hands were covered with the same hair. The fragrance of lavender did little to mask a slight animal odor emanating from the girl.

"Hello, Isabel," Emma said, holding out her hand.

She approached slowly and lay her hand in Emma's. The feel of the hair was soft and silky, the same as the ones she had found on the sofa. Emma's heart went out to this poor lonely creature born into a world where she would always be considered a freak.

"Are you really a relation?" the girl asked in a soft melodic voice.

"I do believe I am, and you must call me Aunt Emma."

"Oh, that's brilliant." Isabel clutched her hands together under her pointed chin.

Emma thought that a strange reply, but she realized it was probably a local use of the word. When she saw the girl nervously eyeing Nate, she turned and introduced him.

"Are you my uncle?" Isabel asked.

"If you want me to be, I shall," Nate said.

Isabel's smile revealed deep dimples. "A family," she said with a deep sigh.

At her side stood a dog with long golden-red hair, its tail wagging in welcome.

"Duchess," Isabel said, "meet my new aunt and uncle."

The dog sat, tail thumping on the floor. Nate reached down and scratched Duchess behind the ears.

"She loves that," Isabel said.

"She's a fine animal," he replied.

"And a friend." A forlorn look and a sigh from Isabel, then she took their hands and led them into the dining room.

Avery Wilkins came in from outside, his forced smile never reaching his eyes, his goatee jutting out at that peculiar angle. Emma wanted to laugh but simply nodded and Nate extended his hand. The man hesitated before he shook it.

The long dining room table was set for six. Emma wondered who the other guest was. Then her gaze turned to an enormous fireplace occupying one complete wall. One could roast an entire hog inside of it. She walked over to the heavy oak beam at the top and fingered the strange markings she had glimpsed on their first visit. "Do these have any particular significance?"

Isabel came up to her and reached to touch them. "They are symbols to keep the witches away. See, that's a cooking pot with bird's feet sticking out. It was supposed to warn the witches that if they came down the chimney shaped like birds, as they often did, they would fall right into the pot."

"Do you think it worked?" Emma asked.

Isabel shrugged. "If people believed it, I suppose so." She looked at Emma with a grave expression on her face. "Anything you truly believe can be real, you know."

Emma bit the inside of her lip and raised her eyebrows. "Yes, it's possible."

"Please sit down," Lindsey said, indicating the two seats across from the fireplace.

Emma noticed the tableware, the gold trim around the edges of the dinner plates peeling off in places, the linen napkins frayed in the corners — all once very grand, but now aging, like the house itself.

"All right, Annabelle, sit down now," Isabel said to the empty chair beside her. "This is my friend," she said to Emma and Nate. "She always sits next to me."

Emma noticed Avery's glowering look. Unpleasant man, she thought.

"Amelia, would you serve dinner now," Lindsey said. "And join us, please."

"No, Davey and I will sit in the kitchen."

Lindsey shook her head. "No matter how I try to include her as part of the family, she keeps herself aloof and persists in act-ing as a servant." She heaved a sigh. "Through the years, we've all come to accept the arrangement."

The dog settled herself next to Isabel as Amelia served roast beef and Yorkshire pudding with roast potatoes and peas on the side.

Emma could feel the tension in the room as they ate in silence. What a strange household this is: a place set for an imaginary friend, Avery Wilkins obviously resenting any visitors, Amelia Perkins insisting on taking a subservient role. She decided it was time to say something uplifting.

"Isabel, would you like me to send you some pictures of my grandchildren?"

"Oh yes, please. What are their names?"

Emma proceeded to tell the girl about her family and felt the tension subsiding.

"Oh how lovely it must be to have children running about. I wish . . ." She left the sentence unfinished.

"Here's the pudding," Lindsey said as Amelia served ice cream. "I'm afraid it's rather simple on such short notice."

"It's just fine," Nate said. "The meal was delicious and quite filling."

After dinner they went into the parlor for a short visit. Emma saw Nate glancing at his watch and signaling her with his eyes as she saw the daylight waning.

"What time is the last train to London?" he asked.

Lindsey looked at the clock. "It leaves in a half-hour, but I'm sure Uncle Avery will drive you back."

"My dear, I live in Cambridge, which, as you know, is in the opposite direction. Besides, I have some business to attend to so I'll take my leave." He said good night and quickly left.

"I don't know what to say," Lindsey said. "He usually isn't so rude. Please excuse his behavior."

"That's all right," Nate said, walking toward the door. "We would rather take the train anyway. It's a pleasant ride."

Isabel looked at them, a wistful expression on her face. Then she cocked her head as if listening to something. "I must go now. The house is calling to me." She quickly walked out of the room followed by the dog.

Lindsey shook her head. "Sometimes she behaves perfectly normally and then sometimes she hears things. I am so worried, but I mustn't burden you with my problems. Thank you so much for listening and coming back this evening. Your visit meant a lot to Isabel."

As they walked back to the station through

the darkening night, Nate shook his head. "That whole situation is sad."

"Yes. The poor little thing living in a world of fantasy," Emma said.

"It's the only world she can survive in. You know," he said, "something's wrong with that whole picture."

"What do you mean?"

"There has to be a reason why that American is so insistent on buying that house. And I don't trust that Avery fellow. Too bad we have to leave with so many unanswered questions. But, I don't suppose we can do anything about any of it."

Don't be too sure of that, Emma's inner voice said.

At that moment they heard the whistle of the train in the distance and quickened their pace.

Chapter 15

That night Emma's fragmented sleep was interrupted by bizarre dreams. The vision of Isabel grew into the semblance of an enormous hairy beast with wild eyes. She woke with a start to hear Nate snoring peacefully at her side.

Oh dear, she thought, letting out a deep sigh. I wish I could get a cup of warm milk and sit in my favorite chair in the atrium. I usually find answers there. Well, tomorrow I'll be able to do just that.

Don't be too sure, her inner voice said.

All right, Guardian Angel, just what do you mean by that?

Wait and see.

Emma was more perplexed than ever. Being as quiet as possible, she walked from one end of the hotel room to the other.

"Just why are you pacing the floor?" Nate's sleepy voice came from under the covers.

"Anxious to get home I guess," Emma lied.

"Come back to bed and I'll hold you 'till you fall asleep."

Reluctantly Emma climbed into bed and nestled in his arms.

"You aren't fooling me, Sparrow. You're worried about Lindsey and Isabel."

"You know me too well." She squirmed until she was in just the right position, her back "spooned" into the curve of Nate's body.

"Go to sleep," he said, yawning. "Everything will look brighter in the morning."

Their plane was scheduled to leave at noon. Emma fussed around the room checking to make sure she had left nothing behind. Her hands itched to pick up the phone and call Lindsey, but she knew Nate would not approve.

"I think that's everything," she said with a sigh. She would be glad to get away from this place and get back home to her family and her plants. But she hated leaving things unfinished, and Lindsey's problems were definitely not over. The ringing of the phone made her jump.

"That's probably the desk," Nate said, picking it up.

Emma saw his brow furrow as he listened. She could hear weeping coming over the wire.

"It's Lindsey," he said, handing her the phone and grunting.

"Hello?"

"Mrs. Winberry, I'm so sorry to disturb you, but someone broke into the house last night." Her voice rose with every word.

"Lindsey, calm down. Talk slowly and tell me what happened." She ignored Nate's violent shaking of his head.

After more sniffling, Lindsey continued. "Someone broke into the library. Isabel is terrified. She says she wants to go to America with Aunt Emma and Uncle Nate . . ."

After a pause Lindsey seemed to regain control of herself. Emma heard her take a deep breath.

"Something woke me, I'm not sure what. I heard Duchess growling. I got out of bed and picked up a cricket bat that I keep for protection."

Emma almost smiled at the picture of Lindsey shouldering the bat against an intruder.

"I heard someone moving downstairs. I called out, 'Who's there? Who is it?' At the sound of my voice Isabel opened her door and Duchess bounded down the stairs barking furiously. Isabel screamed for her dog as I ran after her. I was so terrified I didn't know what I was doing.

"The front door was standing open where the intruder had escaped. Duchess ran after him, but he was long gone. By then Amelia and her son came from their room at the rear, but there was nothing they could do." She stopped for a deep breath.

"What was taken?" Emma asked.

"Nothing that I could see. Whoever it was had been in the library — books pulled off the shelves, desk drawers rifled through as if they were looking for something. But I didn't see anything missing."

"Did you call the police?" Emma was trembling and pacing back and forth until Nate grabbed her in his arms and held her tight.

"Oh yes, they came straight away and searched, checking for fingerprints and footprints outside. One of the library windows had been cleverly removed." She hesitated, then blurted out, "Is there any way you can come over? Isabel is beside herself. She wants you." The last words ended in a whisper.

"Let me phone you back in just a moment," Emma said, disconnecting the call.

Nate let out a breath and crossed his arms over his chest. "Well?"

She told him what happened. "I can't leave, I just can't leave her."

"And why not, Emma? You barely know this girl."

"Because she *needs* me. She needs a friend and I don't think she has any. And besides, she *is* family."

He stood there shaking his head. "Our plane leaves in four hours and we are supposed to go to the airport right now."

"Why don't you go home and I'll stay another few days until this is sorted out." She gave him a disarming smile.

"Oh no. I'm fully aware of all the trouble you get into when you're left alone."

"Nate," she put her hands on his shoulders. "I would never forgive myself if I deserted her and something more serious happened. There's a reason for that break-in." She thought of the strange things that had happened the previous year at the Performing Arts Center and gave a little shiver.

He shook his head and thought for a moment. "Did Isabel really say she wanted to go to America with us?"

"Yes, and that nearly broke my heart." She gave him a pleading look.

"I'll call the airlines and tell them there's been an emergency and we must change our return flight."

"Oh Nate, you're a dear."

He disengaged her arms from around his neck and picked up the phone. "And then, we'll have to call home and tell them we're staying a few more days."

Emma barely heard his end of the conversation.

Guardian Angel, what now?

You can help her. She has no one else.

CHAPTER 16

Nate was uncharacteristically quiet as they checked out of the hotel, hailed a taxi, and began the journey to Roydon. Emma had remembered seeing a Bed and Breakfast along the main street. The hotel concierge had called for them, determined there was a vacancy and made a reservation. After they boarded the train, Emma sat back and watched the countryside. The sun had favored them with an appearance and the recent rain cast a sheen on the leaves and budding flowers on this glorious May day.

I should be home tending to my roof garden, Emma chided herself. But Claude, her neighbor, would take good care of it. He was a fastidious person and, when he made a promise, he always kept it. She wondered how the grandchildren were and missed their chatter and small bodies running around.

All right Guardian Angel, let's get this matter

settled quickly so I can get back to my life. A feeling of unease settled over her when there was no response.

When they disembarked from the train, they pulled their luggage along to the Bed and Breakfast, a quaint cottage with a thatched roof. Rose bushes surrounded the entrance, their fat buds ready to burst into bloom.

A stately looking woman wearing a tweed skirt and brown jumper greeted them with a smile. "Mr. and Mrs. Sandler? I'm Mrs. Rayfield. Do come in."

"Charles," she called. "Come help with the luggage."

A gangly teenager materialized and, without a word, grabbed the suitcases and made his way upstairs.

"After you settle in, you can come down and sign the register," the woman said.

Emma and Nate followed Charles to a large room overlooking a garden showing the first blooms of the season. Flowering bushes abounded here, too. Nate tipped the boy and turned toward Emma.

"Why did she call us Mr. and Mrs. Sandler?" Emma asked.

"I thought that would eliminate the need for bothersome explanations. I'm sorry I've been such a grouch." He put his arms around her and gave her a resounding kiss.

"I can't blame you," she said, a contrite expression on her face. "I do tend to get involved in some rather bizarre circumstances."

"You can say that again."

She frowned, then kissed the cleft in his chin. "And you're always there to help me."

He looked around. "You know, this is a very nice room."

A four-poster bed graced one wall, intricately carved pineapple-designed finials atop the posts. "These furnishings look like genuine antiques," he said, examining the dresser. A mirror framed in gilt hung above it. "I think this is cherry wood," he said running his hand over the smooth surface of a chest of drawers.

"It's lovely," Emma agreed, sitting down in a rocker and looking at the wallpaper, which had an elegantly designed cabbage rose border. An Aubusson rug covered the center of a worn but polished hardwood floor.

"We'd better get moving," Nate said. "The sooner we get things explained, the quicker we can be out of here."

Emma wasn't too sure of that, but she kept her opinion to herself.

Before they left the hotel, they had called

Sylvia and Claude. Emma simply said there were more places they wanted to see before coming home. Then she called Lindsey. Amelia Perkins answered the phone and said Lindsey was lying down.

They went downstairs, registered, and Nate told Mrs. Rayfield they were going to Bellingham House. They both waited for some type of reaction.

"The Bellingham house?" she asked in surprise. "Are you acquainted?"

"Yes, we are," Emma said, noting a look of concern on the woman's face.

"Do you know something about the family?" Nate asked.

"Only the rumors one hears. You know, it's a very old house and, through the years, some strange things have happened, or so I'm told." The woman clasped her hands together.

"Like what?" Nate persisted.

"Well," she hesitated for a moment. "There's a legend that the house has a life of its own." Her eyes widened as she warmed to the subject. "It seems that every fifty years it demands a sacrifice."

Emma stepped back and grabbed Nate's arm.

"You don't really believe that, do you?" he asked, shaking his head.

"If you look back at the history, every half century someone has died mysteriously or — disappeared. There was Joseph Bellingham, Lindsey's grandfather, who was found in the garden. One of the chimney pots fell on his head." Her voice dropped to a whisper. "They say the house killed him." She put her clenched fists up to her mouth and looked from side to side. "And then the gardener disappeared, and then —"

"I think that's enough for now," Nate said. "Thank you, Mrs. Rayfield."

"Of course." The woman composed herself, then asked, "Will you be back for tea?"

"We're not sure," Emma said.

"Let's go," Nate said, propelling Emma toward the door.

"And — do be careful." Again Mrs. Rayfield looked around as if expecting to see someone or something.

"What do you think she meant by that last remark?" Emma asked as they walked at a brisk pace.

"She probably listens to too much gossip. A house as old as that one is bound to have some superstitions surrounding it through the years. And, as far as someone dying there every fifty years, that's pretty much normal. The house didn't kill them."

"I suppose you're right."

"It's the logical male mind."

"Yes, your Lordship." Emma made a little curtsy and began to laugh. "One can make much ado about nothing."

"Yes, especially you." He reached out and gave her a pat on the backside. When they reached the old abandoned white house, Emma hesitated. She felt the same foreboding as the first time, only stronger.

"What's wrong with you?" Nate asked.

"Something about that house bothers me. But I don't know what it is."

"It's your imagination, that's what it is." He took her arm and pulled her along.

At Bellingham House, Emma remembered Mrs. Rayfield's words. She looked at the building but felt none of the negative vibrations she had from the white house. It was just an old house covered with vines. But still . . .

A red Jaguar sat alongside the fence.

"Avery Wilkins is here," Nate said, a frown creasing his face.

"I don't like him, either. Look," Emma said as they approached the door, "someone is digging in the flower bed."

"Probably the housekeeper's son," Nate answered. "A place this size certainly needs a person to tend the grounds."

Amelia Perkins opened the door before

they rang the bell. "I saw you come up the walk," she said. Her face had a strained expression as she squinted through swollen eyes. "Lindsey is in the parlor."

Nate and Emma walked into the same room as last time. Lindsey sat in a chair oblivious to their entrance. She stared out the window, hands clasped in her lap.

"Lindsey," Emma said. "It's Emma Winberry."

She turned and, for a moment, didn't show any sign of recognition, then gave a little shake of her head. "Oh, Mrs. Winberry, what am I to do?" Tears sneaked from her eyes and made their way down her cheeks. "When will this end?"

Emma put an arm around her shoulders in a comforting gesture.

"I see the red Jaguar outside," Nate said. "Is Mr. Wilkins here?"

"Yes, he's looking over the grounds to see if there's something the investigators missed." Lindsey shook her head. "They were very thorough."

"What *did* the police have to say?" Nate asked.

"Not much. They did send over a forensics team and a new detective inspector I'd never seen before. He searched everywhere, but he seemed certain that the only fingerprints they found were probably those of the family. They took all of our prints for comparison. That really upset Isabel. And the ground was so dry outside that there were no footprints. Said they would look into it, but so far, they have found nothing to identify the perpetrators." She held her head in her hands as if it were too heavy to support.

"May we look at the library?" Nate asked.

"Of course, come through." She led the way down a narrow hallway to a medium-sized room on the right.

Books lay scattered on the floor; desk drawers pulled out and their contents emptied; a window boarded up.

"That's how he got in," Lindsey said, pointing to the window. "He cut the glass and took it out."

"Can we touch things now?" Emma asked.

"Yes, the constable and forensics team have finished."

Nate and Emma looked at the books that had been disturbed, picking them up and examining the titles. They were mostly history tomes and biographies. Nate examined the shelving, running his hand against the backboard.

"Do you think someone believes the legend that something is hidden in this house and was looking for it?" Emma asked.

Nate frowned and rubbed his chin. "They'd have to have some idea what they were looking for." He turned to Lindsey. "Are there any books here with the history of this house?"

She looked puzzled for a moment. "I believe there is one, somewhere." She stepped carefully to one section and looked across the row. "Here is a small history of Roydon with some early information about the house. I don't know how helpful that will be." She handed it to Nate. "Wait a minute. I have one of my grandfather's journals. It's in my room. I have been reading through it trying to find some reference to anything hidden. Let me get it for you."

She hurried out of the room and returned shortly with a slim volume. Nate took it and opened it to the first page. Emma peered over his shoulder. The cramped writing was difficult to read.

"May I take this with me? I'll see that you get it back." Nate asked Lindsey.

"Certainly, anything that might help."

As they walked back into the parlor, Avery Wilkins turned toward them. They hadn't heard him come in. He frowned at Emma and Nate. "What are you two doing here again? I thought you had gone back to the States."

"We decided to stay on a few days," Emma said, bristling at the man's rudeness.

"Yes, Uncle, it was so kind of them to change their plans. I do so need their support and Isabel is terrified."

"Don't cringe, Lindsey. You have all the support you need right here in this house." Avery turned to Emma and Nate and his expression softened. "Please excuse my rudeness. We've all had a disturbing time."

Emma had said nothing more during this exchange, just stood to the side watching Avery.

Guardian Angel, something doesn't ring true about that man.

Watch him, the inner voice said.

Emma studied the two. Avery was obviously the dominant one, but Lindsey had said he was a family friend, not a relation. What is he up to? Emma wondered.

"Have you considered a security system?" Nate asked.

"I hardly think that's necessary in a small village such as this," Avery said. "Nothing of any importance really happens here."

"What about the break-in?" Lindsey said. "I certainly consider that important. Someone could have been injured."

She turned to Nate. "Yes, I have been thinking about it, a great deal recently. I plan to call this afternoon and get some details on a security system."

A teenage boy with a severe case of acne came loping into the room. His straight blond hair hung over his eyes. He whipped his head back in a sweeping motion, then made grunting sounds and gestured to Mrs. Perkins who had been standing in a corner.

"Davey," she said. "What is it?" He motioned for her to come with him. "My son," she said.

Avery's eyes followed them as they left the room. "He's mute," he explained, "and a little weak in the head. Does some chores, and a little gardening."

At that moment the doorbell rang. Avery's brows knit in a deep frown. "Now who is that? Amelia," he called. No answer. He stomped out of the room.

"Nasty man," Emma whispered.

Nate nodded.

They heard a verbal exchange from the foyer. "Dr. Lunetti, I'm sorry you made the trip for nothing. There will be no lesson today," Avery said.

A heavily accented voice replied, "My *Bambina Rossa,* she is sick?"

"No, we had some trouble with vandals

last night. Isabel is too upset to sing."

"*Madonna,* I want to see her for just a *minuto.*"

"I'm afraid that's not possible." Avery's voice took on a decidedly unfriendly tone.

Lindsey hurried out of the room. "Ah, Dr. Lunetti, Isabel will be glad to see you."

"Hmm," Emma whispered. "There is definitely some hostility here."

"I wonder why?" Nate pondered.

Avery's voice again. "I told the doctor that Isabel is too upset for a lesson today."

"Why don't we let Isabel decide?" Lindsey's tone had changed.

"Good for her," Emma said. "She's showing a little gumption."

"Isabel," Lindsey called, "Can you come down for a moment? Dr. Lunetti is here."

"I'll bet Avery is boiling inside," Nate whispered.

"Oh, my dear teacher," came Isabel's musical voice, "we had a break-in last night. I was so frightened."

"*Bella mia,* as long as you are all right."

"I want you to meet my aunt and uncle from America."

She walked into the parlor holding the hand of a short rotund man with a mass of white wavy hair and a huge mustache. Laugh lines crinkled around his kind eyes.

"This is my Aunt Emma and my Uncle Nate. Isn't it grand that I have relations?"

The teacher extended his hand to Nate then took Emma's with a bow and a kiss. "So happy my *Bambina Rossa* has a family."

He gave Avery a look that Emma interpreted as dislike.

"Are you ready for a lesson?" he asked the girl.

"Yes, I believe so. I feel so much better now."

"Good," Lindsey said.

"I think we'll be on our way," Nate said. "Here's the number for the bed and breakfast where we're staying."

"Thanks ever so much. We will see you later?"

"You can count on it," Emma said.

Avery stood gazing out the window and didn't turn around to say goodbye.

"I don't trust that Wilkins man," Emma said as they walked back to their lodging. "And what do you expect to find in that book you borrowed?"

"My money genes are prodding me." He grinned at her. "And I don't for one minute believe that break-in was a random act. There's more to it than that. And that American bothers me, too. If a wealthy man wants this house, he has a financial reason, and it's not to turn it into a museum. I wouldn't put it past him to orchestrate the entire thing as a scare tactic, to coerce Lindsey into selling the house. And it wouldn't surprise me if Avery Wilkins is involved in the ploy in some way."

"Why Nate, I do believe you are becoming a detective." Emma took his hand and gave it a squeeze.

"Lindsey and Isabel are decent folks and I don't want to see them taken advantage of. Besides, as you have so often reminded me, they are your family."

CHAPTER 17

"Mrs. Rayfield," Nate called as they entered the B and B.

The woman came hurrying in from the kitchen wiping her hands on a towel. "Oh, Mr. and Mrs. Sandler, have you returned for your tea?"

"No, thank you. We were wondering where we can get some information on the history of Bellingham House." He gave her his most beguiling smile.

"Has something happened over there?" she asked. "I saw two police cars drive in that direction."

"They had a break-in and the police are investigating," Nate said.

"In this village! We never have any trouble here. But," she continued, obviously eager for gossip, "there is that talk of a treasure located somewhere in that house. Supposedly people have been searching for it for years. And," — her eyes widened as her voice dropped — "I told you before about the mysterious deaths and disappearances. They say the house has a life of its own and won't give up the treasure."

"Hmm," Nate said, "very interesting." He rubbed his chin and thought for a moment.

"What do you know about the family?" Emma asked.

"I rarely see anybody, only the housekeeper on occasion, going shopping. Then she just says 'good morning' — never stops for a chat and a cuppa."

"And Lindsey and her cousin?" Emma persisted.

"I've seen Lindsey a few times. She's pleasant enough, sometimes stops for a bit, but," she lowered her voice, "the cousin doesn't go out. She has some type of birth defect; some say she's terribly malformed and doesn't want to be seen. Others say she's mad." She looked around for a moment, as if someone might be listening, and leaned her head closer to Emma and Nate. "I've even heard talk that she might be a werewolf."

"Oh, my! Where did that come from?" Emma asked.

"Someone claims to have seen a hairy creature resembling a wolf roaming around at night." Her body shivered as she rubbed her arms.

Nate shook his head. "Nonsense, those creatures exist only in the imagination. Is there anyone in the village who might have known Lindsey's mother and grandfather? You see, Emma and I are thinking of writing a book and may include that house in the story." He felt Emma pinch his arm but ignored it.

"Oh, authors, how exciting!" All talk of the elusive cousin seemed to be forgotten. "There is an old woman living on the edge of the village. She's lived here ever so long. I believe she came from Cornwall or somewhere thereabouts. She seems to know everything about everyone. And, the library at Harlow might have some reference books."

"Where can we find this woman? Can you call her and ask if she'll see us?"

Mrs. Rayfield laughed. "She has no phone. You'll just have to knock at her door. If she's in the mood, she may talk to you, otherwise, she'll send you off. She's a bit eccentric." She thought for a moment. "As an inducement you might bring her some cream cakes. She does like them."

"And where do we get those?"

"There's a small bakery shop," she pointed out the window, "a ways down. The owner makes them fresh every morning. Tell her I sent you. Now I'll draw you a map."

She went off into another room and returned with pencil and paper. "You cross over the road, then turn left . . ." By the time she finished, she had a reasonable facsimile of a map. "And do let me know if you find out anything interesting."

"Absolutely," Nate said with his most charming smile. "What's her name?"

"Miss Weatherby."

"Thank you."

When they went to their room to freshen up, Emma looked at Nate. "You are becoming an accomplished liar, Mr. Sandler. I wonder how much this Miss Weatherby knows."

"We'll soon find out."

"By the way, what did you make of that story about a treasure?" Emma asked.

"You don't really believe that, do you?" He looked at her out of the corner of his eye.

She shrugged.

"Remember the game Telephone we used to play as kids? A group sits around a table and one whispers something to the kid next to him who passes it on and so it goes around the table."

Emma smiled. "I remember."

"Uh huh. When it got all the way around it bore no resemblance to the original message. That's what I think of the treasure story."

"You're probably right," she agreed.

"Of course I'm right." He tapped his forehead with his finger. "Logic."

CHAPTER 18

Emma and Nate walked down the lanes of Roydon, a village that hadn't changed much in hundreds of years. "It's refreshing to see streets devoid of bumper-to-bumper traffic, to hear the birds singing, and smell the fresh country air." Emma practically danced down the walk.

"It is nice," Nate agreed. "But have you noticed some of the locals staring at us? I guess they don't get many tourists around here. I wonder how that bed and breakfast survives."

"I wonder," Emma said. "We seem to be the only guests there. I did see a flyer in our room advertising some sort of festival. Perhaps that's what she relies on."

"Or, she doesn't need the money and just does it for a lark."

They stopped at the bakery, picked up a half-dozen cream cakes and, as they turned the last corner on the makeshift map, the village seemed to come to an abrupt end.

"Where do we go from here?" Emma asked.

"I guess that way," Nate answered, pointing to a lone cottage in the distance.

They trudged down a weed-grown path to their destination; the thatch on the roof showed wear in too many places. Someone had tried to reinforce the front door, but it hung askew on rusty hinges. One lone rose bush struggled to survive amid the weeds.

"This should be fun," Nate said as he knocked on the door.

A deep bark issued from inside. Nate called, "Miss Weatherby?"

The barking grew louder as a wizened head, resembling a wrinkled apple-doll, appeared in a window beside the door. "Bugger off! If yer sellin', don't want any, an' got nuffin' t' steal."

"Mrs. Rayfield suggested we stop by and see you." Nate held up the box. "We have some fresh cream cakes for you."

"W'o are ye?"

"We're visitors from the United States and would like to know more about this quaint village. We were told that you are the local historian."

"W'o told ye that?"

"Mrs. Rayfield, at the bed and breakfast."

"Nosy ol' biddie."

They stood for a moment, then heard locks turning. The door opened just enough for the apple-doll head to poke out. Behind her the barking continued.

Nate held up the box. "Fresh from the bakery."

"Ye don't look like robbers."

"We're tourists," Emma said, "enjoying the English countryside."

"Don't believe that, but ye might's well come in for a bit. Don't get much comp'ny."

Miss Weatherby was a diminutive woman wearing an old tweed skirt and a heavy wool sweater, though the day was warm. Her feet were enveloped in a pair of oversized Wellingtons with a tear in the right foot, just enough for her little toe to peek out. She motioned to a shaggy gray dog to sit and it instantly obeyed.

Emma looked around the cottage. Unlike the outside, the sitting room was pristine: clean lace curtains graced the windows; a bright flowered sofa and chair looked almost new.

"Never use this room. Might's well sit. Want a cuppa?" Her expression almost dared them to refuse.

"Oh yes," Emma said. "Tea would be delightful."

With a grace that belied her age, Miss Weatherby sauntered out of the room. The old dog trudged behind her.

"This fireplace is interesting," Nate said, looking at some scratches in the oak beam above it. "I wonder if that's supposed to mean something."

"Better not ask," Emma said, "but they do look similar to the ones above Lindsey's fireplace, the ones to warn the witches away. I wonder if every old house has them."

Before long the old woman called them into the kitchen.

"Too old to be carryin' them trays around. Might's well sit in here."

Emma noticed the fine china accompanied by a plate of cookies. She's saving the cream cakes for herself, she thought. She looked around the Spartan room, only a sink, an old stove, a small refrigerator and a few cabinets. The tabletop was scarred and worn in places from scrubbing. An old rug lay underneath it.

With sturdy hands, Miss Weathby poured three cups of strong tea. " 'elp yerself to a biscuit," she said.

As they drank the tea and munched on chocolate biscuits, Emma noticed Miss Weatherby examining them closely through rheumy eyes that sparkled with cunning and intelligence.

"What's yer name?" she asked Emma.

"Emma Winberry."

"A fine proper name. Like it. And w'o's this bloke?" She pointed a gnarled finger at Nate.

"He's my husband." Emma didn't wish to present any impropriety.

"Posh — never 'ad one o' them. Nuffin but trouble."

"Nate is very considerate," Emma countered.

"What kinda name is 'at?"

"It's short for Nathaniel," Nate chimed in, giving her a disarming smile.

"From the Good Book, then. Suppose it's all right. Now what ye want to know?"

"We're friends of Lindsey Bellingham and wondered about the history of the house," Emma said omitting any mention of Isabel.

"Lots o' trouble over there. Knowed the ol' man. Bought the 'ouse. Been empty a long time afore that. Folks feared o' ghosts. Say it be cursed. Naw." She shook her head. A few strands of thin white hair escaped the bun on top of her head, revealing a baby pink scalp beneath. "Don't believe in that rot. 'E was always doin' some kinda work wi' 'is roses — loved 'em, 'e did. 'Ad a orangery in back where 'e worked all the time, mornin' 'till night." She shook her head. "Don't believe in workin' too 'ard. It addles the brain. Say the 'ouse 'ventually killed 'im. Don't believe in that neither. Got kilt from 'is own carelessness. Were fixing the roof. The chimney pot were loose from the wind and fell on 'im. Knocked 'im senseless. Were never the same. Lived a few years, but like a babe. Never said nuffin.'"

"Then why were people so afraid of the house?" Emma asked.

"Superstition."

"What about the gardener who disappeared?"

"Ha! 'E ran off wi' some gal 'e knocked up. That's what 'appened to 'im." She chuckled, but then her face took on a serious expression.

"But sometimes I go walkin' at night wi' the girl 'ere." She patted the dog's head as the shaggy tail whacked the floor. "Funny things sometimes go on in that 'ouse. One time saw somebody lookin' about wi' a torch. Looked in a winda' 'e did. Didn't wait round to see no more. And sometimes there's funny noises like 'owlin'. Gives a person the creeps."

"How long ago was that?" Nate asked.

"Long time." She took a biscuit and munched noisily.

Emma and Nate looked at one another and gave a slight shrug.

"What about the cousin?" Emma asked. "Do you see much of her?"

Miss Weatherby shook her head. "Poor li'l thing. Ran around like a monkey, she did, 'till t'others made fun o' 'er. Then Lindsey's mum locked 'er away and nobody seen 'er since. Poor l'l thing."

Emma and Nate exchanged glances. They weren't going to learn anything more.

"Thank you for your hospitality," Nate said, taking Emma's arm. "We'll be going now."

"Ye can come back if ye want to. The girl 'ere likes some comp'ny." Again the shaggy tail thumped on the floor.

"Thank you," Emma said. "We'll try."

They waved at the apple-doll face that watched them from the window as they walked away.

"Strange old gal," Nate said.

"She's just lonely. If we had more time, we could probably come again and ask her some more questions, but we would have to be specific."

Emma imagined poor Isabel running around the village frightening the other children. They could easily mistake her for a monkey. No wonder Lindsey kept her locked away.

"What are you thinking about?" Nate asked.

"Just wondering how we can help this situation."

"So do I."

Later they returned to Bellingham House. Nothing had changed. Lindsey lay on the sofa, a cold cloth on her head; Avery stood looking out the window, as if expecting someone; Amelia busied herself straightening cushions.

"Anything new from the police?" Nate asked Avery.

"Nothing. So far we have nothing, nothing at all." The man looked older than he had just a few hours ago. His walk was slower, his shoulders more stooped, but something about him bothered Emma. From time to time, he muttered to himself.

Guardian Angel, why don't I trust that man?

She turned to Lindsey who was now sitting up straight. "Was Isabel able to take her music lesson?"

"In a matter of speaking. Dr. Lunetti was very understanding and guided her through the scales, but she wasn't able to do much more."

"She's a very brave girl," Emma said.

Lindsey got up and paced, wringing her hands. "She keeps saying she wants to go to America with you. She believes there are doctors there who can help her."

Emma shook her head but said nothing. She knew it wasn't possible.

"Have you called about a security system?" Nate asked.

"You really don't have to go that far," Avery said in a condescending tone.

Lindsay straightened herself and said, "As a matter of fact I did make the call. The company is sending a man out tomorrow to tell me what would be the best type to purchase." Her eyes locked with Avery's for a moment until he turned away.

Lindsey motioned to Emma to follow her into the dining room. Again Emma walked up to the symbols above the fireplace.

"Do all the houses around here have these symbols?" she asked, running her hand across the rough oak beam. She quickly pulled her hand back, feeling some sort of vibration.

"Did you feel it, too?" Lindsey asked.

"Feel what?"

"The house sometimes sends out messages. If only I knew how to interpret them." She lowered herself slowly into one of the heavy chairs.

Guardian Angel, is everyone in this house mad? But I did feel something when I touched that beam.

The house has something to tell you. Listen carefully, her inner voice said.

"My grandfather restored this house to its original condition," Lindsey said in a monotone. "That's wattle and daub between the oak beams."

Emma ran her hand over the smooth white painted surface. It felt like plaster. "What exactly is this?"

"Oh, it was the only insulation available for centuries, a combination of a certain type of clay mixed with animal dung and horse hair and whatever they had lying around."

"You mean this is original, from the sixteenth century?" Emma found that hard to believe.

Lindsey nodded.

"It certainly is durable. Do the other houses in the area have the same construction?"

"Some do. The newer ones, of course, are built by present-day standards."

Emma sat beside Lindsey and took her hand. It was cold and trembling. "You didn't take me in here for a history lesson. What's on your mind?"

"I'm afraid Isabel is retreating farther into her fantasy world. This morning she told me that she and Annabelle are going away on a long journey, where no one else can follow. I have no idea what she meant. Oh, I don't know what to do."

Emma thought for a moment. "Perhaps you need to consult a psychiatrist or a psychologist."

"I would probably have to take her to London. Can you see her walking down the city streets?"

"No, of course not. What about Harlow or Cambridge? There has to be this type of service available closer than London."

"It would be the same thing, wouldn't it?" Lindsey closed her eyes and gave a long sigh.

"Why don't you lie down for a while? Nate and I will go back to Mrs. Rayfield's. I'll call you later."

"Yes, I believe I shall."

When Emma walked out of the room, Lindsey was still sitting in the chair staring at the blank wall.

I must ask her about her grandfather's work with roses, Emma thought. But this isn't the right time. And what had Miss Weatherby said about an orangery in the back? I believe that was what the Victorians called a greenhouse. I'll ask Lindsey when she's feeling better, though I don't have much time.

CHAPTER 19

"Oh, Mr. Sandler," Mrs. Rayfield called as Nate and Emma returned to the bed and breakfast.

"Yes?"

"A phone call came for you." She looked at Emma and frowned. "Someone was looking for a Mrs. Winberry. When I told them we had no one registered by that name, they asked for Mr. Sandler."

Emma felt her face flush under the woman's gaze.

Nate offered no explanation, just asked for the message. Mrs. Rayfield handed him a folded piece of paper, continued to stare at Emma for a moment, then turned away.

"Come on, Emma, let's go up to the room."

"She looked at me as if I were an imposter. What do you suppose she thinks?"

"I don't care what she thinks and neither should you." He unlocked the door to their room and walked over to the window to read the note.

Emma noticed a deep crease appear between his eyes. "What is it?" She hurried over to him.

"It's from your son-in-law, James. He says to call, no matter what time it is. There's been an accident."

"Oh my God! Who? What?" She sank into the nearest chair, suddenly overcome with weakness.

Nate was already on the phone punching in the numbers to the U.S. He tapped his foot while he waited impatiently for the connection. "James, it's Nate. Sorry, I realize it's early. What happened?"

Emma watched the expression on Nate's face as he listened, just interjecting an "Uh huh" every few seconds.

"We'll catch the next flight home. Goodbye."

Emma trembled as Nate cradled her in his arms. "Susan was injured in an auto accident."

"How bad?" she whispered.

"They don't know for sure yet. She's in the intensive care unit with a concussion and possible internal injuries. They're doing an MRI now." He shook his head and held her tight.

"I think I'm going to faint," she said as spots danced before her eyes.

Nate laid her down on the bed, put a cold cloth on her head, then called the airlines.

Through a fog Emma heard his voice: ". . . medical emergency . . . must get back to Chicago as soon as possible . . . thank you."

He turned back to her. "Are you all right?"

"I think so." She slowly sat up. The spots were gone, but she felt as though she were dreaming. Could this really be happening? Would she wake up soon? *Oh, Guardian Angel, help me.*

"Emma?"

"Yes." She shuddered and gripped the side of the bed. "I'm okay now. What do we do?" She looked at him through tear-filled eyes.

He sat down next to her and put his arms around her. "First of all, we think positive thoughts. You know how resilient children are."

She closed her eyes and nodded, visualizing the pixie face of the five-year-old, the blond curly hair, the sparkling blue eyes.

"You start packing while I go down and settle with Mrs. Rayfield. Then I'll call a cab. The plane leaves in four hours."

When Nate left the room, Emma went into the bathroom, dashed water on her face and went into action mode. She got out the

161

suitcases and threw clothes haphazardly into them. Oh God, Lindsey, she thought. *Guardian Angel, what do I do?*

Call her and explain.

Of course. She dialed the number and waited, sighing impatiently. Finally, Amelia Perkins answered. "This is Emma Winberry. I must speak with Lindsey. It's very important."

"She's taken a sedative and is asleep, Mrs. Winberry."

"Well, please give her a message. We've been called back to the States — a family emergency — leaving in a few hours. Tell her I'll call her from home."

"Yes, ma'am."

She's a strange one, Emma thought as she heard the disconnect. Didn't seem at all concerned about what the emergency might be. Oh, why do I bother with these odd people and their problems?

Because you have to, her inner voice said.

"No, I don't!" She closed the suitcases with a final click and was ready when Nate returned.

Emma felt disoriented when they arrived home. She looked at the clock; it was only a few hours since they had left London. Of course, the time difference. All the way she had thought of every possible scenario. Now she trembled as she heard Nate's voice speaking on the phone.

"Calm down, Sparrow," he said, pulling her down on the sofa and holding her shaking hands. "She's stable. They thought at first that she might need surgery, but aside from a mild concussion, a fractured pelvis, and a bruised kidney, she's all right. There's no internal bleeding."

Emma winced as he enumerated each injury. They all sounded so serious to her.

"Remember," he said, squeezing her hands, "children heal very quickly." He took a tissue from the box on the end table and dabbed at her eyes. "If you're not too tired, we can go to the hospital and see her for a short time. Stephen and Pat are there with her. The others were there earlier."

"Let me wash my face and comb my hair and I'll be ready." She gave a deep sigh and threw her arms around him. "I don't know what I'd do without you."

He smoothed down her unruly hair. "I'll always be here for you. I'm afraid you're stuck with me."

"And I won't let you go." She clung to him, then gave him a weak smile and headed for the bathroom.

■ ■ ■ ■

As they entered Northwestern Hospital Emma stared with a feeling of trepidation. She'd had entirely too many encounters with hospitals in the past few years. She saw an attendant wheeling a woman through the lobby, a cast on her left leg. A man walked beside her carrying a bouquet of flowers.

Happy things do happen in hospitals, her inner voice said. *And they far outweigh the tragedies.*

Emma nodded as she heard Nate ask for ICU. He took her arm and led her to a bank of elevators. Her legs felt like lead, as if she were trudging through a sea of mud. Neither spoke as they rode up to the appointed floor.

When the door opened Nate had to lead her by the hand. This wasn't real, wasn't happening. Any moment she would wake and find out it was all a dream.

Before Emma knew it her oldest son, Stephen, had his arms around her. She heard his dear voice, ". . . condition stable . . . out of ICU soon . . ." She studied his careworn face, dark circles around his eyes, three days' growth of beard.

"Oh Stephen, how did such a thing happen?"

164

"Let's sit down," Nate said. "I'll get some coffee."

When the three were seated, each sipping the bitter brew, Stephen told them the whole story. "Susan was just leaving the playground with a group of children. Two adults were there supervising. Suddenly a car, out of control, swerved around the corner and plowed into the group." He stopped for a minute, rubbed his eyes, and took another swallow of coffee. "One little boy was killed," he whispered. "Three others are here, one still in critical condition. Susan was lucky. She was in the back."

Nate shook his head as Emma cradled her son in her arms. "But she's going to be all right?" she asked.

"Yeah, that's what the doctor said."

"What about the driver?" Nate asked.

"He's in police custody, no license, blood alcohol level through the roof — the works."

"I hope they lock him up and throw away the key," Nate said bitterly.

"Oh they will," Stephen said. "There were plenty of witnesses."

"And the other prisoners will make him wish he were dead," Nate added, clenching his fists.

At that moment Pat came out of the unit and walked up to the trio, a smile on her face. She grabbed Emma and Nate's hands. "She's asking for a hot dog."

Stephen folded his wife in his arms and held her trembling body.

"Mr. and Mrs. Winberry." A smiling young man in a white coat, wearing a stethoscope around his neck, came toward them.

He looks way too young to be a doctor, Emma thought.

The older you get, the younger they look, her inner voice said.

"Your daughter is doing extremely well. We're moving her out of ICU and onto the pediatric ward in the morning."

"May we see her?" Emma asked. "I'm her grandmother."

"Certainly." He led Emma and Nate through the double doors and to a cubicle across from the nurses' station. The sounds of bleeping, the blips on monitors, and the occasional alarm attested to the struggle between life and death in this unit.

Emma's heart ached as she gazed at the tiny body, lost in the large bed, tubes snaking into her bruised arms, wires attached to the doll-like chest.

"Grandma," the child croaked, trying to raise her arms.

Emma sat carefully beside the bed and took the little hand in hers, then kissed the swollen cheek.

"A car came off the street," Susan lisped, a bewildered look on her face.

"I know, dear. Your daddy told me."

"It's not supposed to do that."

"No, it isn't. But sometimes drivers are not careful. That's why children have to stay far away from the street."

"My guarding Angel saved me," she whispered.

"That's what Guardian Angels are for," Emma said, swallowing the lump in her throat.

"When can I go home?" the child asked.

"As soon as the doctor says you're well enough."

Susan's eyes began to close and her hand went limp.

"She's under sedation," a nurse whispered as she adjusted the intravenous drip.

Emma hadn't even noticed her come in.

"We'd better leave," Nate said, taking Emma's arm.

"She *is* going to be all right?" Emma asked the nurse, needing her reassurance.

"She's doing fine. Try not to worry too much. Children recover much faster than adults."

"What about the others?" Emma asked.

"They're all stable."

All except the one who died, Emma thought. Those poor parents.

CHAPTER 20

When they returned to their condo, Emma collapsed in her favorite chair in the atrium. The adrenaline rush had subsided and been replaced by jet lag. She looked out over the lake and murmured a prayer of thanksgiving. Her granddaughter would recover. Her arms hung down along the sides of the chair and her head lolled as she dozed.

What about Lindsey Bellingham? Her inner voice asked. *Is she going to be all right? And Isabel?*

Guardian Angel, I can't worry about them. I have my own family to consider and my own life.

But she is *family. She's your niece, remember?*

Emma's brain could hold no more. Without another thought, she fell asleep.

"Emma, wake up," Nate's voice called through a fog.

"Huh? Wha?"

"You've been asleep for two hours. You're going to have a crick in your neck. Let's have a bite to eat and then we'll go to bed."

Emma rubbed her neck as she watched him carry in a tray with two cups and two cheese sandwiches.

"You are a dear," she said, feeling her stomach grumble. When had she eaten last? "What time is it?" Outside she saw stars twinkling in the dark sky. A sliver of a moon hung over the placid lake.

"Ten o'clock. I'm ready to hit the sack." He sat in a chair next to her and took a generous bite of his sandwich, a swallow from one of the cups and made a face. "Ugh! Warm milk. How can you drink this stuff?"

"It helps you sleep. I think it's tryptophan, or something like that."

He shrugged and finished the milk. "If you say so."

After their snack, they put the dishes in the sink and stumbled into bed.

When Emma woke the next morning she again felt disoriented. Where was she? The hands of the clock on the bedside table pointed to five. She went to the bathroom then climbed back into bed. Had it only been yesterday that she was in England? Slowly she recalled the events of the last twenty-four hours and shuddered. Susan would recover. That was all that mattered.

She lay there dozing on and off, visions of Lindsey and Isabel invading her fitful sleep. Finally, she swung her legs over the side of the bed, slid into her fuzzy slippers and quietly left the bedroom. She looked back at Nate snoring peacefully. I envy him, she thought. I wouldn't care if I snored, if only I could sleep like that.

The sun was just putting in its appearance as she started making a pot of coffee. She did some yoga stretches as she waited. I must get back to my routine. Getting stiff. With a cup of brew in hand, she padded into the atrium and settled down, trying to sort out her thoughts.

She looked lovingly at her plants. Claude had done an excellent job of caring for them. They literally begged to be put out onto the roof garden. She'd better call Claude and tell him they were back. He and Thomas were such caring neighbors. She knew they would be upset when she told them of the accident. She would call her other children, too — later. She heaved a sigh. All she wanted was to make her mind a blank and leave it that way. But that wasn't going to happen.

What about Lindsey and Isabel? Her inner

voice asked again.

What about them? There's nothing more I can do, even if I were still in London.

Perhaps there is.

Guardian Angel, sometimes you try my patience. I can't see the solution to every problem.

Oh yes, you can. You have the gift.

Emma let out a deep sigh and added *Call Lindsey* to her mental list.

When Nate finally woke, they had a leisurely breakfast and both agreed that this trip had been more arduous than expected.

"Well," he said, yawning, "now we can concentrate on the big fundraiser for the Midwest Opera."

Emma cringed. She had forgotten all about that. They had both made the commitment to help in planning this affair.

"With the way prices are skyrocketing, Midwest needs as much money as we can raise. James wants to add another production year after next, and you know what that will cost."

Emma simply nodded. "I wonder how Susan is this morning?"

"Why don't you call? Maybe she's been moved. We can go over there with a gift, something to make her laugh."

Emma immediately went to the phone and returned in a few moments, her face wreathed in smiles. "They're moving her now. Oh Nate, you have no idea how relieved I am."

"Come here," he said. He pulled her down on his lap and kissed her neck. "My Sparrow, your family is as dear to me as if they were my own." He patted her backside. "Let's get dressed and go shopping — see what's of interest to little girls in today's complex world."

When Emma and Nate arrived at the hospital, she with a new doll in her arms and he carrying a case of play cosmetics, they found Susan in a two-bed room on the pediatric ward.

"Grandma." She lifted her thin arms now devoid of needles and sporting only a few Band-Aids. "I'm all better," the child said.

Emma swallowed the lump in her throat. "I can see that. Look what we brought you." She placed the baby doll in Susan's arms and the child immediately began cooing and singing to it.

"What are you going to name her?"

Susan screwed up her face for a moment then looked at the little girl in the other bed. "I'll call her Sandy, like my new friend.

Sandy, this is my Grandma and Grandpa Nate."

A small bruised hand sneaked out from under the covers and waved.

"She can't talk," Susan said. "The doctor had to put wires in her mouth 'cause she was in a bad accident, just like me."

Emma flinched as she remembered her former neighbor, Tracie Adams, whose jaws had been wired after an injury.

Susan continued her chatter. "But she's all better now too, aren't you, Sandy?"

The girl gave a wan smile and nodded.

Nate bent over, kissed Susan's pale cheek and put the makeup case on the bed.

"Ooh — now I can be all beautiful. Thank you. Grandma, please help me put on some lipstick and look, there's paste-on stars, too. You can have one, Sandy, if you want."

And so the visit went, satisfying Emma that her granddaughter was on the mend. As they left the room and walked down the corridor, they ran into Stephen and Pat talking to the doctor.

"Thank you so much, Doctor." Pat held a list of instructions in her hand. She turned to Emma and Nate, her face beaming. "We can take her home tomorrow if she continues to improve as she has. Isn't that marvelous?"

"Yes." Emma sighed with relief. Suddenly she felt drained, as if the past week had sapped her of all her strength.

Emma procrastinated for the next two days. Her Guardian Angel kept nagging at her to call Lindsey, but every time she reached for the phone, she thought of something else she should be doing.

Emma Winberry, the inner voice scolded, *call Lindsey now. Remember, she's family too.*

With a reluctant sigh, Emma looked up the number, checked the time, and took the phone into the atrium. The lake was especially turbulent: waves crashing against the shore; no boats braving the elements. Was this some sort of omen? She punched in the number and waited.

"Bellinghams," a voice answered. She recognized it as Mrs. Perkins.

"Hello, this is Emma Winberry calling, may I speak with Lindsey?"

"Yes, ma'am, one moment."

Not a very talkative woman, Emma thought. Didn't even acknowledge that she knew me.

Lindsey's distraught voice came over the line. "Mrs. Winberry, I'm so glad to hear from you. What happened? Why did you leave in such a hurry?"

Emma told her about the accident and Susan's condition. "But she's recovering nicely, thank you. Went home from the hospital yesterday. It's such a relief." Emma hesitated before asking the next question. "Have the police found out anything yet?"

"No, they're still searching for clues and finding nothing. And I don't much like this new Detective Inspector. He asks too many questions."

"Isn't that his job?" Emma asked.

"I suppose, but some of them seem irrelevant. And he insisted on going over everything again, both inside and out. It was a bit disconcerting."

"Hmm," Emma said. That seemed a bit odd. Why send another detective out for a mere break-in? "Lindsey, did the first Inspector, what was his name, Allenby? Did he tell you to expect someone else?"

Hesitation from the other end. "Now that you mention it, he said he would contact me if they had any leads. Said nothing about sending another man out."

"Did he have proper identification?" Emma asked.

"Oh yes, I wouldn't have let him in if he hadn't."

I don't want to alarm her, Emma thought, but it sounds like overkill. "I suppose they're just being thorough," she said.

"Yes." Lindsey's voice sounded weak and unconvincing. "I suppose."

"How is Isabel?"

"She's so frightened, afraid even to go out into the garden. She misses you, too. She was somewhat relieved when the security system was installed. The man who came out suggested magnetically operated door and window contacts covering the first floor. There is also a panic button, connected to a central station that notifies the police. It does make us all feel safer."

"I'm glad to hear that. Be sure to keep it activated at all times," Emma cautioned.

"Oh I do, always."

Silence on the line.

"Is there something you're not telling me?" Emma asked.

"I received another threatening phone call this morning. This time the caller was more specific. Said Isabel is in mortal danger if I do not comply."

"But what do they want you to do?"

"It's very strange. First they asked for a quarter of a million pounds. When I said there was no way I could raise that kind of money, they said they would settle for 100,000 pounds."

"Hmm," Emma said. "They sound like

real amateurs. Professionals usually steal something of value, then ask for money for its return. Did you tell this new Detective Inspector all this?"

"Oh yes, but he's brushing it off. Says that as long as they have nothing to bargain with, I should ignore the threats."

Something about that didn't ring true as far as Emma was concerned. But, as Lindsey said, the police had nothing to go on.

"Have you considered selling the house to that American and being done with this whole affair?" Emma asked.

"I've considered it quite seriously. Uncle Avery is urging me to do it, too. And some money problems have surfaced." She hesitated a moment as if trying to decide how much to tell Emma.

"You see, I told you about the trust fund. It isn't earning as much as it did in the past and I will run out of money before long. I may have to seek some form of employment."

A warning light popped in Emma's head. Something sounded fishy. "Lindsey, what bank holds the trust?"

"Why do you ask?"

"Just curious," she lied.

"The HSBC, an international banking service. It's very reputable."

"I'm sure it is. Please keep me updated, and do be careful."

"I shall, and thank you for everything."

After Emma hung up she sat back pondering the situation. *Okay, Guardian Angel, what now?*

Don't trust Avery.

Is he siphoning funds from the trust? Emma wondered. I'd better ask Nate what he thinks.

While they ate a lunch of cream cheese and avocado sandwiches, Emma told Nate about her conversation with Lindsey and her suspicions about the trust.

"I wouldn't put anything past that man," Nate said, wiping cream cheese from his chin.

"Is there any way you can check on it?" Emma asked. "You have so many contacts in the business world."

He reached for her hand. "My dear, I was never involved in banking and these types of records are not easily available. Lindsey needs to demand an audit of the fund and how it's being spent: how much goes to household expenses and how much the trust is earning. Why doesn't she control it herself? I'm sure it was set up so that when she reached a certain age, the control would revert to her."

"That's a good question." Emma screwed up her face. "I'll ask her the next time I phone."

CHAPTER 21

Emma tried to resume her life and put Roydon on the back burner but her Guardian Angel kept nagging at her.

You must help Lindsey and Isabel.

How?

Go back. There's a way.

Nonsense, she thought, Nate and I are immersed in planning this fundraiser. He'll never consider it. She kept mumbling to herself as she rearranged the dust on the wooden surfaces in the living room.

"You're mumbling," Nate said, "what's on your mind?"

"Oh my Guardian Angel keeps telling me I should go back to Lindsey. I know it's ridiculous, but . . ."

"No buts," he interrupted. "It's out of the question. Besides the cost we have commitments, remember? Now put that active imagination of yours aside and come on. We're supposed to be at a planning meeting in a half-hour."

"You're right. I'll quick change and be ready in a jiffy."

As they closed the door to the condo, Emma heard the phone ringing but decided to let the answering machine do its job.

The meeting lasted inordinately long; members of the committee couldn't decide on the appropriate venue for the affair. After two boring hours the president made a decision and closed the meeting.

"I swear," Emma said as she climbed into the car. "Some folks make 'much ado about nothing.' I thought either one of those hotels would be fine."

Nate simply grunted. He was just as annoyed as she was. They stopped for a quick lunch then went home.

When they opened the door the phone was ringing again. "I'll get it," Emma said. She picked up the instrument and looked at the caller ID, unknown caller, probably someone asking for a donation. "Hello," she said in an uninviting tone.

"Oh Mrs. Winberry, thank God I finally reached you. I've been calling and calling." A sob, then a hesitation.

"Lindsey? What in heaven's name is wrong?"

"Isabel has gone missing!"

"What do you mean?"

"She was in the garden with Duchess, her dog, and now she's gone." She began blubbering so that Emma could hardly understand her.

"Calm down. Talk slowly and tell me what happened." She ignored Nate's questioning look.

After more sniffling, Lindsey continued. "Remember, I showed you the walled garden where Isabel spends time reading and playing with Duchess. She has just started going outside again since the break-in. Shortly after breakfast she went out and, when Amelia went to call her for lunch, she found the dog lying unconscious on the ground, the gate open and Isabel — gone." More sobbing.

"Did you call the police?" Emma asked, vaguely recalling the walled garden.

"Oh yes. Detective Inspector Allenby came straight away. He said that since the gate is open and the dog was drugged, it appears to be an abduction. The forensics team is still out there looking for prints and clues. Oh dear, I can't bear this."

What about the other Inspector? her inner voice asked.

"Lindsey, did the other Inspector come out with him?"

She hesitated for a moment. "No, as a matter of fact, I haven't seen him or heard from him since the first visit. When I asked Detective Inspector Allenby about him, he didn't seem to know who he was."

That didn't sound right, but Emma wasn't about to alarm her any further.

She visualized poor Isabel in the hands of strangers doing who knows what to her. She slumped into a chair.

"Is there any way you can come back here?" Lindsey begged. "I need you."

"I'll try," Emma said. "Call me in the morning."

Emma turned to Nate standing with his arms folded across his chest, his face creased in a frown. "Now what?"

"Isabel has been kidnapped."

"Oh dear God. That poor helpless little thing."

"I must go back, Nate. I simply must."

"We have the opera fundraiser to plan and my brother is coming from Florida. I have to see him. There's a serious problem with some of his investments and he indicated that there were some family issues." His brows knit together; his lips pursed.

She looked at him with determination. "I didn't say *we;* I said *I.* Please, Nate, let's not argue about this." Her eyes pleaded with him.

He blew out the breath he had been holding. "You are not going back there alone. You have the tendency to get into too much trouble."

"I wasn't thinking of going alone," she said, although she hadn't thought of taking a companion. "I'll ask Gladys if she wants to come with me."

"Well —" he hesitated "— at least she's grounded and level headed." Then he walked up to her and took her in his arms. "Sparrow, I almost lost you twice. I couldn't bear to go through that again. I love you and I need you. My life would be empty without you."

"Oh, Nate." She cradled his face in her hands. "My Guardian Angel won't let anything happen to me. I just want to give Lindsey moral support through this trying time. Now that I'm convinced that she's related, I feel obligated to be there for her, and she has no one else."

"She has Avery Wilkins for moral support."

"Humph. I don't trust that man. He rarely makes eye contact. I think he's hiding something."

"I know what you mean, I didn't like him

either. I'm sure I'll regret this, but I know how stubborn you are. Call Gladys."

Emma punched in the number and waited impatiently while it rang five times until someone finally answered.

"Hello, Gladys? I was just about to hang up."

"Don't be so impatient. I was in the bathroom."

"Oh, sorry. How are things out East?"

"Great. Am going to be a grandma again any day now."

Hmm, Emma thought, she had forgotten about the imminent birth of Gladys's third grandchild. They talked about family and Susan's accident and quick recovery.

Then Gladys asked, "What was the real reason for the call, my friend? I always know when you're holding something back."

Emma told her everything that happened while they were in the U.K. and then her rash promise to Lindsey. "I wondered if you wanted to come with me."

"God, Emma, if it weren't for the baby coming, I would love to go. But I promised to help. The other child is only two and is hell on wheels."

"I understand. Nate will have a fit when I tell him. He's adamant about my not going alone."

"I don't blame him. I wouldn't want you to go alone either. Can you get someone else?"

She heard the concern in her friend's voice. "Not to worry. I'll find somebody."

After the call, Emma paced through the atrium, the living room, the kitchen and back again. What would she tell Nate? Everyone she thought of had other obligations.

"I could ask Maria," she muttered out loud, "but she would attribute everything to the *malocchio.* It would never work."

How about Tracie, the girl who lived next door. The one you nurtured? Her Guardian Angel asked.

Tracie? Of course.

Yes, she should be out of school for the summer and a trip abroad would be a wonderful experience for her. She's the right person, I feel it. I'll call her.

At that moment she heard Nate's voice. "Well, what did Gladys say?"

"Her daughter's having a baby and she promised to help. I've decided to ask Tracie."

"Tracie?" His voice mirrored his surprise.

"Yes, she's been studying and working so hard that a short vacation will be good for her and she's a bright girl. I believe she can help." She gave him a disarming smile.

He simply let out a frustrated breath and shook his head.

CHAPTER 22

Isabel woke, dazed and confused. Where was she? She looked around the darkened room, a small amount of light issued from a window somewhere in the distance. She was lying on a mattress of some kind. Slowly she pulled herself up to a sitting position — light-headed, with stars in front of her eyes — then flopped back, breathing rapidly.

Her foggy mind tried to remember what had happened. Playing in the garden with Duchess. Something happened. What? Duchess lying on the ground — someone opening the gate — a hood over her head — rough hands — couldn't call out — consciousness slipping away. She looked down at her clothes. She was still wearing her jeans and the oversized sweatshirt with the Covent Garden logo that her music teacher had given her. She felt her arms — they were kind of heavy, but nothing hurt. She looked down at the long red hairs sprouting through the straps of the red sandals on her feet. Nothing had changed there.

As her eyes adjusted to the gloom, Isabel saw something resembling bars. She managed to raise herself off the mattress and hobble up to them. Grasping one after another she made her way around the entire structure. She was in a cage! Oh my God, what's going to happen to me?

"Help," she called, but her voice sounded weak, even to her ears. Would Lindsey and Uncle Avery be able to find her? Over and over she called for help until she fell back onto the mattress and cried in fear and exhaustion.

Annabelle, where was she? Oh, there in a corner outside the cage. "Annabelle, come here and help me." No answer. "Why don't you come to me?" Still no answer.

Voices — what were they saying? A door opened; someone switched on a light. Isabel squinted at the sudden burst of illumination.

"Well, it looks like our 'monkey-girl' is awake. I wonder if she can talk or just hoot." His cruel laugh made Isabel wince. "She's got clothes on just like a real person. Maybe we should take 'em off."

"Leave her be," another man said. "We're

only supposed to keep her here 'till we get instructions."

The first man didn't seem satisfied. He sniffed, then wrinkled his nose. "Smells like an animal. I wonder if she's got normal female parts."

His lewd laugh made Isabel cover her ears with her hands. But she had seen his face. Something looked strange, like ink spilled down the right side.

"Look at that red hair. It's all over her. Maybe she's got a red arse like some o' them monkeys in the zoo."

The second man grabbed the first one by the shirt collar and pulled him away from the bars. "I said leave her alone. Now go get her some water and something to eat. If she dies we don't get paid."

The two men left the room but didn't turn off the light. Isabel looked around. In one corner of the cage sat an old-fashioned chamber pot. A chair with a cane seat stood in another corner. The mattress was the only other item.

Like an animal in the zoo, she thought. That's all they think of me. Lindsey and Annabelle are the only ones who understand that I'm a human being with feelings and hopes and dreams that will never come true. And now even my friend is avoiding me. If only Aunt Emma and Uncle Nate had taken me to America with them, this never would have happened. I won't eat or drink anything, then maybe I'll die. That would be best — for everyone, especially me.

CHAPTER 23

After much discussion and a few minor arguments, Emma finally convinced Nate that she would be entirely safe.

"All right, but you'll call me every day. I'll get a converter for your cell phone so you can charge it over there."

She reached across the table and squeezed his hand. "You do realize that I must do this, don't you?"

"Knowing you, I'll never hear the end of it if you don't. But promise me you won't get involved in anything dangerous."

"I'm only going to support my newly found niece. You know that if kidnap victims aren't found within the first forty-eight hours, they're usually not found at all or . . ." She didn't finish the sentence. "Lindsey needs a life of her own. She's been as much a prisoner in that house as Isabel. I can help her work through anything that happens."

"If you put it that way, I suppose it's safe enough. But I'll miss you every minute you're gone." He put his arms around her and held her close.

"You'll be so involved with the opera fundraiser and your brother's visit you won't even notice my absence." She kissed the cleft in his chin. "And, I'll be back before you know it."

They finished their breakfast with no further discussion about Lindsey and walked along the lakeshore, basking in the morning sunshine.

Emma punched in Maria's number and was greeted by her cheery voice. "Hallo."

"Maria, *come stai?*"

"*Bene, bene.* Good to hear your voice, Emma. How was your trip?"

Emma had told her they were going to France and London. She decided not to go into details, just gave her the highlights.

"*Bene, bene,*" Maria kept saying.

Then Emma told her about Susan's accident and how their trip was cut short. Of course, the superstitious Italian attributed the accident to the *malocchio* and advised the child to wear a clove of garlic around her neck for protection. Emma kept agreeing with her, smiling at the image of Susan in the schoolroom reeking of garlic.

"Maria, is Tracie home? I would like to talk with her."

"*Si, si,* I get her."

A moment later Tracie's voice came through the phone. "Mrs. Win, how nice to hear from you."

Emma asked about school and if her classes were finished for the semester.

"Took my last exam on Friday. What a relief. Now I can work all summer and save some money."

"How about going out to lunch with me? I want to talk to you about something."

"Okay. When do you want to go?"

They made a date with no further explanation. Emma knew the girl was probably full of questions but she thought it better to explain everything in person.

As Emma sat on a bus headed for the north side of the city. She thought back two years when she had first met Tracie. The girl had lived in the condo next door with her aunt and uncle. Emma and Nate had helped her get her life in order. There was no comparison between the anorexic seventeen-year-old with multiple piercings on her face and body and the beautiful self-assured girl she was going to see.

Emma had purposely been vague about inviting her to lunch. She was eager to see what kind of response she would receive, knew in her heart the girl would jump at the chance to go abroad. Tracie had been living with Emma's dear friend Maria, but when she finished her education and had a real job, she had told Emma she would find an apartment of her own. She had casually mentioned a young man. How serious was it? Emma wondered, but she didn't pry.

When she reached her destination, motherly Maria threw open the door to the Chicago bungalow.

"Emma, I no see you in so long." She smothered Emma with hugs and kisses. "Come in, come in. Tracie is almost ready."

Maria fussed and led Emma into the spacious kitchen where every Italian family congregated. "Sit, sit. You want coffee?"

"No, thank you. Tracie and I are going out to lunch and I'll have some there." She read the question in her friend's eyes. It wasn't fair to leave her fretting and wondering. "I want to take her on a vacation," she whispered. "But it's a surprise."

Maria nodded. "Good. She works too hard, that one."

At that moment a lovely young lady walked into the room, her oval face framed

196

by shining brown locks. Emma remembered when that hair was three different colors, but that was another lifetime.

"Tracie." She got up from her chair and enfolded the girl in her arms. The anorexic body had filled out into a perfect female form. "You look wonderful."

"You look pretty good yourself, Mrs. Win." Tracie returned the hug.

They left Maria with Emma promising to come back soon for a proper visit. As they walked toward the bus stop, Emma turned toward the girl. "I have a favor to ask of you."

"Anything. After all you and Mr. Nate did for me I'll do anything you want. You saved my life."

"Don't be melodramatic, dear. You needed help and we were there, that's all. Let's not dwell on the past. Look to the future." She took a deep breath and looked at Tracie.

"I need to return to London and Nate can't come with me. So I want you to come as my companion."

The girl's eyes opened wide in amazement. "Oh my God! London. I always dreamed of going abroad but I never thought . . . when would we go?" Then her forehead wrinkled as she looked away. "But

I don't have enough money for a trip like that."

"No problem. All expenses paid." Emma grabbed her hand and gave it a squeeze. "I'll tell you all about it over lunch."

Just then the bus came and they boarded going south toward Water Tower Place. Emma could see that Tracie was thinking. Every so often she closed her eyes and smiled. When they were seated in a café, each with a sandwich in front of her, Tracie asked, "Can we see all the places I've heard about: the Tower of London, Buckingham Palace, the museums? How long will we be gone? What kind of clothes do I need? What is the weather like there?"

"Hold on a minute. I'll answer all your questions, but first, I have to tell you something about this trip."

The girl sat forward, listening intently as Emma recounted everything that had happened up to the phone call two days ago.

"Wow," was all Tracie said.

"So you see, it isn't exactly a sightseeing trip, but we will go to those places you want to see." Emma sat back. She hadn't realized she had drunk three cups of coffee and was feeling wired. She picked up her sandwich and took a bite.

"No," Tracie said. "It's more important

that we help rescue this poor girl. After all, you rescued me, now it's payback time. Whatever I can do to help, count me in."

Emma felt tears stinging her eyes. She was so proud of the way Tracie had matured and found meaning to her life.

"How long will we be gone? I have to tell them at work." She had a part-time job at the beauty salon where Maria's granddaughter, Connie, worked as a stylist.

"I'm thinking two weeks at the most." Emma sincerely hoped that would be enough time to clear everything up, one way or another. She shivered at the thought. "You'll need a passport," Emma said. "You don't by any chance have one, do you?"

"It's a funny thing, but I do. When I was thinking of running away, I took some money from my uncle's stash and applied for one. He never found out about it and I'm ashamed to admit it. But I wasn't thinking too straight back then."

"I understand completely," Emma said. "That makes things simpler."

"But the picture." Tracie rolled her eyes. "It doesn't look like me at all."

"I'm sure we can have another picture taken. Let's stop at the Post Office and ask. They'll be able to help us."

Emma paid for the lunch and they headed

for Water Tower Place where they went on a shopping spree and bought Tracie whatever she would need for the trip. Emma freely handed over her credit card.

"I'll pay you back," the girl said.

Emma gave her a look. "Don't even consider it. After all, you're doing me a favor, remember that. And, Tracie, don't tell Maria anything about Lindsey or Isabel. You know how she worries."

"Gotcha. Boy, what would my English professor think of that." They both began to laugh as they walked on to another store.

"Let's go in this book store and get a beginner's book on sign language," Tracie suggested.

"Whatever for?"

"The housekeeper's son who doesn't speak. My psychology professor said that when someone loses one of the senses, the others become more acute. If I study some signs, I might be able to communicate with him better."

"But he can hear and responds with grunts and scribbling," Emma said. "Now that you mention it, I did see him and his mother communicating with their hands. Perhaps they do that when they don't want anyone else to know what they're saying. Good thought."

"He may feel a kindred spirit if I can make a few signs. I'll bet he knows more than anyone else about what's going on in that house. Besides, I may have a deaf student one day and I should know something about the language."

"You're becoming a detective already. That's an excellent idea." She took the girl's hand and looked into her eyes. "I am so proud of you. You were on the brink of self-destruction and look at you now, becoming a regular Sherlock Holmes."

"I owe it all to you and Mr. Nate and I'll never forget that."

Emma blinked a number of times. "Come on, let's see what we can find."

CHAPTER 24

When Emma got home, Nate gave her a look she couldn't interpret.

"How was your visit with Tracie?"

"Great. She's eager to go along. The dear even bought a book on sign language so she'll be better able to communicate with the housekeeper's son. She thinks he probably knows what's going on."

"What makes her think that?"

"I don't know, something her psychology professor said. Anyway, she's excited about doing some sleuthing." She expelled a breath as she plopped in a chair. "I'm weary. We went shopping, too."

"I don't doubt that. Now relax a minute. We had a call from the U.K. while you were gone."

Emma sat forward. "Isabel?"

"They received a ransom note. Whoever took her wants 100,000 pounds or they're threatening to sell her to a traveling carnival."

"Oh my God." Emma sat back and visualized Isabel on display to a gawking crowd.

"I know," Nate said. "The thought is chilling."

"So they've made good on their threat. That's an indication that Isabel is alive, don't you think?"

Nate shrugged. "Who knows?"

Emma jumped out of the chair. "Come on, show me how to order airline tickets on the computer. I have to get back there."

"Let me do it." He walked into the study, Emma right behind him, and fired up the computer.

"Tracie will need a passport," he said. "How long will that take?"

"She has one, just needs the picture updated. We stopped and had another one taken. Her new passport will be ready in three days."

"What did that cost you?" he asked, eyebrows raised.

She held up her hands. "Only a few dollars."

"When did she get a passport?"

"I'll tell you about that later, now what's available in the next few days?"

Within minutes he had the British Airlines website up and began looking at flights. He punched in dates to check the fares. "You're in luck. If you leave before Memorial Day, you can get a better fare. High season begins around May 30. Then the fares go up."

"That should give us just enough time."

"Give me your credit card," he said with a sigh of resignation.

Emma handed him the card and soon the printer spit out the electronic tickets.

"I made it for two weeks. You might as well do some sightseeing. After all, Tracie has never been abroad. You know, this trip is going to cost you a bundle."

"Oh Nate, you are a jewel. I don't care about the money. And I promise to stay out of trouble. As I said, I'll just be there to lend moral support."

He grunted as she rushed out of the room to call Tracie.

Her next call was to Lindsey. "I'm coming back," she said. "Now tell me about the ransom note."

After expressing her relief that Emma was returning, Lindsey told her that the note had been slipped under the door sometime during the night. The authorities had examined it, but there were no fingerprints.

"By the way," Emma said, "What happened to the dog?" She was almost afraid to ask.

"Duchess is fine. She was drugged, not poisoned, thank God. Isabel would be devastated if anything happened to her."

When Emma hung up, she wondered if there was actually anything she could do to help find the girl.

Okay, Guardian Angel, you're sending me back there. I hope you have a plan, because I haven't a clue.

Just observe. The answers will come.

"I certainly hope so," she mumbled as she lay on the bed suddenly overcome with weariness.

Within the next few days Tracie had a new picture on her passport and they were packed and ready to leave.

Nate was unusually quiet as Emma bustled around the condo checking on last-minute chores and making lists. "Nate, do you have Mrs. Rayfield's phone number? I can't find it anywhere."

"With the way you're throwing things around, I'm not surprised." He walked into the bedroom and returned with a card, a little dog-eared, but the name and number were clear. "Here."

"Why are you scowling at me like that?"

"The more I think about this venture, the more unsettled I feel." He took her in his arms. "Sparrow, I really don't want you to go."

"Oh, Nate." She put her hands around his face and kissed his chin. "I must. Lindsey needs me and so does Isabel, if she's still alive," she whispered.

"I need you, too. I wish we had never gone abroad. Then you wouldn't be involved in all this."

"But we did and I am." She gave him another kiss and picked up the phone, punched in the country code and the ten digits. The answer came on the second ring.

"Rayfields."

"Mrs. Rayfield, this is Emma Winberry. My — husband and I stayed with you when we visited Roydon a few weeks ago."

"Oh yes, you had to leave rather suddenly, some emergency if I remember."

"Yes, but everything is all right now." She didn't want to go into any details. "I'm returning next week to do more research," she lied. "And I wonder if you have a room available."

"Oh dear, I'm so sorry. We're renovating, you see. There was a leak in the thatch and the entire roof needs to be redone. I'm afraid I won't be able to house any guests for quite some time."

Emma hesitated. She hadn't expected that. "Are there any other bed and break-fasts or inns in Roydon?"

"Oh dear no. You would have to go to Harlow for that."

"Thank you very much." She put the phone back on the charger with more force than necessary and turned to Nate.

"I heard enough of your side of the conversation, so what now?"

"I'll phone Lindsey and see what she has to say."

Again Emma punched in the required numbers and waited. She heard the double rings over and over until she was ready to disconnect.

"Hello," a harried voice answered.

"Lindsey? It's Emma. You sound distraught."

"I'm so glad you called. We received another letter with the same threat, only this time they've given us a time limit — one week. Again there were no prints and no way to trace it. I'm about at the end of my tether."

Emma heard an intake of breath and a groan. "I'll be there day after tomorrow, but Mrs. Rayfield can't put us up. Do you have any suggestions?"

"Why you can stay here, of course. Is Mr. Sandler coming with you?"

"No, he has commitments. I'm bringing a friend, Tracie Adams."

"Fine. I'll have two rooms ready for you. I'm about ready to sell the house to the American and offer those people all the money to get Isabel back."

"Don't do anything until I get there."

CHAPTER 25

Isabel retreated to a corner of her cage, sat on the floor and pulled her knees up to her sunken chest. She had refused to eat for the past three days, drank only enough water to quench her thirst. The smell of her unwashed body disgusted her. Only the full chamber pot sent out a worse stench.

She looked at Annabelle in the opposite corner, standing motionless, like a store mannequin. "Annabelle," she called, "can't you help me?"

No answer. "Where are Lindsey and Uncle Avery? Oh, Aunt Emma, why did you go away? Please come back and save me."

Suddenly the door burst open. Another man accompanied the man with the stain on his face. He wore a large brimmed hat pulled down over his eyes.

"This place is a pigsty!" the man shouted. "Empty that stinking chamber pot and give this creature a shower and some clean clothes. Then force her to eat, no matter what you have to do. She's no good to me dead." He slammed the door as he left.

His voice sounded familiar, but she couldn't place it. Isabel was certain she had heard it before.

Grumbling and complaining, the first man opened the cage and wrinkled his nose at the smell of urine and feces as he took the chamber pot outside.

When he returned he held a nightdress and a pair of socks in his hand. "Take off them clothes!" he yelled.

Isabel shook her head.

"Take 'em off or I'll rip 'em off ye!"

Tears streamed down her face as she obeyed.

"Well look at that. I never would 'a believed it. Just like a monkey." He laughed as he threw a bar of soap into the cage and aimed a hose at Isabel. The jolt of cold water made her jump, but it felt good to have a wash. She soaped her entire body and stood there being hosed down like an animal.

That's what I am, an animal, not a real person at all, she thought as her tears mingled with the water.

Obediently she dried herself as best she could with the rags he threw at her. Then she quickly put on the clean nightdress. She had to admit that it felt better.

Before long he returned with a tray of food. It smelled wonderful, not like the slop they had given her before. Shepherd's pie, her favorite, a glass of real milk, and a blueberry tart. She felt ravenous but when she began to eat her stomach contracted after just a few bites. She lay back and waited a while, then ate a little more. But there was no way she could finish everything no matter how much she wanted to. She did hide the blueberry tart under her cot. She would try later. Clutching her stomach, she lay on the cot hoping she would go to sleep and never wake up again.

CHAPTER 26

"Are we going to rent a car, Mrs. Win?" Tracie asked, her voice brimming with excitement. "I can drive." Nate was navigating the traffic to the British Airways terminal at O'Hare Airport.

"Heavens no," Emma answered. "They're all flip-flopped over there."

"Flip-flopped?"

"What she means," Nate explained, "is that the driving mechanism and steering column are on the right side of the car. And they drive on the left side of the street."

"That's what I said. It's all flip-flopped. And," Emma continued, "there are all kinds of signs painted on the pavement telling you to look right or look left. Your life is in peril trying to cross a street in London."

"Emma, you're exaggerating. It's not that bad, but there is a lot of traffic, and pedestrians do not have the right of way."

Tracie sat quietly, apparently digesting this

piece of information.

"Lindsey said she would have a car pick us up at the airport," Emma said to ease her obvious discomfort.

"You mean somebody will be holding up one of those signs with your name on it?"

"That's exactly what I mean."

"How cool is that," the girl said, sitting back and bouncing on the seat.

Emma glanced at Nate and saw the smile on his face.

"Now Tracie," he said, "I want you to keep an eye on Emma and see that she doesn't get into any trouble."

"I'm on it, Mr. Nate — Sherlock Adams." She began to giggle.

"We're only going there to be supportive, that's all. I promised not to get into any trouble."

Nate let out a breath as he pulled up to the terminal. "I've heard those words before."

"We're on our way, Tracie," Emma said as they settled in their seats on the jumbo jet en route to Heathrow Airport.

"I'm so excited." Tracie gazed out the window as the plane pulled away from the gate. "I have to pinch myself to make sure I'm not dreaming."

Emma felt a lump in her throat as she remembered her goodbye to Nate, the forlorn look on his face, the promise to call every day. She checked her seat belt and settled in for the seven-and-a-half-hour flight.

All right, Guardian Angel, this is all your doing. Now help us set things right so I can get back to Nate and my family where I belong.

You belong where you are needed, her inner voice said. *You have the gift.*

Pooh to the gift. I don't want it.

She closed her eyes and tried to concentrate on the task ahead, tried to "see" Isabel. Where was she? Was she in pain? Was she still alive?

Emma's head began to ache as she opened the book on her lap and tried to read. She thought about the obstacles that they were about to encounter. With a sigh she wriggled in her seat, but couldn't get comfortable. Next to her, Tracie was making motions with her hands as she studied the book on sign language. Emma looked over and glanced at a picture of hands pressing against lips. She leaned a little farther and read that it meant "thank you." So many different positions of hands and fingers meaning different things.

I could never learn that, she thought, but

Tracie is young and full of promise. She studied the beautiful girl, her smooth skin, taut and healthy, her luminous saddle-brown hair falling in a gentle wave across her face.

You led her here, her inner voice said, *saved her from a life on the street.*

No, I didn't. She paused for a moment. *But, perhaps, I did. And now I have to do the same for Isabel.*

With those thoughts, Emma closed her eyes, finally began to relax, and fell asleep.

When the plane landed at Heathrow, Tracie was bouncing with excitement. "We're really in London, Mrs. Win. I can hardly believe it."

Emma didn't answer, unsure of what awaited them.

By the time they retrieved their luggage and waited in the line through customs, Tracie was visibly tired. "Look at all these people."

"Yes, this is one of the busiest airports in the world," Emma answered.

She looked around for the driver Lindsey had arranged to take them to Roydon.

"There he is," Tracie said, jumping up over heads in front of them. "It says Winberry."

"Good," Emma sighed. "I'm beat."

They pulled their luggage over to a man who looked Middle Eastern. "You are Winberry?" he asked in a heavy accent.

"Yes," Emma said.

"This way, please."

He took Emma's roll-along and led them to the car park and the waiting vehicle. The two women climbed into the back seat while the driver stowed their luggage in the boot.

"You are going to Roydon?" he asked.

"Yes, Roydon."

"I take you there the quickest way."

The car lurched ahead as they fastened their seat belts.

When they pulled into the village, Emma remembered approximately where the house was in relation to the train station. She directed the driver to go to the left along a road that looked familiar. As they passed the high wrought iron fence surrounding the abandoned property, she again felt a chill and a sense of foreboding. Why? What was it about this house that disturbed her so?

Then the driver called her attention to the sign with the picture of Henry the Eighth. "Is this where I turn?"

"Yes, yes, go left." Emma felt that something about that old abandoned house might be important. She would ask Lindsey about it again. Then she spotted Bellingham House. "Pull up to the gate, right here."

He stopped the car, opened the boot and began pulling out their luggage as Davey, Amelia Perkins's son, came hesitantly toward them.

"Davey, do you remember me?" Emma asked as she alighted from the vehicle. She stretched her back and Tracie followed suit.

The boy nodded but his eyes were glued to Tracie.

"This is my friend, Tracie Adams," Emma said.

The girl held out her hand but Davey stood unmoving and continued to stare at her, his eyes wide, his mouth open. "That's all right. We'll get acquainted later." She grabbed a suitcase and the boy took another, following close behind.

Emma turned to the driver. "How much is the fare?" she asked, opening her purse.

He waved his hand and shook his head. "Already paid."

She took out a ten-pound note and handed it to him, knowing it was a long ride back to London. It was a good thing they had quite a few British pounds left. They would come in handy now.

"Thank you, thank you," he said removing the last bag. Then he got back into the car and drove away.

Emma grabbed the handle of the case, pulled it up and began rolling it toward the house just as Lindsey came running out.

"How glad I am to see you, Mrs. Winberry," she said, wrapping her arms around Emma.

"You've lost more weight, my dear," Emma said, holding her out at arm's length and looking at the sagging clothing, the skirt pulled tight with an old leather belt, the sweater drooping at the shoulders. "And I think it's time you dropped the Mrs. Winberry. It's much too formal. How about just Emma, or Aunt Emma if you feel more comfortable with that."

"Oh yes, I would love to call you — Aunt," she said.

"Good."

Lindsey turned to Tracie and extended her hand. "And you are Tracie. What a lovely girl, welcome. Come in, both of you. It looks like it might start raining any minute now."

The sky had been overcast during the ride from London. Now dark clouds, heavy with rain, made the early afternoon seem like nightfall. Tracie was all eyes as she walked into the house taking in the wattle and daub between the heavy oak beams and the old planking on the floor.

"Wow," was all she could say.

"Amelia, will you please put out the tea while I take our guests to their rooms. I'm sure they need a pick-up. Davey, help with the luggage."

The boy's eyes never left Tracie as he followed them up the narrow staircase, a bag in each hand.

"Aunt Emma," she hesitated for a moment, a fleeting smile crossing her face, "you may take this room." Lindsey led them into an airy room with a four poster bed, a chest of drawers and a wardrobe. A cool breeze from the open window blew the lace curtain about. "Davey, close that window. It's beginning to rain."

She turned to Emma. "I aired out the rooms for you. They haven't been used in quite a long time. The bathroom is down the hall." She led them to a medium-sized bathroom with the necessary plumbing fixtures. "I'll have to show you how to work the shower. I believe yours in the States are a bit different."

Emma gripped the woman's trembling hands. "Calm down. I'm sure we'll figure it out. We're here to help, understand?"

She nodded and walked into another room, a little smaller. "Tracie, you may have this room. Oh dear, the rain is coming in."

Tracie walked to the open window and closed it as a gust of wind blew in large drops of water. "This is just great," she said, running her hand over the ornate wardrobe. "It even has a fireplace."

"All the bedrooms have fireplaces," Lindsey replied. "When this house was built there was no such thing as central heating. We've since had it installed, of course. The fireplace in the sitting room is the only one we occasionally use."

"What's this little room off in the corner?" Tracie asked.

Next to the fireplace, heavy oak beams framed a narrow doorway.

"Oh, that's a priest's hole. It used to have a door on it but Grandfather removed it. We mostly use it for storage."

Tracie looked confused. "I don't understand. What's a priest's hole?"

Lindsey sighed. "Back in the sixteenth century monarchs were always declaring which religion their subjects could practice. When Henry the Eighth declared that the Protestant religion must be practiced throughout the land, Catholics, who still held masses in secret, had a concealed room in their homes to hide the priest."

Emma shook her head. "What fools we are. People have been killing each other in the name of religion since time began and I don't see it stopping in the foreseeable future."

With those words, a streak of lightning creased the sky followed by a clap of thunder that literally shook the house. The three women cringed for a moment.

"These storms usually pass rather quickly," Lindsey said. "As soon as you two are settled in, come down for tea."

"We will, and please don't fuss," Emma said.

Lindsey gripped her hand. "I'm so glad you're here." Then she turned and left the room.

Tracie ran her hand over the smooth wattle and daub between the heavy oak beams. "I can't believe we're actually in a house that's five hundred years old." She turned to Emma, her deep brown eyes wide with wonder. "If these walls could talk, I wonder what they would say."

"Some people around here believe that this house does just that."

"Do you believe it?"

"I don't know, but I do know that old

houses retain some vibrations from the past. Now, what do you think about Lindsey?"

Tracie's expression became serious. "That woman really needs us, Mrs. Win. I hope we can do something to help her."

Emma nodded. "So do I. Now I'll use the bathroom first."

After Emma tended to the call of nature, she went back to her room and wondered just what she and Tracie could actually do to find Isabel. She kept visualizing every possible scenario, one worse than the other.

Guardian Angel, you got me into this situation, now you had better be around to help.

CHAPTER 27

After Emma and Tracie hung up their clothes and splashed water on their faces, they made their way down the narrow, steep staircase to the parlor.

"Please sit," Lindsey said, beginning to pour tea. A tray sat on a small table next to the sofa. "You must be in need of some refreshment. Have some bread and butter and cakes." She set only a cup of tea beside herself.

Emma and Tracie filled their plates and enjoyed the sweet tea and the food. They sat back, each feeling the effects of the time change.

"It should be the middle of the night back home, right?" Tracie asked, stifling a yawn.

Emma nodded. "It takes a couple of days to adjust."

Lindsey sat silently looking at the floor.

"Now tell me what has been happening since the last time we talked," Emma said.

"Nothing. Absolutely nothing. The police still have not found Isabel, and it's driving me to distraction." She rubbed her face with her hands as if trying to wash it all away.

"No further communication?" Emma persisted.

Lindsey shook her head. "I don't know what to do. The week extension they gave us is almost up. I'm about ready to sell this house to that American and offer all the money to the kidnappers if only I knew how to contact them."

"What does Mr. Wilkins say to that?"

A deep crease formed between Lindsey's eyes. "That's the strange part of all this. At first he encouraged me to sell and now he's completely reversed his position. I don't understand him anymore." She rubbed her hand across her eyes. "He used to be such a caring person, but lately, a change has come over him. He's adamantly against my selling, but it isn't his house now, is it?" She looked up and, for the first time, Emma saw a look of defiance and determination on the woman's face.

"Why is he so against selling?" Emma asked.

"The same old excuse. He says the income from the trust isn't doing well, and this house is the only asset I have left. But I could live a long time on the proceeds from the sale, even after I pay off the kidnappers, and I'm certainly capable of getting a job if necessary. I've been thinking about it a lot lately."

Emma bit the inside of her lip and frowned. "Something doesn't make sense. Lindsey, why aren't you handling that trust yourself? Usually when the recipient reaches a certain age, he or she takes over the management."

"I'm beginning to regret that I didn't do just that. Uncle Avery convinced me that I had no knowledge of banking nor investing and he could do a better job."

I'll bet, Emma thought. Well, I might as well say what's on my mind. "Do you think he's taking money from the trust for himself?"

Lindsey looked at her through tear-filled eyes. "I don't know. It is possible. I've wondered about that very thing, been such a dependent fool all my life."

Emma reached out and took her hand. "Call the bank and ask for an audit of the money to see exactly where it's going."

"Can I do that?"

"Of course you can. It's your money. And, I suggest you don't tell Avery Wilkins about it."

Tracie had edged out of the room while Emma and Lindsey were talking. She felt that she shouldn't eavesdrop on this conversation and the dining room intrigued her. Emma had told her about the huge fireplace with the witches' symbols carved into the oak.

As she walked into the room she felt someone behind her. Pretty sure who it was, she turned to glimpse Davey ducking behind the door. "Come out, Davey. I won't bite you. I want to be friends, please?" She made the sign for friends, fisting her hands and interlocking the right and left index fingers.

Gradually the blond disheveled head peeked around the doorway and stared at her, a surprised look on his face. Tracie smiled and held out her hand. "Come on. I want you to show me these markings on the fireplace."

He inched over to the heavy beam and grunted as he ran his hand over the carvings. Then he began to sign rapidly.

"Wait a minute," Tracie said. "I'm just learning to sign. Maybe you'll help me."

He nodded vigorously and gave her a broad smile, his acne-covered face almost handsome.

"That's better. My name is Tracie and I'm here to try and help Mrs. Winberry find Isabel."

Slowly he shook his head, the corners of his mouth drooping.

"You don't think anyone will ever find her?" Tracie asked.

He shrugged and held out his hands, palms up.

"He doesn't know nothing, Miss."

Tracie turned to see Amelia Perkins scowling at her son.

"You, young man, are supposed to be working in the garden and tending to your chores, not standing about gawking."

The boy gave Tracie a forlorn look and ran out of the room.

"I'm sorry he's bothering you, Miss."

"No, not at all. You see I'm studying to be an art teacher and would like to learn to sign, in case I have a deaf pupil someday."

"Oh, he can hear, and he's not as dumb as everyone thinks, just pretends to be. He's got eyes like a hawk, that one has. He don't miss too much that goes on around here, and there's some mighty funny things goin' on, I must say." With that she turned and left a startled Tracie standing there.

■ ■ ■ ■

After a short nap, Emma and Tracie went out into the garden for a look around. The rain had stopped and the air had a fresh clean smell.

"What are we looking for?" Tracie asked.

"I have no idea, but we have to start somewhere." Emma shook her head. "Everything's overgrown. Look at that flower bed filled with weeds. This place has been sorely neglected." The gardener in her wanted to start pulling weeds right now, but that wouldn't help find Isabel.

They walked toward the rear fence. "Didn't you say they had a gardener?" Tracie asked.

"Supposedly he left in a hurry." Emma remembered what old eccentric Miss Weatherby had told her and Nate. Perhaps another visit with the woman might shed some light on things.

"Look at this vine," Tracie said, fingering a vigorous winding plant totally obscuring the fence, its tendrils reaching out for anything else to latch on to.

"Ugh." Emma frowned. "I've never seen anything like this before. It seems to be running wild and taking over everything it can climb onto. I'll ask Lindsey what it is."

"I heard you," Lindsey said, coming up behind them. "It's called Russian vine. Another name for it is the silver lace vine, although I can't imagine why. Grandfather was trying to grow a species that wouldn't be quite so invasive. He did succeed, somewhat, with the one growing on the sides of the house. We've been trying to get rid of this for years, but it keeps coming back. It grows wild around here and takes on a life of its own. It won't allow anyone to kill it." Her eyes were almost as wild as the vine.

Emma was examining the thick stem twisting at the base of the plant. "It's the size of a small tree; would almost require a bulldozer to dig this stuff up."

"I gave up long ago," Lindsey said in defeat. "We keep it trimmed back the best we can, but with the gardener gone . . ." She left the sentence unfinished.

"Over there is what's left of grandfather's orangery." She led them to a pile of rubble, mostly stone, broken glass and pottery shards. "As you can see, the vine is taking over here, too. It seems to be covering up the past." She looked off into the distance at puffy clouds floating across the sky.

As her eyes met Emma's, she heaved a deep sigh. "Perhaps the past should be forgotten. I think this place has become too much for me. Even though I promised Mum I would never sell it, I simply can't handle it alone anymore."

Emma didn't know quite how to respond to this. She, too, felt it was time for the woman to move on.

"Oh, look at this beautiful dog," Tracie said as Duchess came up to them slowly wagging her tail. Tracie stooped down and began petting and crooning to the animal. She was rewarded with a thorough licking of face and hands. "Good girl."

Duchess responded to the sound of the girl's voice and wagged her tail more vigorously.

"That's the most animated I've seen her since . . ." Again Lindsey wasn't able to finish the sentence. "Aunt Emma, what shall I do?" Lindsey grabbed the fence for support, the vine automatically twining around her fingers.

"Right now I want you to lie down and let me think. What did you learn from the bank?"

"They're going to look into it straight away."

"Good. There must be some explanation for everything that's been happening here."

■ ■ ■ ■

"Lindsey, Tracie and I are going for a walk around the village," Emma said.

Tracie gave her a quizzical look and Emma responded with a slight shake of her head.

"Are you sure you're not too weary from your journey?" Lindsey asked.

"No, not at all," Emma lied.

All right Guardian Angel, I am exhausted, but I'm relying on you to direct me to the answers.

As they walked toward the church, Tracie looked at Emma. "We're not just going for a walk, are we?"

"No, I want to go back to see Miss Weatherby."

"Who is she?"

Emma told her about her previous visit with Nate.

"If she didn't know anything then, what makes you think she'll tell you something now?"

Emma held up her finger. "That was before Isabel went missing. Things have changed drastically and it won't hurt to ask."

They walked along in silence, their brisk

pace slowing to a stroll. Emma gazed at the quaint houses, each with a well-tended flower bed, but was in no mood to appreciate them.

"Aren't you tired, Mrs. Win?" Tracie asked.

"Yes, I am, but we only have a few days. I don't know what the kidnappers will do when the week is up." She felt a shiver, though the warm sun had quickly replaced the rain.

"Wait a minute. We have to stop here first," Emma said, noticing the miniscule sign: *Baked Goods for Sale.*

"Hello," Emma called. As they opened the door a tinkling bell alerted their presence to the owner. Emma remembered the friendly rosy-cheeked woman from the previous visit. She came in from a back room wiping her hands on a tea towel.

"Afternoon," the woman said. "What can I do for you?"

"Do you have any cream cakes?" Emma asked.

"I just have these three. If you'd like, I'll wrap them up."

"Yes, please." She noticed Tracie looking at the plump cookies filled with raisins and nuts. "And I'll take two of these cookies."

"Oh yes, they are my best sellers. Three

cakes and two biscuits." She figured out the amount on a paper bag with a stubby pencil. "That'll be one pound, six pence."

Emma handed her a two-pound coin and pocketed the change. The woman thanked her and they proceeded on their way. She took the cookies out of the bag and handed one to Tracie. "For energy."

"Why did she call them biscuits?" Tracie asked, biting into the chewy confection.

"Beats me. Cookies are biscuits and I have no idea what actual biscuits are called, if they even have them. And, by the way, all desserts are referred to as 'pudding.' "

Tracie raised her eyebrows and Emma simply shrugged.

"They sure talk different around here," Tracie said.

When they reached the end of the village proper, Tracie turned to Emma. "Where to now?"

"See that overgrown path leading to the dilapidated house down there?"

"Uh huh."

"That's where we're going."

As they trudged through the weeds, their steps slowed even more, each overcome with weariness.

They finally reached the house and Emma grabbed the worn banister. "Be careful of that step," she warned. It slanted at a precarious angle. As she knocked on the door, the apple-doll face peered through the window.

"Who are ye?"

"Miss Weatherby, it's Emma Winberry. I was here a couple of weeks ago and you invited me to come back." She held up the bag containing the cakes.

The face disappeared and in a moment the door opened with a complaining squeak. A half-smile creased the sagging face when the woman recognized Emma. "Weren't expectin' no comp'ny," she muttered. "Might's well come in and sit for a bit." She was dressed in the same clothes with the Wellingtons on her feet. Emma wondered if she owned any real shoes.

Again Emma marveled at the contrast between the neat interior and the neglected exterior of the house. The old dog lay by the fireplace, lazily thumped her tail and let out a low woof. Tracie knelt beside her and began petting and crooning to the animal. The tail thumped harder.

"She's goin' blind," the old woman said. "Can't barely hear nothin' neither."

"Miss Weatherby, this is my friend, Tracie Adams."

Tracie stood and extended her hand. "I'm

happy to meet you."

The woman declined the hand and frowned. "What kind 'o name is that?"

"It's really Teresa, but I like Tracie."

"Humph. You young people always changin' things. But I 'ave to say you're a pretty girl and you got good manners. And the girl here seems to like ye." She pointed to the dog.

Emma handed her the bag with the cream cakes and noticed her eyes light up.

"Sit down and I'll put the kettle on." She lumbered out of the room rubbing the small of her back.

Emma looked at Tracie. "It would be rude to refuse. In this country, if you're not sloshing around full of tea, you're in the loo getting rid of it."

Tracie giggled. "Such funny words." Then she turned her attention back to the dog who had risen painfully from her place and plopped down next to Tracie.

After a cup of tea and a few stale biscuits, Emma looked closely at Miss Weatherby. "Something has happened at Bellingham House. Isabel has gone missing."

The woman took the news in stride. "Not surprised. Somethin' bad about that place."

"The kidnappers want a great deal of money or they threaten to send Isabel off to a traveling carnival."

"Might's well kill the poor li'l thing."

"We need your help. Did you see anything unusual, anything at all, or do you have any idea where they might be hiding her?"

Miss Weatherby sat back, closed her eyes and thought for a moment. "There were a big car went down the road 'bout a week ago. Girl and me was walkin'."

"What kind of car?"

She looked at Emma as if she were daft. "I don't know 'bout cars, but it were big, like one o' them foreign jobs."

Emma remembered the American driving an expensive green Rolls Royce, an unusual vehicle in this part of the country. *Guardian Angel, is he involved?*

"Did you notice what color it was?" Emma asked.

The woman screwed up her face. "Think it were green, yep, green."

"All right, that's good to know. Now can you think of any place where they might hide the girl?"

"Well," she hesitated for a moment. "Somethin' peculiar 'bout that big ol' empty house."

"Which house is that?" Emma asked.

"The big one wi' the fence 'round it, on 't edge o' t' village. Been for sale more'n a year now. Me and the Girl was walkin' of an evenin'. Saw lights bouncin' around, like someone wi' a torch. Was whisperin', too. Weren't none o' my business, so I turned around straight away."

"When was that?" Emma asked, sitting forward.

Miss Weatherby frowned and thought for a moment. "Some time last week, I think. Yep!" She slammed her hand on the arm of the chair. "It were last week."

"We'll check that out," Emma said, getting up. "And thank you so much. If you see anything out of the ordinary, will you contact us at Bellingham House?"

Miss Weatherby let out a frustrated sigh. "Now 'ow 'm I supposed to do that? Got no phone 'ere."

"Oh, that's right." Emma, now feeling the effects of the time change, was deflated by those words.

"So ye'll just have to come back and ask me now, won't ye?" She gave Emma a smug look. "And don't fergit the cream cakes."

CHAPTER 28

The following morning Emma felt disoriented and weary. *Guardian Angel, I'm too old for this running around trying to solve other people's problems.*

Lindsey is not other people. She is family. And you are never too old, you only think you are.

"Ugh," she said, struggling with the shower. "Now how in the world does this thing work?" Lindsey had shown her the previous night, but Emma had been too tired to comprehend. Finally, her efforts were rewarded with a spray of cold water. Emma cringed and drew back until the warm water began to flow. By now she was wide awake and yearning for a cup of coffee.

As she walked out of the bathroom, she encountered a bright-eyed Tracie.

"Good morning, Mrs. Win. Isn't it great? Here we are in England. I still can't believe it."

"I need coffee," Emma said as she sniffed in vain for the strong coffee aroma to waft up the stairs.

"We'll probably get tea," Tracie said, ducking into the bathroom.

Emma quickly dressed, made the bed and descended carefully down the steps. She found Lindsey sitting in the kitchen drinking a cup of tea and staring out the window.

When she heard Emma, she turned. "Good morning. Did you sleep well?"

"Yes, just fine. How about you?"

"I seem to be in some sort of trance these days. I sleep a few hours, thanks to the tablets the doctor gave me, then wake up to find Isabel still gone. I just want this nightmare to be over." She rubbed her eyes with both hands. "I miss her so much."

"I understand. I remember my feelings after my husband died. I'm sure you're feeling the same loss."

Lindsey nodded.

"Do you have any coffee around here by any chance?" Emma asked, sorely needing a caffeine jolt.

"I have instant. Will that do?"

Lindsey looked so eager to please that Emma didn't have the heart to tell her she disliked instant. For a woman who ground her own coffee beans, it was a poor substitute for the real thing. "That's fine." She sat down in a chair and tried to look alert. A couple of days to adjust, she kept telling herself over and over, just a couple of days.

"Here, I'll let you spoon in the amount you like," Lindsey said, switching on the electric teapot. Her motions were like those of a robot moving automatically from one spot to another.

Emma put two teaspoons of the dark powder into a mug as she heard the automatic pot switch off. Lindsey poured the boiling water into the cup. At least it smells like coffee, Emma thought as she poured in a generous amount of milk. She took a sip and smiled. It was passable, but barely.

Better get to the business at hand. "I want to ask you about that abandoned house down the road."

Lindsey appeared surprised at the question. "Oh, that's been for sale for ever so long. No one lives there and, obviously, no one wants it. It's terribly neglected and overgrown. That nasty Russian vine is taking over the place." She poured herself another cup of tea. "Would you like some toast? I'm afraid breakfast is rather informal around here. I haven't felt much like eating recently."

"I'd like some toast," Tracie said, walking

into the kitchen. She wore one of the new outfits Emma had bought her, a roomy sweatshirt over cargo pants with six pockets.

"My, don't you look smart," Lindsey said, a rare smile crossing her face. "You look like you're going exploring. It's good to have a vibrant young person around. I feel I'm absorbing some of your energy."

"Take all you want," Tracie said, a huge smile on her face. "I've got lots more."

"I'm sure you do. Tea?"

"Sure. Tea and toast sounds good."

Emma turned her attention back to the abandoned house. "Is there any way we can get in there?"

Lindsey thought for a moment. "An estate agent in Harlow has the keys, but the place is empty."

"I'd still like to have a look around. Something about that place intrigues me. Tracie, suppose we walk over after breakfast and do a little snooping."

"Great. I'll take notes."

"Whatever for?" Lindsay asked.

"Mrs. Win's friend is always asking her to write a book. Maybe she will someday."

Emma shook her head. "Her husband has a small publishing company in New York. I keep telling her that I'm not a writer, just a nosy woman."

"Inquisitive," Tracie corrected.

Emma smiled. She was so pleased with the progress the girl had made.

After breakfast, Lindsey took Emma aside. "I'm going into London this morning. When I called the bank, they asked me to come down and verify my signature on some papers transferring funds. I don't like the sound of it one bit. I can't believe a man I've trusted all my life would try to cheat me." Her forehead wrinkled into a frown, her hands balled into fists.

"Check it out. You must stand your ground," Emma said, patting her shoulder.

"You will be all right on your own for a few hours?" Lindsey asked.

"Don't worry about us. We're going to search around a bit, see if we can uncover anything the police may have missed."

"They were quite thorough."

"Still, you never know."

"Tracie, before we leave, I have to call Nate. He'll worry if I don't." Emma pulled out her fully charged cell phone and punched in the numbers. He answered on the second ring.

"Hi, Honey, it's me."

"Sparrow, I miss you already. How is everything over there?"

242

She told him about their visit to Miss Weatherby's and her noticing the car, but she omitted their plans to investigate the empty house. Better to tell him that after the fact.

"Lindsey's gone into London to talk with the bank about the trust."

"Good. It's time she managed that herself."

"How is the planning for the fundraiser going?" Emma asked, eager to change the subject.

"A few glitches, but then aren't there always? We couldn't get the singer we wanted but the program chair is checking on someone else."

"That's good. We'd better not talk too long. You know how much these transatlantic calls cost on a cell phone."

"I don't care how much it costs," he said, a wistful note in his voice. "I just need to hear from you every day to make sure you're all right. And don't fret, I'll pay for everything."

"You're a treasure, but don't worry. We're fine."

"You know I will until you're back here where you belong."

"Yes, and I hope it will be soon. I love you."

"Love you, too."

When she disconnected Emma felt a tug at her heart. She had caused Nate so much anxiety in the past few years. *What am I doing here so far away from him? I should be home.*

Finish the job, her inner voice said. *Then you can go home.*

A short time later, Emma heard the phone ring. She looked around for Amelia, but the woman was nowhere in sight. The persistent sound continued. *I'd better answer it,* she thought, picking up the instrument. *It might be the police with some news or a ransom call.* That thought made her cringe.

"Hello, Bellingham House."

"Hello, is Lindsey there?" a masculine voice asked.

"Not at the present. Do you care to leave a message?"

A hesitation, then, "Yes. Tell her Derrick Saunders called. I'll be in London for a few days on business. When will it be convenient to call her back?"

"She should be here later this afternoon," Emma said.

"Thank you."

When she put the phone back on the charger, Emma wondered who this Derrick Saunders was. Lindsey hadn't mentioned anyone by that name. Could he be someone involved in Isabel's disappearance? Anything was possible. She should write down the message but couldn't find a pen and paper. I'll remember, she thought, as she hurried out the door calling, "Tracie, I'm ready."

The girl was out in the garden romping with Duchess. "She's a great dog," Tracie said, running up to Emma. "Okay, let's go sleuthing."

Emma grinned. "You're really getting into this, aren't you?"

"You bet I am."

They walked down the road at a good clip, enjoying the cool, crisp early summer weather.

"I get the distinct feeling that someone is following us," Emma said.

"I'll peek." Tracie slowly turned her head. "I think it's Davey. He just ducked behind a tree."

"He's a strange one," Emma said. "You know he's smitten with you, don't you?"

Tracie blushed. "He's sweet."

"He stares at you like a moonstruck lover."

"Oh, look at this rose." Tracie stopped and buried her nose in an orange-red cabbage rose in full bloom. "I've never seen anything like it. Take a sniff, Mrs. Win."

"That's a prize winner," a woman said,

standing at her open door.

"It's lovely," Emma said. "And such a beautiful fragrance."

"I haven't seen you before," the woman said. "Are you visiting someone in the village?"

"Yes, we're staying at Bellingham House."

The woman drew back at the mention of Lindsey's home. "They've never had visitors before that I can remember," she said.

"Lindsey and I have recently discovered that we're related," Emma explained, giving the woman a winning smile.

"Hmm, how surprising." She frowned, then turned and walked back into her house.

"What a strange reaction," Tracie said.

"A lot of superstition surrounds that house," Emma mused. "When Nate and I stayed at the bed and breakfast, Mrs. Rayfield, the owner, said the house had a life of its own."

"You don't believe that, do you?"

"Of course not, but you know how gossip escalates."

They walked along in silence, the carefree mood replaced by one of foreboding as the vacant house came into view. Emma turned quickly. "Davey, come on out. We know you're there and we need your help."

The boy popped out from behind a bush

and loped toward them, a sheepish grin on his face. He whipped the hair out of his eyes with a toss of his head.

"Listen carefully, this is very important. I have a feeling that this old house has some clues as to where Isabel might be. Do you understand?"

He nodded vigorously. Eagerly he began to grunt and sign.

"Wait a minute," Tracie said, "Slow down. Remember, I'm just learning."

He smiled at her and blushed. Then he pointed to his eyes and held up two fingers. He put the thumb of his right open hand on his forehead and then on his chest.

Tracie bit her lip, trying to remember the meaning.

Davey repeated the motions, more slowly.

"You saw two men. Is that right?"

Another vigorous nod.

"Were they here, on this property?" Emma asked. She was rewarded with a grunt and another nod. "When?"

He opened his hand twice.

"About ten days ago?"

Another nod.

And Miss Weatherby had seen someone sneaking around and heard whispering. There was definitely something strange going on here.

Davey pointed to the house, then led the way. The front gate sported a new padlock but he led them around the back. There the old iron fence was covered with Russian vine, obscuring it completely.

The boy searched around, then found the spot he was looking for — an area where the vine had been cut. He pointed to a section of fence lying on the ground.

"Good work," Emma said.

The boy lowered his head, obviously embarrassed by the praise.

"The ground is trampled here as though someone has been going in and out." Emma scrutinized the area but saw nothing else. "Let's have a look in the windows."

Quietly the trio made their way through weeds and brush along a trampled path to the house. It appeared forlorn and deserted. Emma felt as if the house wanted to tell her something.

Guardian Angel, now I'm getting loony like some of the folks around here.

Listen. You know that walls absorb the vibrations of things that happen through the years, her inner voice said.

"Be careful," Emma cautioned. "If there is someone in there, they may not be friendly."

Davey bravely waved the women to stay

back and walked up to the rear of the house. He peered into a window at the side, turned and shook his head.

Emma and Tracie followed and tried the door, but it was locked. Cautiously they went around the entire house and looked in all the windows. Nothing. Then Emma spotted something on the ground. She picked it up to reveal a fresh candy wrapper.

"This would indicate to me that someone's been around here. But who?"

"It could be kids sneaking around, couldn't it?" Tracie said.

"Yes, but then it could also be someone else."

After thoroughly checking the outside of the house and the surrounding area and finding nothing more, they retraced their steps.

"Look over there," Tracie said. "More of that vine growing over a mound."

"The stuff is everywhere," Emma said. "We'd better go back now. I'll ask Lindsey if the police searched this house and suggest they go over it again." She sniffed and wrinkled her nose as they made their way back to the opening in the fence. "It smells like an outhouse around here," she said and thought nothing more about it.

Davey placed the fingertips of both hands

on his chest and rocked his hands in and out sideways.

"What does that mean?" Emma asked.

Tracie shrugged. "I have no idea."

Isabel listened — voices, very distant, but they were women's voices. Someone was out there, maybe looking for her. She tried to call for help, but no sound came. Her voice was hoarse from screaming and crying.

"Come back!" she croaked, as the voices faded in the distance.

Oh God, I never hurt anyone. Why are they doing this to me? Because I'm a freak. That's why I'm in this cage. Please, just let me die.

She looked in the corner at Annabelle standing there. "Annabelle, why won't you talk to me? You just stand in that corner. Sometimes you laugh at me. You were the only friend I had. Now I have no one."

CHAPTER 29

Emma frowned when she saw Avery Wilkins's car in front of the house. What does he want? She wondered.

Davey ran to the back and into the garden shed as Emma and Tracie entered the house to face Wilkins's scowl.

"What are you doing back here?" he demanded. His pursed lips caused the goatee to jut out at a forty-five-degree angle, giving him a comic appearance.

"You don't have to be rude," Emma said, pushing Tracie behind her. "Lindsey asked me to come back."

"Where is she?"

"She went into London." Emma's expression was all innocence. "Said she had some business to attend to."

A deep furrow appeared between his eyes. "What kind of business?" The strange goatee bounced with each word.

Emma had to control herself. The man

looked ludicrous. "I have no idea."

"She could have consulted me. After all, I am her uncle."

"I don't believe so," Emma said. "I was under the impression that you were a family *friend.*" She emphasized the word *friend.* "*I,* on the other hand, *am* her aunt."

Avery stood glaring at Emma, his hands twitching at his sides. "I hope she isn't doing anything stupid."

"That remains to be seen. I'll tell her you called."

Avery stormed out of the house and gunned his car as he sped down the road.

"He sure was mad," Tracie said.

"Hmm. I think he's afraid he's going to be in deep trouble if Lindsey uncovers any mismanagement of the trust." A smile lit up her face. "Now, let's search for that so-called hidden treasure."

The rest of the morning Emma and Tracie spent searching the library, the parlor, dining room, and bedrooms. Isabel's room was especially poignant: dolls, stuffed animals, pink ruffled curtains at the window. Dried lavender lay liberally sprinkled around the room, but a slight animal smell lingered. It appeared to be the room of a child, a child who would never grow up. Emma tried to concentrate, to connect with the girl. Where are you, Isabel? Are you still alive? That thought lay heavy on her heart.

"Since Lindsey is out, I think we should wait until she gets back to look in her room," Emma said, unwilling to invade the woman's privacy.

"Amelia," Emma called from the top of the stairs, "how do we get up into the attic?"

"Oh Mrs., it's too dangerous. You'll have to climb the ladder. What are you lookin' for?" She came slowly up the stairs, panting with every step.

"I have no idea," Emma said, "but we must rule out the possibility that the old tale of something hidden might be true. I thought that fresh eyes might uncover a clue."

Amelia shook her head. "We've searched and searched for ever so long."

"Still, I would like to have a look around the attic."

"You have to lay this ladder against the wall."

Tracie grabbed one side of the ladder and Emma the other.

"Then you climb up and push that door back."

"I'll do it," Tracie said, scrambling up the rungs.

"Be careful," Emma cautioned. She stood at the bottom gripping the ladder with all her strength.

"Okay, I'm at the top," Tracie said.

"Push the door back," Amelia instructed.

"Ugh!" Dust fell as the heavy wooden door moved on rusty hinges. With a shove, Tracie pushed it backwards. It hit with a thud. "Okay, I'm going in here now." The girl's head disappeared into the maw of the dark attic, followed by the rest of her body.

"What's up there?" Emma called.

"Lots of stuff. But it's dark and I can't see too well."

"I'll get a torch straight away." Amelia hurried down the hall and returned in a moment with a large flashlight. "We keep these around for when the electrics go out."

"I'm coming up," Emma called. She held the flashlight in one hand and handed it to Tracie when she had climbed halfway up.

"Give me your hand, Mrs. Win. I'll help you."

"I'm quite all right. Just get out of the way so I can get through."

"Oh, the phone." Amelia hurried down the stairs to answer it.

"Whew!" Emma dusted off spider webs

and shivered. She remembered the previous year when she and Nate had investigated the storeroom in the basement of the Performing Arts Center. Here she was, 3,000 miles away, doing something similar.

"Where shall we start?" Tracie asked, looking around.

"I wish we knew what we were looking for." Emma stared at the number of old toys, a broken hobbyhorse listing to one side, boxes with clothing spilling out and cast-off lamps and small tables. "Why do people keep all this junk? It's a fire hazard. Let's start by checking these boxes."

"There's a window here," Tracie said, walking up to a grimy pane. "I'll wipe away some of the dirt and maybe it'll give us more light." She took a rag from one of the boxes and began wiping away years of dust and dirt.

"Does it open?" Emma asked.

"I think so." Tracie turned a latch and pushed the window up, letting in fresh cool air.

"Here," Emma said, "prop it open with this piece of wood. That's much better. It's stuffy up here. If we pull the boxes near the window, we won't need this flashlight." Emma switched it off and began searching.

After an hour they had found nothing but

old clothes, some of them molding from an apparent leak in the roof. Emma examined the floor. It looked like the roof had been leaking for quite some time. Boards were rotted and she was certain that the water must be seeping into one of the bedrooms below. The house did need a lot of work and would certainly take a considerable amount of money to renovate. Perhaps Lindsey *should* consider selling it.

"Be careful not to step on those rotting boards," Emma cautioned. "They look like they might just give way and I don't want you falling through the floor."

"Okay, but I don't think there's anything up here, Mrs. Win." Tracie straddled the hobbyhorse, putting her weight on one side to keep from falling. She picked up an old doll with only one arm. "It's sort of sad looking at all this stuff. Once it was new and some child played with it."

"Look at this," Emma said, picking up what appeared to be an old ledger. She went to the window and examined the notations inside. "This must have belonged to Lindsey's grandfather. She said he was a botanist. These seem to be schedules of grafting of various rose species."

"Aunt Emma, *what* are you doing up there?" Lindsey's voice floated through the opening.

"Searching, but not finding much," Emma answered. She had had enough. "Here's a ledger that apparently belonged to your grandfather."

"Do come down and have some tea and bring the ledger. I'm sure it's nothing of any importance, but I'll look at it. I do have something to tell you."

"Tea again." Emma raised her eyebrows and smiled at Tracie. "Coming," she called.

Tracie closed the window then they carefully climbed down the ladder, closing the attic door behind them.

"I think you two need a washing-up." Lindsey smiled, looking at them with a shake of her head.

"Absolutely. We'll clean up and change our clothes and be down shortly." She handed the ledger to Lindsey and went into her room.

A half-hour later they sat in the kitchen sipping tea and munching on sandwiches and biscuits.

"Did you find out anything at the bank?" Emma asked.

Lindsey's face took on a pained expression as she pulled on her earlobe. "The banker showed me papers transferring small sums of money over the years. Only Avery's signature was on the transfers. You see, the way the trust was set up, either one of us could handle the money." Her voice caught in her throat. "I trusted him without question. What a fool I was."

"How much did it amount to in all?" Emma asked.

"One hundred thousand pounds." Her voice dropped to a whisper. "I can't believe he would cheat me like that. He was always so solicitous."

"Con men usually are," Emma said, remembering Nate's words. "So, what are you going to do?"

"I signed papers placing the trust in my name only, so the transfers will stop immediately. I should have done that a long time ago."

Emma toyed with the cup in her hand. "Are you going to take legal action?"

Lindsey covered her face with her hands. "I don't know."

"You should, you know."

Lindsey didn't respond.

"At least confront him with the theft."

"Yes. I need to think about this. Too much is happening all at once. I'll consider speaking with a solicitor, but now I need to have a lie-down." She got up from her chair and slowly walked out of the room, halting every few moments to grab something for support. Amelia took her arm and helped her up the steps.

"Mrs. Win, this is all so wrong. That man should go to jail." Tracie's face was set in a determined frown. "When people you trust turn on you . . ."

Emma knew the girl was remembering her own treatment at the hands of her own uncle. She took Tracie's hand. "We'll help her sort it out."

After lunch they sat in the parlor, each woman with her own thoughts. Emma was about to tell Lindsey about the phone call when she saw a car pull up outside, one she didn't recognize. She watched from the window as a short pudgy man with a shock of white hair and a mustache to match alighted from the vehicle and walked toward the house. As he came closer, she recognized him as the music teacher.

Duchess barked and wagged her tail as Amelia opened the door. "I'll tell Lindsey you're here."

Emma walked into the foyer and extended her hand. "Dr. Lunetti, how nice to see you again."

He scrutinized her for a moment, his mustache twitching. Then his eyes lit up in recognition. "Ah, the *zia* from America." He put down his package and gripped Emma's hand in both of his. "How is my *Bambina Rossa?* Is she well now? I bring her a present. I no get a call for a lesson."

"I'll let Lindsey explain," Emma said as she led him into the parlor.

"Oh Dr. Lunetti," Lindsey extended her hand, "I meant to call you, but so many things have happened that it slipped my mind." She lowered herself into a chair as if standing were too much of an effort.

Emma's eyes sent her a message — *tell him the truth.*

"I think you had better sit down, Doctor," Lindsey said, clearing her throat and sitting up straight.

His concerned look turned into one of fear. "Something bad happened? What?"

"Yes, something terrible. Isabel has gone missing. Someone took her out of the garden."

His eyes opened wide as saucers. Then he whispered, *"Madonna,* the *malocchio."*

Emma suppressed a grin hearing her friend Maria's voice saying the same words.

"What can I do to help? They want money? I got some. I give it for Isabel."

Lindsey's lower lip quivered. "That's very good of you." She stifled a sob.

"The police are looking?" he asked, his kind eyes filled with unshed tears as he turned from Lindsey to Emma.

"They're doing all they can," Lindsey said, knowing how lame that sounded.

At that moment Avery Wilkins burst into the room. No one had seen his car return. "What's going on here?" he demanded. "Why is Lunetti here?"

Lindsey addressed the music teacher, who seemed completely befuddled. "Dr. Lunetti, I think it would be best if you leave now. I'll call you as soon as we have any news."

"*Si.*" He handed her the package. "For my *Bambina Rossa,* when they find her." His voice broke with the last words. He pulled out a large white handkerchief and wiped his eyes.

Lindsey stepped back as Emma escorted the man to the door. Then she stood in the foyer and listened as Lindsey's voice took on a venomous tone that surprised even Emma.

"Avery Wilkins, how dare you barge into *my* house and insult *my* guests. You seem to have forgotten that this is still my house and under my control. And for your information, as of today, so is the trust fund."

He appeared to shrink. All the bravado had disappeared. He looked at her like a trapped felon with no way out.

"I made a trip to the bank and discovered something very interesting," Lindsey continued, her hands balled into fists. "Do you care to explain, or would you rather speak with my solicitor?"

"Lindsey, you're getting upset for nothing. This business with Isabel has unnerved you. You don't understand investing, my dear." He tried to take her arm, but she pulled away.

"Perhaps not, but I do understand theft. Now get out of my house. Call me only when you've made restitution." Her eyes blazed with anger; her face turned red.

"You'll regret this, Lindsey. Whatever I did, I did for your benefit."

"Explain it to the bank."

He turned and left the house with the little dignity he had left.

"I'm proud of you," Emma said, walking into the room. "I know that was a difficult thing to do." She handed her a tissue. Lindsey's heart-wrenching sobs broke Emma's heart.

"I've trusted him . . . all my life . . ."

Emma guided her to a chair.

"Aunt Emma, what shall I do?"

"If only the answer were that easy," Emma said. "I lived in an old house near Chicago for many happy years. I raised my family there and, after my husband died, I kept the house because it had so many memories. As the years went by it became increasingly more difficult to keep the place up — costly repairs, the garden, too large to handle, stairs to climb every day. When I decided to sell it, I realized that I took the memories with me. I have never regretted that decision."

"Then you think I should sell to the American?"

Emma thought carefully. She had to choose exactly the right words. "When Tracie and I were in the attic, we noticed the floor rotting from a leak in the roof. It must be coming into one of the bedrooms."

"Yes," Lindsey said. "It leaks into the priest's hole. In fact, some of the wattle and daub has softened from the frequent dripping. I must have it repaired."

Emma nodded. Now that she had her thinking, she persisted. "And the garden needs so much work it will take an entire team to set it right."

"Yes, yes, and as you say, the stairs, they're steep and treacherous."

"You don't have to sell to the American, you know. There may be other buyers."

"But the more important problem is, how

am I going to save Isabel?"

Perhaps you can't, Emma thought. "Don't make any decisions just yet. Think about it. The answer will come in time."

But time was exactly what they didn't have.

Chapter 30

Later that afternoon, the phone rang. Oh dear, Emma thought, I forgot to tell Lindsey about the call. I do hope it isn't more bad news.

"Amelia, I don't want to speak to anyone unless it concerns Isabel," Lindsey said.

"All right." She came back into the room with her hand over the mouthpiece to the phone. "It's Mr. Saunders."

"Derrick?" Lindsey's eyes lit up in surprise. "I'll speak to him." She turned to Emma and Tracie and excused herself, taking the phone into the library.

A short time later she returned, her eyes red-rimmed, as if she had been crying.

"I'll go up to my room," Tracie said. "Have to write a letter."

Lindsey sat, staring at an empty teacup.

"Do you want to tell me about him?" Emma asked.

She gave Emma a wan smile. "Yes, I

believe I do." Then she sat back and looked up at the ceiling.

"Derrick and I have known each other since we were children. His grandparents lived here in Roydon and he spent his summers with them." She smiled, as if remembering years past. "As we grew up, we became very fond of each other, in fact, we fell in love. Those were wonderful carefree years, running in the fields, holding hands, stealing a kiss when no one could see us." She blushed at the memory.

"Later, after Isabel came to live with us, Derrick asked me to marry him. He was going to Devon to become a hotel manager. He was full of plans and promises." Her pained expression touched Emma's heart. She took her hand and squeezed it.

"I knew Mum wasn't well and I was torn between my loyalty to her and Isabel and my love for Derrick. So, I refused his proposal." Tears ran freely down her cheeks. She sniffed and wiped them away with her hand.

"Some time later I heard that he had married. I was happy for him but devastated by my lost love. Can you understand that?"

"Oh, yes," Emma said. "One never quite gets over something like that." She hesitated for a moment. "Why is he calling now?"

"He's in the area and wants to see me before he returns to Devon."

"What did you tell him?"

"I told him about Isabel's abduction and how upset the household is. But I did ask him to come for dinner tonight. Do you think that was the right thing to do?"

"Of course." Emma bit the side of her lip as an idea materialized. "You know what, I think Tracie and I should have a picnic outside and let you two be alone."

"Oh no, that wouldn't be right."

"Oh yes, it would. Whatever he wants to say should be said in private. If you want to discuss it with me later, that's fine."

Lindsey pulled on her left earlobe. "Perhaps that would be best."

"Now, you lie down and rest," Emma ordered, "while I tell Amelia you will have a special guest for dinner." At least something positive is happening in her life.

Emma and Tracie sat outside in the cool evening air enjoying their picnic of cheese sandwiches and lemonade. Emma had insisted on preparing it herself. They were both getting tired of shepherd's pie and roast beef with Yorkshire pudding.

"Gosh, Mrs. Win, this tastes good," Tracie said, downing the last bite of her sandwich with a swallow of lemonade. "I really miss a good hot dog."

"So do I," Emma agreed. "I can't wait to get back to my own cooking."

"Oh look," Tracie said, "they're coming out."

A smiling Lindsey approached them, holding the hand of a tall, thin man. Emma looked into his rather plain face, deep blue eyes, a long nose, and a mouth just a little too large.

"Aunt Emma, Tracie, I would like you to meet Derrick Saunders."

"How do you do," he said in a soft melodious voice.

When he shook Emma's hand, she noted the firm, determined grip. Something about his demeanor inspired confidence. "Please join us," she said. "We've been enjoying this lovely evening. It makes me a bit homesick for my roof garden."

Derrick smiled. "I can understand that. I was just telling Lindsey about the house in Devon that I purchased last year." He turned to Lindsey with an expression that conveyed a message. "Perhaps when this nightmarish situation has been resolved, she'll agree to pay me a visit."

"I would like that," Lindsey said, "very much."

"Now I had better take my leave. You will keep me informed?"

"Yes, definitely."

He said goodbye and Lindsey walked him to the road where he had left his car.

"He seems nice," Tracie said. "Oh look, he's kissing her."

"Hmm." But didn't Lindsey say he had married? I wonder what happened to his wife? Emma pondered. "Come on, Tracie, let's clean this up and go inside. It's getting a little chilly."

Later that evening Lindsey knocked on Emma's bedroom door. "May I come in?"

"Of course." Emma closed the book she had been attempting to read. "Sit down here, next to me. Derrick seems like a fine man."

"Oh yes, he is." She sat on the edge of the bed and clasped her hands together. "Seeing him again — all the old feelings resurfaced, for both of us." Her eyes shone with a new luster.

"I'm glad for you," Emma said. The poor thing certainly needs something uplifting in her life.

"He told me that the marriage didn't work out. They divorced three years ago, no children. He's been busy establishing himself and now he's bought a lovely home." Her voice dropped to almost a whisper. "He said he still loves me."

"My dear, don't let this opportunity slip away again. If you do, you'll regret it all your life."

She nodded. "I know. He even said there would be a place for Isabel."

"That's very generous of him."

"Oh, my head is spinning. So much has happened so suddenly." She got off the bed and began to pace. "Do you think it's a sign that I should sell the house and leave? After we find Isabel, that is."

"Yes, I do Lindsey," Emma said. "But don't try to sort anything out tonight. You're exhausted. Get some rest and the answers will come when your mind is clear."

"I suppose you're right. Thank you for being here. You've brought out a part of me that I've suppressed all these years." She squeezed Emma's hand.

"You just needed a nudge," Emma said.

After she left, Emma sat back, rethinking everything.

All right, Guardian Angel, is it a sign? I do want everything to turn out right for Lindsey and I want to go home. But will we ever find out what happened to Isabel?

Be patient, her inner voice said. *It isn't over, yet.*

CHAPTER 31

The next morning Emma slept later than usual. When she ambled downstairs, she found that Lindsey had gone on an errand. Emma looked all over for Tracie, but couldn't find her. "Amelia, have you seen my friend, Tracie?"

"Yes, she went off for a walk with Davey. He's teaching her to sign. He's quite taken with her, you know." She gave Emma a rare smile.

I suppose there's no harm in that, Emma thought, but something bothered her. Why didn't Tracie wait for her?

Nonsense. She's not a child. She can go walking in this peaceful village if she wants to. Emma yawned, realizing how tired she still was. She ate a bite of breakfast then picked up her book and settled in a chair.

"What are you trying to tell me, Davey?" Tracie was totally frustrated by her inability to understand his signs.

He grunted and mimicked writing. Tracie took the pen and tablet she used for note taking out of her pocket and handed them to him. Painstakingly he printed something and handed it to her.

She squinted at the uneven letters. "I think I know what you mean. There's a root cellar or something like it near that old house covered with that awful Russian vine."

He nodded vigorously and made motions with his hands indicating a mound.

"Yes, we saw that. It's where I smelled that . . . oh my God. I know what that smell was — number one and number two."

He looked at her questioningly, obviously not understanding the words.

"Come on," she said, racing toward the old house, Davey close behind.

The sun was high in the sky when they reached the broken fence. Tracie stopped when she spotted a small panel truck driving slowly toward the gate. "Behind this tree. Hide." She grabbed Davey's hand and pulled him behind the trunk of an ancient oak.

They watched as a man got out, opened the padlock, then got back into the truck and drove through.

"Look," Tracie whispered, "he's parking

behind the house so no one sees him." By now she was trembling with excitement and — fear.

He walked over to the mound of Russian vine, not thirty feet from where they hid. Then he seemed to disappear.

"Where did he go?" The two crept out from behind the tree and spotted the trapdoor. He had pushed the vines away and pulled the door back. "We've seen enough," Tracie whispered. "Let's get out of here."

"What's yer hurry?" Rough hands grabbed them both, one by each arm and twisted them behind their backs.

"Ow, let go of me," Tracie yelled.

"Hey, Mort, there's two kids up here nosin' around," he called to his companion. In a moment the other one appeared from the mound of vines.

Where had the second man come from? Hadn't they noticed two men in the truck? By now Tracie was terrified.

"Well, what ye' know." The second man grabbed Tracie and held her while the first one took both of Davey's arms and twisted them behind his back. He grunted in pain.

"Don't hurt him," Tracie yelled. "Let go of us. We were just taking a walk. We'll go about our business and pretend we never saw either one of you."

"Oh ye' will, 'eh?" He laughed, but the sound was more of a growl. "Ye talk like a bloody American. And a purty one, too." He grabbed her chin and pulled her close. In the bright light Tracie saw the port wine mark streaking down his face.

"My friend will call the police if we don't come back soon and they'll put you both in jail." Tracie tried to keep her wits about her and examine the man's face closely. She was sure she could draw a reasonable likeness of him if she had to.

"Don't get cheeky wi' me, gal." He turned to his partner, "What'll we do wi' these two?"

"Let's toss 'em down there wi' t'other one for now till we talk to the boss."

"He ain't gonna like it."

"I'll get rope o't the truck and we'll tie their hands and feet. Hold this other one, too."

"Hurry up, 'for somebody sees us."

"Help!" Tracie screamed as loud as she could.

He slapped her hard across the cheek. Remembering the assault by her uncle, Tracie flew into a rage — stomped on his instep and kneed him in the groin.

"Ow!" He let go of Davey who pummeled him more.

"Run, Davey, run!" Tracie yelled. Within seconds the boy disappeared into the brush. The thug writhed on the ground as Tracie gave him one more stomp, then she turned to get away — too late.

The other thug grabbed her and twisted her arms behind her back. "Wildcat, huh? We'll see how feisty ye' are when yer down in t' hole." He shoved a rag in her mouth and quickly tied her hands and feet. Then he pushed her into the dark space, almost throwing her down the stone steps. "Cool off down there fer a bit." He closed the door with a thud and Tracie was left in total darkness.

Isabel crouched in terror as she heard voices and someone struggling. Were they here to save her? When she heard a body tumbling down the stairs, she trembled, then risked calling out.

"Is someone here?"

Tracie shook her head to clear her thoughts. She took a whiff of the animal smell and the odor of excrement. Her stomach lurched. With some difficulty she managed to spit out the rag.

"My name is Tracie," she said. "Are you Isabel?"

"Yes, have you come to save me?"

"I'm tied up. Where are you? I can't see anything." As her eyes began to adjust, Tracie saw a window almost obscured by the vine but admitting a tiny bit of light.

"I'm in a cage," Isabel sobbed, "like an animal."

Oh God, Tracie thought, what am I to do? Did Davey get away? She was just able to make out the bars and a huddled form behind them. "Listen, Isabel, if I can get myself over to the bars, can you reach out and untie the rope?"

"I'll try," the weak voice responded.

Tracie managed to roll her body over to the cage without too much difficulty. "All right, my hands are right up to the bars. Reach through and untie the knots." She felt the feeble fingers struggling with the rope.

"Hurry. They might be back any minute."

"I'm trying."

As Isabel frantically worked at the knot, they heard voices. Oh God, please make it be the police, Tracie prayed. But she knew it was too soon. Davey would be just getting back by now, if they hadn't caught him, too.

The door opened and Tracie was blinded by a flashlight shining directly in her eyes. Before she could react, she felt a cloth clamped over her nose and mouth, a suffocating smell, and soon, total darkness.

Emma looked anxiously out the window. Where were Tracie and Davey? They had been gone for quite a while. Amelia had a concerned look on her face, too.

Lindsey had returned and now paced back and forth. "This house is cursed," she muttered over and over.

"Here comes Davey," Amelia shouted, hurrying to the door.

The breathless boy fell into the room landing on his hands and knees, his breath coming in gulping gasps.

"Where's Tracie?" Emma almost screamed the words. Her mind conjured up all kinds of scenarios, one worse than the other.

The woman helped her son stand and hugged him to her, his tears and sobs soaking her jumper. "Now, son, calm down and tell me what happened."

Lindsey brought a glass of orange juice that the boy swallowed in two gulps. Then he began to sign, slowly at first, then faster and faster.

His mother grabbed his hands. "Slower, Davey. I can't read what you're signing."

He nodded, fell into a chair and started over while she translated as he went along.

"He and Miss Tracie went back to the abandoned house to investigate a root cellar there." She stopped for a moment as the boy hesitated.

Emma wanted to pull the words out but knew she was powerless. Was Tracie hurt? Had she fallen? Worse yet . . .

He commenced to sign again, faster this time.

"They saw a vehicle coming and hid behind a tree. A man opened a trapdoor hidden by the vine when another man grabbed them. They fought but Tracie was captured and told Davey to run for help."

She turned terrified eyes to Lindsey. "Oh Lord, call the police."

With trembling hands, Lindsey grabbed the phone.

Emma heard her words as if from far away. Tracie was in danger and it was her fault. She had brought the girl here. If anything happened to her, Emma would never forgive herself.

Guardian Angel, this is what comes of meddling in other people's business.

But it is your *business,* her inner voice reminded her. *Lindsey is family.*

"Aunt Emma?" She realized Lindsey was saying something. "Are you all right?"

Emma shook her head. "Yes, just shocked is all."

"Shall we go out there or wait for the police? They'll be here in ten minutes."

"If we go out there without proper authority, we might make matters worse," Emma said. "Let's wait."

Emma kept staring at the clock as the seconds ticked by. Amelia held her distraught son, telling him how brave he was. Lindsey simply stared at a blank wall.

Emma jumped as she heard the siren exactly seven minutes after the call. They ran outside and, in as few words as possible, explained what happened. The police took off toward the abandoned house.

"Amelia, you and Davey stay here," Lindsey said, "in case anyone calls. Come on, Aunt Emma, we'll follow in my car."

Emma needed no encouragement. She was out the door and in the car in seconds. She heard Davey grunting and crying, but his mother held him firm.

It took but a few moments to reach their destination. On the way Emma saw doors open and people outside staring, apparently wondering what had happened to disrupt their tranquil existence.

When Emma and Lindsey alighted from the car, a constable held them back. "You can't go any closer, I'm afraid. This is a crime scene and we don't want to contaminate it now, do we?"

They held their breath until the other policeman came up out of the cellar shaking his head. "Empty, but there's lots of evidence down there. Get forensics," he called to his partner. Then he walked up to Lindsey and Emma. "Ladies, I believe this is where they held the missing girl captive. There's a cage down there with evidence that someone or something has been living in it."

"A cage." Lindsey leaned heavily on Emma. "They kept her in a cage?" Her voice faltered in disbelief.

"Apparently they moved her along with the other young lady. I'll need accurate descriptions of both of them. As soon as we collect all the evidence, Detective Inspector Allison will come over to speak with you. If you have pictures of the missing girls, it will be a great help. Now you'd best go home. There's nothing you can do here. Let us do our job."

The women stood motionless for a moment. Then, in a voice she barely recognized, Emma said, "Come on, Lindsey, let's go back and . . . wait."

CHAPTER 32

Tracie's mind tried to sort out what had happened. She couldn't remember much. She and Davey had gone to the abandoned house. Yes, it was coming back to her now — the car, the trapdoor, the man who grabbed her, then — nothing.

Where was she? God, she was thirsty, would love a glass of lemonade. What was that sound? Whimpering. Then she remembered. Isabel, a cage, a rag over her face. She shook her head to clear away the fog.

He must have drugged me, the bastard. She was getting angrier by the minute. After the experience with her uncle, she had vowed that no one would ever hurt her again. And yet here she was, but where? She felt the ropes around her wrists and ankles, pulled with all her might, but they wouldn't give. The whimpering again.

"Isabel, is that you?"

"Yes."

The voice was so faint she could barely hear it.

"It's me, Tracie. Do you know where we are?"

"No."

"Are you tied up?"

"Yes."

Tracie tried to see, but the darkness was complete except for a bit of light coming from under what must be a door. She squeezed her eyes shut then opened them, hoping to adjust somewhat to the dark. No good. She would just have to feel her way.

"Isabel, talk to me so I can estimate where you are. Maybe I can get over to you and we can untie each other."

"All right. What shall I say?"

"Anything." Then Tracie had an idea. "Why don't you sing me a song. Lindsey said you have a lovely voice."

"I'll try, but I'm awfully thirsty." After clearing her throat, Isabel began to sing a plaintive melody.

"Good, keep singing." Tracie rolled herself over what felt like a hard wooden floor until she came up against a soft body.

"Oh," Isabel said.

"I'm here. Now let's see if I can untie you." She felt around for the girl's hands and felt hair. At first she recoiled but, realizing it was Isabel, began working at the knot. "Let me know if I hurt you."

"Go ahead. You can't hurt me anymore than I already am."

Poor thing, Tracie thought. She was all the more determined to free the girl and get her back to Lindsey. As Tracie worked at it, the knot finally began to yield. She pulled and pushed until her fingers bled; her wrists burned but she kept at it, ignoring the pain.

"There," Isabel said. "You did it. My hands are free."

Tracie let out an exhausted breath. She realized she wasn't quite over the effects of the drug.

"Let me get your hands now," Isabel said, a note of hope in her voice.

It took twice as long to untie Tracie, but at last both girls' hands were free. Quickly they untied their ankles.

"There." Tracie took the girl in her arms, ignoring the animal odor, and said, "Don't be afraid. Other people once shunned me, and Mrs. Win, your Aunt Emma, saved me. I'm sure she'll save both of us now."

Isabel nestled in Tracie's warm embrace. "It's so good to have someone with me. I've been alone for so long. Even Annabelle won't talk to me anymore."

Tracie stroked Isabel's hair and held her,

then realized they had no time to lose. "Come on. Let's see if we can get out of here." She crawled to where the light shone and touched the outline of a door. Cautiously she stood up and listened. No sound from the other side. She searched for a handle or a knob, but found nothing. She threw all her weight against the door but it wouldn't budge. They were bolted in from the outside.

Emma and Lindsey sat immobile listening to Detective Inspector Allenby.

"We found quite a lot of fingerprints that could be helpful in identifying the abductors."

"You said there was a cage there," Lindsey said, raising her eyes to the Inspector. "Did they keep Isabel locked inside?"

"I'm afraid so. But it was large enough to walk around in. It held a cot, a stool and a chamber pot. We found long red hairs on the cot."

"Those will be Isabel's." Lindsey's voice trailed off and her eyes took on a vacant expression.

"Did you find anything that might belong to the other girl, my friend Tracie Adams?"

"No, we didn't. There were some strands of rope left behind. Apparently they tied the girls before moving them. Also a cloth smelling of chloroform. These may all give us some clues."

"So you have no idea where they may have taken them?" Emma persisted.

"We're doing a house-to-house canvass of the village asking people if they saw an old truck or anything unusual."

"How do you know it was a truck?"

"The boy described it in sign language to his mother. Who in the village would own an old truck?" He directed the question to Lindsey.

She shook her head and pulled on her earlobe. "There are a few businesses that have small trucks, but everyone would recognize them." Then she thought for a moment, and remembered something. "I don't know if this means anything, but the American has been driving around in a Rolls Royce."

The inspector raised his eyebrows. "Tell me more about this American."

"I gave an accurate description to the other Inspector after the break-in," Lindsey said.

"Who? What was this Inspector's name?"

"I don't remember him telling me his name, but I believe I did tell you about him. He was rather brusque, said he was from Harlow. Come to think of it, I'd never seen him before and I haven't seen him since."

Detective Inspector Allenby frowned. "And he didn't give his name?"

"Not that I can recall."

"Did he show you his warrant card?" the Inspector persisted. "And was he here with a constable?"

"He did show me an ID of some sort, but I didn't look at it closely. And, he came alone."

The Inspector frowned. "I'll look into it. Now, tell me about the American."

"As I told you when Isabel went missing . . ." Lindsey wiped away a tear. "He has offered to buy this house numerous times. Wants to turn it into some sort of museum."

"Did you tell him about the National Heritage and their rigid restrictions?"

"I did, but he persisted. Said he knew how to get around such regulations."

"Where can I find him? Did he give you a business card?"

"Yes, I have it in my room. I'll get it for you."

While Lindsey was gone, Emma suggested to the Inspector that he might want to question Avery Wilkins, a family friend. She turned up her nose. "He seemed to be very chummy with the American."

The Inspector wrote down the name.

"He also embezzled a large sum of money from Lindsey's trust fund," she blurted out.

"This is all very interesting," he said, writing in his notebook.

"And Inspector, don't think I'm daft, but there is supposed to be something of value hidden somewhere in this house. Could all this be tied together?"

Oh Guardian Angel, have I gone too far? He's going to think I'm balmy.

"Is there any basis in fact to this so called hidden treasure?"

"No, just talk."

"Perhaps that's all it is, but I will speak with this American and Mr. Wilkins. One of them may be able to shed some light on all this."

"Oh, another thing I just remembered," Emma said, sitting on the edge of her chair. "I was visiting Miss Weatherby who lives off at the west end of the village. She claims to have seen a big foreign-looking car driving around recently."

"I'll question her also," he said, again jotting down in his notebook.

Emma bit the side of her lip. "She'll be more cooperative if you bring her some cream cakes."

He frowned and tilted his head to the side.

"She's a bit eccentric," Emma added.

Just then Lindsey came into the room with the card and handed it to the Inspector.

JULIAN DUNCAN
WORLD-WIDE IMPORTS

The address and phone numbers were based in New York.

"This may prove interesting. I'll phone his office and see where he might be staying. Now give me an address where I can contact Mr. Wilkins."

Lindsey gave Emma a questioning look, then gave the Inspector Avery's address and phone number.

"Thank you, ladies. I'll be in touch."

Amelia led him to the door as Lindsey turned to Emma. "You don't think Avery is mixed up in this, do you?" She grasped a chair for support.

"I wouldn't put it past him. I haven't trusted that man since I first met him and neither should you," Emma insisted. "Detective Inspector Allenby didn't seem to know anything about the other Inspector. He became noticeably upset. I think there's more to this other man than meets the eye. And Allenby knows it."

After the Inspector left, the reality of the

situation finally hit Emma like a fist. Her knees buckled as she sank into a chair. She was helpless and despondent, worried about Isabel and Tracie. Oh why did I ever come here?

CHAPTER 33

The ringing phone made both women jump. They heard Amelia's voice answering.

"Mrs. Winberry," she called, "it's for you."

"Me?" Oh my God, I forgot to call Nate. What shall I tell him?

Tell him the truth, her inner voice said.

She made a face as she took the phone. "Hello," she answered in a voice as controlled as she could muster.

"Emma, why haven't you called me?" Nate's irate voice came over the line.

"Oh Nate, there's been some trouble."

"I knew it. The minute I let you out of my sight something happens. Tell me."

She took a deep breath, eased herself into a chair and, in a halting voice, told him the whole story, even about Tracie being missing.

"I don't know what to say," he answered. "If my brother weren't coming tomorrow, I would come over there on the next flight."

291

"No, no, the police are working on it and there's nothing any of us can do but wait."

"Have there been any more calls from the kidnappers?" he asked.

"None." Then Emma thought of something. "There's one thing you can do, though."

"Name it."

"See what you can find out about World-Wide Imports, Julian Duncan owner; that's the American's business." She gave him the address and phone number of the New York office. She had the foresight to copy it from the business card before Lindsey handed it to the Inspector.

"That's the man we saw sleepwalking *au naturel* at the hotel, right?"

"Yes." Then she remembered something else. "Didn't you write down the license plate on his fancy Rolls Royce the first time we were here?"

"Come to think of it, I did. Hang on a minute, I'll find my notebook."

"Lindsey," Emma said, "quick, give me a piece of paper and a pen."

"I'm back," Nate said as Emma positioned a notepad on her lap.

"Okay, let's have it."

He read off the plate number and Emma copied it down. She read it back to him. "I think the police should have this. Now try not to worry too much. I'm doing enough of that for both of us. The worst part is the feeling of helplessness. If I could only do something."

Nate let out a frustrated sigh.

"I promise to call you tomorrow with a progress report."

"And don't you forget."

After they said goodbye, Emma showed the license plate number to Lindsey.

"Brilliant," she said.

"Call Detective Inspector Allenby and give him that number," Emma said. "He may be able to pull it up and see if there has been any trouble in the past."

While Lindsey made the call, Emma went out in the garden. It was a perfect evening, the sky filled with stars, a full moon casting shadows on the bushes. I should be enjoying this but my heart feels like a lead weight in my chest, she thought. She walked around as if in a trance trying to get her emotions under control and her thoughts in order.

That American keeps flaunting his expensive car around the village. He seems to be sending a message saying I can buy anything I want. But I don't think he would be so blatant if he were the kidnapper. I believe someone else has the girls. Julian Duncan certainly doesn't seem to need the money. No, he wants the house for some other reason. Perhaps there really is something of value hidden here.

Tracie, where are you? Are you hurt? Are you and Isabel together? She tried desperately to make some connection with the girls.

Oh Guardian Angel, what am I to do? Are they safe? She sat on a lawn chair and dropped her head in her hands.

They are not far away, her inner voice said.

But where?

Have faith. It won't be long.

Emma wasn't sure just exactly what that was supposed to mean, but it did give her some comfort.

"I think we're in some sort of storage shed," Tracie said. Since she was wearing cargo pants, she had pocketed certain items she thought might be useful: a pad of paper and pen, a candy bar and a penlight. She had forgotten about that. She pulled it out of her pocket with trembling fingers, clicked it on, and shone it around. A small animal scurried from a corner and burrowed into a straw bale in another corner. Tracie ignored the fact that it might be a rat. They had to find a way out.

In another corner Isabel crouched, her head in her hands. She raised it to the light. "You have a torch," she said.

"Yeah. Look, there are some tools in here." Tracie ignored her burning wrists, sore from the ropes, and began assessing what might be useful. She felt something furry touch her hand and jumped. Then she realized it was Isabel. She put her arm around the girl and gave her a hug.

"Sorry. I guess I'm a bit jumpy. Here's a broken hoe. Might be a good weapon." She put it aside. "And here's a screwdriver." Tracie examined the old tool. The tip was partly broken off, but still usable. "Maybe we can loosen the hinges on that door. Here, hold the light." She hurried to the door and tried to fit it into the slot of one of the rusted screws.

"Hold that light closer so I can see." The slot was crusted with something that Tracie would rather not identify. She scraped it out until she could fit the tip of the screwdriver in. But no matter how hard she turned, the screw didn't budge. It was rusted in solid.

She let out a frustrated breath. "We need some WD-40."

"What's that?" Isabel asked.

"Oh, it's something we use in the States to loosen rust, but, since we don't have any, we'll have to think of something else." Tracie took the light from Isabel and began examining the boards of the shed.

"What are you looking for?" Isabel asked.

"I'm not sure. This place looks pretty old. Maybe some of these boards are rotted and we might be able to kick them out."

"You're so clever." The girl joined Tracie in the search. "The ones at the bottom are more likely to rot because of the moisture."

"Now you're the clever one," Tracie said, getting down on her hands and knees and working her way around the shed.

"Here's one," she said excitedly. "Hand me that old hoe and I'll try to knock it loose."

For the next half-hour Tracie pounded with the hoe and kicked at the board with her foot until she finally managed to free one end. "Now we're getting somewhere." She worked with renewed vigor but only managed to free that one board. The others held tight. It seemed hopeless.

"At least we can see outside." She looked out at the blackness of the night: no stars, no moon, no sounds.

Isabel grasped her hand. "The only good thing that's happened in all this is meeting you. I wish you would never leave me." Then she began to sob.

Tracie couldn't say a word. She held her for a long time, then they split the candy bar and curled up against the bale of straw, neither caring whether there were rodents inside. They soon fell into an exhausted sleep.

Emma was beside herself with worry. She had brought Tracie to the U.K. for an adventure and led her right into danger.

Lindsey sat listlessly in a chair in the corner of the parlor. Neither of them had eaten much dinner.

"Lindsey," Emma said, "I've been thinking. The American doesn't need your money and he certainly doesn't want this house for a museum. He has another agenda."

"Do you think he kidnapped Isabel to coerce me into selling him the house?" Lindsey said. "I've asked myself that over and over."

Emma shook her head. "I don't think so. If he had, why would he drive that expensive car around the village. I'm sure everyone has seen it by now. No, someone else took Isabel."

"But how do we find her? The police seem to be getting nowhere. They haven't been able to trace the phone calls. Each time the call comes from a different train station."

"Aren't there security cameras in those stations?" Emma asked.

"Oh yes, but the caller is careful to stand away from the camera. All they can say is that it appears to be a man."

Lindsey got up and began to pace, wringing her hands. "If I do sell the house to the American I can give the money to the kidnappers and get Isabel back."

"And then what?" Emma asked. "Where would you go?"

"Well, Derrick did say he wants me to come to Devon and would find a place for Isabel."

"What did he mean by 'find a place'?"

Lindsey sighed. "Oh I don't know, but it's some hope, isn't it?"

Emma nodded.

Lindsey didn't seem able to tolerate much more as she crumpled into a chair and held her head in her hands.

Emma put her hands on the woman's shoulders and began to massage the tense muscles.

"Oh, that feels good."

"I've been thinking about something," Emma said. "The last time you talked with Detective Sergeant Allenby did he say anything more about the detective who came after the break-in?"

"No, and when I asked, he was evasive, as if he didn't want to discuss it."

"Hmm." Emma thought for a moment. "You said he was very thorough in searching the house, particularly Isabel's room."

"Yes. What are you thinking?"

"Just wondering who the other officer really is and if he might be involved."

CHAPTER 34

Tracie opened her eyes and felt disoriented. Was this a teddy bear in her arms? She shook her head as the memories of the past twenty-four hours came flooding back. She lay paralyzed with fear. Then she saw the light sneaking in from the board she had kicked loose. She looked down at the sleeping figure cuddled next to her. The heart-shaped face resembled a porcelain doll but the hair surrounding it destroyed the illusion. A strong animal smell filled her nostrils.

"Poor little thing," she whispered. What cruel fate had destined this helpless girl to live her life as a freak? I have to be strong for her, but I'm scared, really scared.

What was that crackling sound? Tracie looked around and saw something move. A mouse had found the discarded candy wrapper and was pulling it into the bale of straw. She shuddered.

I can't let Isabel know how frightened I am. Have to keep her from freaking out on me. We have to get out of here before those thugs come back.

"Isabel, wake up. It's morning and we've got to find a way out of here."

Isabel rubbed her eyes and stared at Tracie. "Don't let them get me," she pleaded. She sneezed and began to cough, followed by a groan.

"Come on, let's try and knock out more boards." Tracie grabbed the hoe and pounded on another board while Isabel yelled out the opening for help until her voice gave out.

After a futile attempt, Tracie dropped the tool. "It's no use." Then she put her finger to her lips and listened. "Somebody's coming."

"Oh no, they're back," Isabel sobbed as she coughed again.

"No, I hear a dog barking." A wet nose pushed through the opening and snuffled. "Help!" Tracie shouted.

"Oo's in there?" a strange voice asked.

"We're being held prisoner. Please let us out."

They heard someone fiddling with the lock on the door.

"Can't open it. Got to get me shotgun."

301

"Wait!" Tracie yelled. "Please, call the police!" She flipped onto her stomach and looked out the opening to see an old woman lumbering away followed by a dog. "She's walking away, but at least someone knows we're here."

"Did she say shotgun?" Isabel asked, clutching Tracie's arm.

"I think so. Oh, if she can only get back here in time." Something about the woman seemed familiar. She sounded like Miss Weatherby, but Tracie wasn't quite sure. Her mind was still in a fog.

"I'm so thirsty," Isabel said.

"Me too, and hungry."

"And my throat is sore," Isabel whined.

"I hope you're not getting sick." Tracie touched Isabel's face and forehead. "You feel kind of warm." She put her arms around the girl in an attempt to comfort her, but Tracie became more anxious as the minutes passed.

After what seemed like hours they heard the dog barking again. "I think she's back," Tracie said, looking out the hole.

"A'right now. Stand away from t' door. I'm gonna shoot off t' lock," the old woman said.

The girls crouched in a far corner and covered their ears with their hands. A shot rang out and clanged against the lock, shaking the shed, followed by a second one. Then silence. Tracie and Isabel didn't move. The smell of gunpowder filled the small room. They looked up as the door swung open and a wizened old woman, wearing a headscarf, stood there holding a huge gun. It was Miss Weatherby. Tracie was sure of it.

"Well, come out. What ye waitin' fer? That's what ye wanted, ain't it?"

The girls scampered outside and breathed in the fresh air. "We have to get away before those two men come back," Tracie said.

"Come on. In the woods. I'll hide ye."

None too soon they hid in a wooded area covered with more Russian vine. They watched as an old truck pulled up to the shed. The woman motioned to the dog to be quiet. Tracie shivered as she saw two men jump out and examine the lock.

"Damn!" one of them shouted. "They're gone. We ain't gonna get paid if they get away. They're probly headed fer the village. Let's head 'em off." They jumped back into the truck and sped down the road.

Tracie's heart thudded against her chest so hard she was sure the others could hear it.

"Miss Weatherby? You are Miss Weatherby, aren't you?"

The woman looked at Tracie with a critical eye but didn't acknowledge her. "Come wi' me," she said, leading them through the thick woods to a small house set back from the main road.

Suddenly, Tracie remembered exactly where they were. She saw Miss Weatherby's cottage in the distance. They hurried along as quickly as they could. Tracie was ready to sprint, but she saw how the old woman was beginning to wheeze. She wanted to help her but hesitated. Mrs. Win had told her that Miss Weatherby was an independent woman living out here all alone and didn't seem to need help from anyone. Tracie paced herself to the old woman's speed. She pulled Isabel along. The girl was coughing and sniffling.

When they reached the house, Miss Weatherby cautioned, "Be careful o' them steps. Some o' 'em are loose."

Tracie took Isabel's arm and led her up the right side of the stairs next to a shaky railing. When they entered the house Tracie recognized it as unchanged since the last time she was here. A milk bottle holding fresh flowers sat on the end table.

"Sit down. I'll make ye' a cuppa." The woman walked into the kitchen as the girls sat down on the flowered sofa, each letting out a deep sigh.

"Oh," Isabel said, relief audible in her voice, "I can hardly believe we've been rescued."

Tracie frowned. "We're not safe yet. I've been here before with Mrs. Win and we're pretty far from town. As soon as Miss Weatherby comes back we'll ask her how we can get back and call the police."

Isabel nodded eagerly, then began to cough. When the spell abated, she leaned her head back and dozed.

Soon the old woman returned pushing an old tea cart with squeaky wheels. "Ain't been used in a long time, but can't carry no tray. 'Ere ye' must be 'ungry, too."

Isabel's eyes opened wide. She eagerly took the plate Tracie handed her with buttered bread and biscuits. Miss Weatherby prepared the tea and handed each girl a mug.

"This tastes so good, ma'am. We were so hungry and thirsty," Tracie said through sips of tea and bites of bread.

They ate every crumb and each drank two mugs of tea. Then they sat back and looked at their savior.

"By the looks o' ye,' yer Isabel, right?"

"Yes, I was kidnapped. Can you call Bellingham House please and Lindsey will come and take us home?" Her cough sounded worse and she began to wheeze.

"Ain't got no phone," she answered.

"Do you remember me, Miss Weatherby?" Tracie asked. "I was here with Mrs. Winberry not too long ago."

"Aye, I remember ye'. Ye'r Teresa but ye' call yerself som'at else."

"Yes, Tracie, but you can call me Teresa if you want to. Now how are we going to get away? Those men will be looking for us and they'll probably come here." She felt Isabel grab her arm.

"Don't ye' worry. I got a root cellar where ye' can hide and I got me shotgun. I ain't afraid to shoot, neither." She looked at the two bedraggled girls. "We better get ye' some 'ealin' salve fer them rope burns. Them buggers tied ye' up, didn't they?"

"Yes," Isabel said, starting to cry.

Tracie put her arms around the frightened girl. "It's all right. Miss Weatherby will take care of us." But how effective was an old woman with a shotgun against two strong men?

CHAPTER 35

Emma watched the clock as the hands seemed to move in slow motion. She knew the police were still canvassing the houses in the village. So far, no one had seen the girls.

Lindsey lay on the sofa, calm from a mild sedative the doctor had given her. She had been near hysteria before Amelia called the family physician.

Davey sat at the window and stared out at the rain coming down in sheets. His face reflected the sadness that Emma knew he felt. His hands moved in signs that Emma thought might be a prayer. Her heart went out to the boy. He was besotted with Tracie and was now devastated by her disappearance.

Emma jumped as a streak of lightning flashed through the sky followed by a crash of thunder, shaking the house. Lindsey stirred and murmured, "The rain will come in — priest's hole — must put bucket . . ."

"Hush," Emma said. "Davey and I will take care of it." She turned to the boy, his hands still moving.

"Davey, come with me. We must check the leak in the priest's hole." She was eager to do anything to help relieve the tension in her body.

Obediently he fetched a bucket and followed Emma upstairs.

When they entered the bedroom, the water was soaking a hole in the wattle and daub. "Oh dear," Emma said. "This is literally crumbling."

Davey placed the bucket on a shelf above the soaked insulation. Chunks of clay and other substances that Emma would rather not identify fell to the floor. She removed a few sticks and hairs, which fell apart in her hand. Then she noticed a space behind the wall, probably caused by the constant dripping of water.

"Davey, can you bring me a flashlight?"

The boy looked at her, not comprehending. Of course, she thought. They don't call them flashlights.

"A torch. Can you find a torch?"

He nodded and ran out of the room. Emma waited, not wanting to put her hand down the hole. Anything might be down there.

When he returned, she stood on tiptoe and shined the light down into the opening. There was definitely something at the bottom. The boy tried to look in but wasn't tall enough.

Emma looked around. "Davey, bring that stool over here, please."

He did as she asked then climbed on to it. She handed him the light.

"Can you see what it is?"

He shook his head then carefully reached in. Emma watched the concentrated look on his face, hoping that it was nothing alive. When he finally pulled out his hand, he handed her something round. It appeared to be some type of coin.

Emma hurried into the bathroom and washed the clay off of it, revealing a shiny metal that looked like gold. She rubbed it with a towel then held it up to the light. United States of America spanned the top of the coin. Below it was printed twenty dollars above a double eagle design. The other side depicted the figure of the winged victory with the date: 1933.

This is an American coin, she thought, and I'll bet it's worth a bundle. But what's it doing here, in Roydon? This is obviously why Julian Duncan is so eager to buy this house. Somehow he must suspect this coin is hidden here.

She looked at the boy whose eyes stared at the gleaming gold, wide with wonder. "Davey, it's very important that we don't say anything about this except to Lindsey. Do you understand me?"

He nodded and signed something that Emma didn't understand, but responded to anyway. "Not even your mother."

She was rewarded with a smile and another nod as he placed his index finger to his lips.

"Good boy," Emma said, giving him a hug. He drew back then hugged her in return.

"You go downstairs and wait for me. I'll be down in a few minutes. It's almost tea time I believe." She smiled as the boy nodded and bounded down the steep steps.

Now where shall I hide this? Emma pondered.

Why not where you found it? her inner voice said.

"Hmm, good call." She took one of her knee socks out of the dresser drawer and wrapped the coin in it, then put it in a small drawstring bag she used to carry jewelry when she traveled. She tucked it back into the opening in the wattle and daub, making sure the string of the bag hung over the side.

Then she took her cell phone from the charger and punched in her home number. She fidgeted while she waited — two — three — four rings. Nate answer, I must talk to you.

"Hello," his breathless voice came over the instrument.

"Where were you?" she asked, trying to control her anxiety.

"I was just walking in the door. Have they found Tracie and Isabel?"

"Not yet. The police are doing a house-to-house canvass of the village but it's raining buckets here and I don't know how far they've gotten." She paced back and forth as she stared at the relentless downpour. "I'm worried sick."

"So am I and I feel so helpless. My brother indicated that he has a serious problem with some investments he made. And, there's trouble with the marriage. I feel that I have to be supportive of him right now."

"Of course you do. No question about it." She thought for a moment. "Nate, have you found out anything about the American, Julian Duncan?"

"Not much." He sighed. "His business seems to be legit. From what my contacts tell me, he's a bit eccentric, has a fleet of expensive cars and is an avid coin collector."

"That's it!" Emma exclaimed.

"What's it? What do you mean?"

She whispered into the phone. "Davey and I were putting a bucket in the priest's hole to catch the rain. There's a serious leak in this roof. To make a long story short we found a coin in a hole in the wattle and daub; the wall is crumbling from all the water." She described the coin in detail. "I think that's what Duncan is after."

"Whew!" Nate said, letting out a breath. "I don't know much about coins but it does sound like a collector's item. I'll call a few dealers and see what I can find out. But if it's an American twenty-dollar gold piece, how did it get to Roydon?"

"That's a good question."

"And," Nate continued, "what does it have to do with Isabel's kidnapping?"

"I don't think the two are related. I believe somebody else took Isabel for an entirely different reason. I haven't figured that out yet. Let me know if you learn anything about the coin. Now I hear Lindsey calling me. Talk to you soon. Love you and miss you."

"Me, too."

CHAPTER 36

Isabel lay on the sofa alternately shaking with chills and burning up with fever. Her breathing filled the room with wheezing.

"Poor lil thing," Miss Weatherby said as she put cool cloths on the girl's head. " 'Ere, drink some 'ot tea." She held Isabel's head and spooned sweetened tea into her mouth.

"She needs a doctor," Tracie said, looking anxiously at the girl's gray color.

Outside the rain poured down as lightning streaked across the sky and thunder shook the cottage.

"Ain't gonna get no doctor in this. I'm gonna put a mustard plaster on 'er chest. Best thing." The old woman retreated into the kitchen while the dog sat next to Isabel licking her hand and whining.

"Am I going to die?" Isabel asked between wracking coughs.

"Absolutely not." Tracie thought for a moment. Got to get help — right now. "Listen,

Isabel, I'm going to go to the village and get Lindsey. She'll take you home and call a doctor."

"You can't . . . go . . . out . . . in this storm."

"Yes I can. I'm strong and healthy. All I'll do is get wet. Been there before." Tracie looked down at the pitiful figure covered with blankets.

"What if . . . they come back . . . looking for me?"

"Not to worry," Miss Weatherby said, pushing a cart into the parlor. "I'll hide ye' in't root cellar wi' the 'tatoes and onions." She proceeded to put a flannel on Isabel's chest. Pungent fumes rose from the cloth.

"Smells bad," Isabel complained.

"Aye, but it'll do ye' good." She pulled the blanket up over the plaster and tucked it around the girl's neck.

"She's breathing easier already," Tracie said.

The old woman nodded. "Nothin' works like 't old remedies." She turned to Tracie, her wrinkled face furrowed in a frown. "Now what was ye' sayin' 'bout goin to t' village?"

"This is my best chance to get help. No one will be looking for us in this storm."

She jumped as a crash of thunder rent the air.

"Ye'r right 'bout that. Ye'r a plucky gal, ain't ye'?"

"I've been in tight scrapes before and I'm not afraid." Tracie tried to hide the fact that she was terrified; that wouldn't help anyone.

"Don't believe ye', but yer right. Better git going."

"You will take care of Isabel?" Again Tracie looked at the helpless girl.

"Aye. Got me shotgun and ain't afraid to use it." She went to an alcove and returned with a dark-colored slicker. "Put this on. Keep ye' a might dry, and stay away from 't road. Them buggers might be about."

"I will."

Tracie glanced one more time at Isabel, whispered a prayer, then slipped out the door.

Emma went quietly down the stairs and into the parlor where Lindsey sat sipping a cup of tea. She helped herself to a cup and drank it automatically, wasn't sure if she had put sugar in it or not and didn't really care.

"Have a biscuit," Lindsey said.

"No thanks. Lindsey, I have to talk to you about something important."

"There's nothing more important than getting the girls back."

"I agree, but Davey and I found something." Emma looked around to make sure Amelia and Davey weren't in the room. She heard the woman in the kitchen talking to her son. Quickly Emma told Lindsey about finding the coin and her conversation with Nate.

"I can hardly believe it," Lindsey said. "That does explain why the American is so eager to buy this house, but how did the coin get here?"

"That's a good question. Now we have to keep it secret. For now, I think we should leave it where it is. And, above all, don't tell Avery Wilkins."

Lindsey shook her head. "I haven't spoken to him since the day I went to the bank. I feel so betrayed." Her face contorted in grief and helplessness. "My life is falling apart, Aunt Emma."

Emma sat on the sofa next to her and put her arm around her shoulders. Both women sat there watching the storm rage outside . . . watching and waiting.

As Tracie carefully crept down the old stairs, she clutched the banister for support. Wind whipped at her face; the rain came down so hard she could hardly see in front of her.

Good, she thought, if I can't see anything, no one will be able to see me. But which way do I go? She stood for a moment, totally disoriented. As if on cue, the rain slackened and Tracie could just make out the low shapes of cottages in the distance. She turned and saw the woods behind her. Okay, toward the houses. Mrs. Win is always talking to her Guardian Angel. I hope, if I have one, she's watching over me.

Slowly she began plodding toward the village, keeping well away from the road. It was totally dark, no moon, only clouds and rain. Intermittently the water abated somewhat, but for the most part, it kept coming down in a steady sheet. Even with the flashlight she could see very little — just vague shapes of trees and bushes. She walked slowly, careful to maintain her footing. Her slow progress frustrated her. Isabel is so sick and still in danger, and those thugs might be close by.

Suddenly when she tried to put her right foot down, there was nothing there. She turned to see a ravine — too late. She tried to plant her feet on solid ground, but could find none. She grabbed a bush and clung to it. As her hand began to slip, she reached out to another bush, dropping the penlight.

"Damn!" She felt a searing pain as a thorn stabbed into her palm. She could gain no ground with her feet. They kept slipping and sliding along the muddy hillside. Finally, gravity pulled at her and she was forced to let go. Her body tumbled, rolling over and over until she reached the bottom, landing with all her weight on her right foot.

"Oh God," she moaned. "Where am I now?" A throbbing started in her right ankle and grew stronger by the minute. Oh boy, I hope I didn't break anything. She moved all her other parts. The rest of her body seemed to be only scratched and bruised. Tracie pulled herself up on her hands and knees and grasped around for the flashlight, but it was gone.

When she tried to stand, her right leg buckled under her, the throbbing in her ankle growing worse by the minute. I guess I'll have to crawl, she thought, but when she looked up, the incline was too steep.

Tracie sat there, feeling miserable and frightened. I've failed, let Isabel down. Nobody will find me 'till morning and then it might be too late.

What was that? Voices? She hunkered down low and listened.

"My mum is gonna be cross."

"Mine, too. I told ya' we should'a gone

back when it started raining."

Someone was trudging through the brush getting closer and closer. There were at least two of them. They sounded like young voices, certainly not those of the thugs. Shall I call out? I have to, can't possibly get back to the village on my own.

"Help! Help me! I'm hurt."

"What was that? Sounded like somebody callin' for help," one voice said.

"Where are ya?" another voice asked.

"Over here. *Please* help me." Tracie looked up into the faces of two young boys peering down at her.

"Bloody hell! It's a girl," one of them said. "How'd you get here?"

"Never mind that now. I think I've sprained my ankle and I *must* get to Bellingham House. It's a matter of life and death."

"Better grab her arms," the first boy said.

She felt each boy take one of her arms and pull. "Ow!"

"Sorry. Yer stuck in the mud."

"It's all right." Tracie tried to stand but fell right down again.

"Easy now," the boy said.

"I can't put any weight on my right ankle," she groaned.

"Jeffrey," the first boy said, "put her left

arm around yer neck and I'll take the other one. Can you hop?"

"I think so," Tracie said.

"Okay, my house is just down the road. It's the closest place to go."

Laboriously the boys took most of Tracie's weight on their shoulders while she hopped on her left foot. The rain had let up a little, making visibility better. They dragged her around to a more gradual slope and finally reached the road. Tracie looked both ways half expecting to see the old truck that had transported her and Isabel. But nothing moved. The road was slick with water running down the slight incline.

"There's my house up ahead. And there's my mum, at the window," the lead boy said.

"Maybe she won't be so cross when she sees we rescued somebody," the other boy said.

"I hope so," the first one said.

When they reached the three steps, Tracie felt she could go no farther. "Wait a minute. Let me catch my breath."

The door opened and an imposing-looking woman stared down at them. "George Burrows, you're in a world of trouble staying out in this weather. And who have you got there?"

"Please ma'am," Tracie said, raising her

rain-soaked head, "these boys saved my life. I sprained my ankle and couldn't walk. Have to get to Bellingham House. Matter of life and death." With those words she collapsed on the steps, unable to move.

"I swear, young people. Got no sense at all. Lift her up boys and bring her by the fire before you all catch your death."

Tracie felt herself carried into the house and set down on the floor before a warm crackling fire.

"Jeffrey, you'd better get on home, right now," the woman commanded.

"Yes'm."

"And George, go change your clothes and bring me some towels and a dressing gown from my room."

"Yes, Mum."

Tracie heard footsteps running up a stairway. She turned to the woman who shook her head.

"You're an American, aren't you? What are you doing here and out in this weather?"

"I was kidnapped . . . with Isabel . . . locked in a shed . . . Miss Weatherby rescued us . . . have to get to Lindsey . . . phone . . ."

"Wait a minute. You're making no sense at all. The phones are out, my dear. I'll make a cuppa hot tea and change your wet clothes and then you can tell me all about it."

"No time," Tracie pleaded, but the woman was gone. She snuggled closer to the fire and felt the throbbing in her ankle getting stronger. Oh God, how can I help Isabel? Was that a vehicle she heard passing on the road? She wasn't sure. A crash of thunder obscured all other sounds as the rain pelted the windows.

Tracie lay in a state of semi-consciousness — waiting.

CHAPTER 37

Emma looked over at Lindsey, who lay dozing on the sofa, her right arm and leg hanging off as if she were about to fall to the floor. Emma closed her eyes and tried to relax, but she kept visualizing the girls, restrained and frightened. Did they have food and water? Were they in another cage somewhere?

If Tracie is harmed in any way, I'll never forgive myself for putting her in danger, she thought.

Why am I not also worried about Isabel?

Because she's not your responsibility, her inner voice said.

Oh, Guardian Angel, lead us to them before it's too late.

They are safe. Have faith.

Emma took some comfort in those words. Of course, her mind could be conjuring up just what she wanted to hear, but her celestial guardian had never let her down.

She must believe.

And what about this coin? she asked herself. It should be in a safety deposit box in a bank. I don't trust anything in this old house.

Just then the wind whistled through the rafters in the attic; it almost sounded like a plaintive wail, as if someone were calling. Emma shivered. She would be glad to get away from here and back to her normal life. She looked out the window and continued her lonely vigil.

Mrs. Burrows returned with a cup of sweetened tea. "Come now, my girl, open your eyes and drink this. It will do you good."

Tracie looked up at the strange woman. Where was she? Her ankle throbbed to the rhythm of a drum. She squeezed her eyes shut then opened them again as the memory of the last twenty-four hours resurfaced.

"Oh, my ankle," she moaned.

"Drink the tea then I'll get you out of those wet clothes and tend to that ankle," the woman commanded.

Tracie did as she was told, the tea soothing her and sending its warmth through her chilled body. Her clothes clung to her like a clammy cocoon.

"But Isabel, she's in danger . . . must help

her." Tracie's eyes were wide with fear.

"We'll take care of you first," the woman said. "Lift your arms and I'll take this shirt off you."

With difficulty Tracie obeyed and felt immediate relief to be rid of the wet garment. Then off came her bra. Mrs. Burrows discreetly covered her chest with a towel. She took off Tracie's shoes and socks then the cargo pants. They were more difficult. Tracie sat up and slid them down, wincing with each movement.

"There," Mrs. Burrows said, wrapping her in a fleece dressing gown and rubbing her wet hair with the towel. "You should be nice and warm now."

"Yes, thank you. That's much better." She boosted herself off the floor putting her weight on her left foot and lay down on the sofa.

Mrs. Burrows put a pillow under her right foot and shook her head. "That looks like a bad sprain."

Tracie looked down at her swollen ankle, now turning a dark shade of purple. "Do you think it's broken?"

"Don't know. You need a doctor for that, but I'll bind it and put some ice on it to ease the swelling." She smiled and caressed Tracie's cheek. "Then you can tell me all about what happened."

Tracie grabbed her hand as she was about to leave the room. "Please, can you call Bellingham House? It's an emergency."

The woman loosened Tracie's hand. "My dear girl, all the phones are out. I tried to call Jeffrey's mum earlier but got no signal at all. Nobody's going anywhere 'till morning. Now lie back and try to relax."

Oh God, Tracie thought. How am I going to get word to Lindsey? Isabel was so sick. What a mess.

After Mrs. Burrows had wrapped her ankle and put an ice pack on it, she handed Tracie two tablets. "Take these. Will dull that pain."

"What are they?"

"Paracetamol." To Tracie's raised eyebrows, she explained, "Something like your acetaminophen in the States. Now, tell me what you were raving about when George brought you in."

Tracie let out a breath and lay back. Then she told Mrs. Burrows the whole bizarre story.

The woman's eyes widened. "If you didn't seem like a sensible girl, I'd say you'd been sniffing something." She walked over to the window. "The rain is letting up and I think it will be sunrise soon. In a bit I'll get

George up and send him off to Bellingham House.

"There comes some fool speeding down the road in a truck. Where could he be going at this hour?"

Tracie froze. "Which way is he going?"

"Away from town. There's nothing out there."

"Oh yes there is. There's Miss Weatherby's cottage — and Isabel."

Isabel muttered in her delirium . . . the two men back . . . taking her away. She screamed as she woke from a troubled sleep, her body clammy and trembling.

"There, there," Miss Weatherby said, stroking her face. "Calm down, child. Now I don't want to scare ye' but I see a truck comin' this way. I'll 'ave t' 'ide ye'."

Isabel sat up, eyes wide with terror. "Where?"

"Come on. No time to tarry. Got to get ye in t' root cellar."

Isabel dragged herself off the sofa and leaned heavily on the old woman. This can't be happening, she said to herself. No . . .

"Come on, 'urry."

Miss Weatherby sat her on a kitchen chair and pushed the table aside. She pulled up a worn throw rug from the floor to expose the door to the cellar. With a strength that belied her appearance, she pulled up the door and quickly lowered Isabel down into the dark space. The dog was beginning to growl a warning.

"Take this torch and 'ide 'mid the 'tatoes and onions," she commanded.

"You won't leave me here, will you?" Isabel begged.

"Not to worry, child. I be back."

With those words the door closed over Isabel's head. She was alone in the dark. She switched on the torch and looked around. The comforting odor of onions filled the dry cool room. Isabel nestled among them, closed her eyes and prayed.

A few minutes later she heard raised voices. Whose were they? Certainly not Lindsey and Aunt Emma. The dog barked furiously then was silent. It must be someone she knows, Isabel thought.

Then she heard a gruff voice shout. "The girl, where?"

What was that loud noise, a gunshot? Someone yelled followed by a thud, as if something heavy had fallen to the floor.

Someone walking from room to room. "Gotta be here." Those men. They were searching — for her.

Oh God, please don't let them find me.

And where is Miss Weatherby? Is she hurt? Isabel scrunched lower and covered herself completely with potatoes and onions. She held her breath, didn't dare to make a sound.

She heard what sounded like swearing as the footsteps finally retreated. She heard a motor start and a vehicle drive away. Were they gone? Then — silence. She waited a long time then pushed herself out from under the vegetables. "Miss Weatherby," she called. No answer. Louder. Still no answer. She reached up and pounded on the door. No one came. She was trapped down here. Would it be her tomb? The chills started again and Isabel fell to the ground, unfeeling and uncaring.

CHAPTER 38

Emma and Lindsey each sipped a cup of tea as they watched the eastern sky streak with pink. The rain had swept the area clean, and fresh air streamed in through the open window.

Emma took a deep breath. She felt as though she hadn't slept in a week. She wanted to get up off the chair and walk about, but her limbs wouldn't respond. She watched Davey outside sweeping fallen debris from the sidewalk. Everything seemed to be happening in slow motion. Suddenly he turned and ran into the house signing and grunting excitedly.

Amelia hurriedly opened the door for her son. "What is it, Davey?"

She nodded as she interpreted his signs and turned to Lindsey and Emma. "A lad from the village is running this way."

Lindsey jumped up from her chair, followed by Emma. They hurried to the door to see a boy opening the gate.

"Who is it?" Emma asked.

"George Burrows. He lives in a cottage just at the edge of the village," Lindsey answered.

The boy ran up to the women, panting and blowing. He bent over, grasped his thighs with his hands and began talking in halting breaths. "Found a girl . . . sprained ankle . . . Miss Weatherby . . . Isabel . . ."

"Wait a minute, George, we can't understand you," Lindsey said, grasping his shoulders.

He took a deep breath, pulled a note from his pocket, and handed it to her.

"It's from Tracie," Lindsey almost shouted.

Emma grabbed her arm, her legs almost buckling under her. She craned her neck to read.

"Isabel is at Miss Weatherby's cottage. Tracie is safe with Mrs. Burrows, has an injured ankle. She says we must go directly to get Isabel. She saw a truck driving that way." Lindsey turned to Emma. "They're alive, thank God!" She grabbed onto Emma for support. "But we must leave immediately."

"Yes, yes," Emma said, flooded with relief.

"George, you go inside and have a cuppa tea and some biscuits," Lindsey instructed.

"We'll go directly to Miss Weatherby's."

Davey took George by the arm and led him into the house as Lindsey and Emma ran to the car.

Oh God, Emma thought, Tracie is safe. I am so grateful. "Shouldn't we call the police?" Emma asked.

"I don't want to wait for them," Lindsey said. "I want to go straight away."

Emma pulled her back and handed her the cell phone. "Call them. We'll meet at Miss Weatherby's cottage."

"Yes, I suppose you're right."

As Lindsey made the call, Emma had a disturbing premonition. What would they find? Her sixth sense told her something was terribly wrong, but she didn't know what.

The women climbed into the car and Lindsey raced through the sleeping village. It was barely dawn and most people were just awakening. A few curious eyes peered out of windows, but, for the most part, all was still. Her hands gripped the steering wheel, her body tensed forward watching the rutted road as the car splashed through puddles.

When they reached the gravel road to the cottage, water and debris forced Lindsey to slow to almost a crawl.

Emma wanted to get out and run, but she knew she wouldn't get there any faster.

"This is as far as I can go," Lindsey said. "We'll have to walk the rest of the way."

They got out of the car and sank into a pile of mush, water filling their shoes.

Oh God, Emma prayed. Let us be there in time.

"Look," Emma said, as they plodded through thick weeds and deep gouges in the road, "tire tracks."

Lindsey grabbed her hand. "Aunt Emma, I'm so frightened."

"So am I."

Not a sound issued from the cottage, no apple-doll face watching from the window, no dog barking.

Guardian Angel, this silence is terrifying. I'm afraid of what we'll find inside.

Hurry, they need help, the inner voice said.

The door stood ajar. "Miss Weatherby," Emma called. "Are you here?"

No answer.

Carefully they pushed the door open.

"Oh my God," Lindsey said as they stared at the bodies of the old woman and the dog lying on the floor.

Emma knelt and felt for a pulse. "She's alive, but that's a nasty-looking wound on her head." She pulled her cell phone out of her pocket and handed it to Lindsey. "Call for an ambulance. You know how to direct them."

While Lindsey made the call, Emma tried to revive the woman. She groaned, but that was all. Then Emma looked at Miss Weatherby's faithful dog. The lifeless body lay next to its mistress. She shook her head and went into the kitchen to get something to wash the blood off the woman.

"They'll be here in about ten minutes," Lindsey said. "I'll look for Isabel."

"What was that sound?" Emma said putting her finger to her lips and listening. There it was again. A vague pounding coming from the kitchen. They hurried into the room.

"Lindsey, help me," a muffled voice called. It was coming from below the floor.

"Isabel?"

"I'm in the root cellar," a hoarse voice called.

Quickly they moved the table and pushed the rug aside to reveal the door. Emma grabbed the handle and pulled it up.

Tears streamed down Lindsey's cheeks as she looked into the face of her cousin. "Oh, thank God."

"Quick, pull her up," Emma said, reaching for one of the girl's hands. Lindsey took the other and soon she had Isabel in her arms, comforting and soothing the girl.

The welcoming sound of the siren screamed in the distance.

When the police car arrived followed closely by the ambulance, Emma hurried to the door to let them in. The paramedics immediately dealt with Miss Weatherby, checking her vital signs and her pupils and starting an intravenous drip.

The constable sat with Lindsey and the sobbing Isabel, asking questions.

"Detective Inspector Allenby has been following this case," Lindsey said.

"Yes, ma'am. I'll see that he gets a full report."

Lindsey got Isabel under control and the girl answered as many questions as she could but, within minutes, she broke down again, sobbing hysterically.

"Constable, may I take her home?" Lindsey begged. "She needs a doctor as soon as possible."

"Perhaps she should go to hospital," he suggested.

"No," Lindsey said. "That's out of the question. We have our own physician who tends to her. You do understand, don't you?"

"Yes, I do. You take her and I'll be along to Bellingham House later to question her further. I'll phone for a constable to meet you there to search the premises. I doubt the kidnappers would return there but one never knows."

"Thank you. Now you'll probably get a more coherent report from the other girl, Tracie Adams. She's at Burrows'." She quickly gave him the directions.

Emma turned to Lindsey. "You take Isabel home and I'll accompany the constable to Mrs. Burrows's house as soon as Miss Weatherby is safely on her way to the hospital. Will that be all right?" She directed her question to the policeman who nodded.

"I'll call for an investigative team to come and examine the premises here," he said, taking out his cell phone.

A moan issued from the old woman as the emergency crew lifted her onto the stretcher. "Me dog," she whispered, half opening her blackening eyes.

Emma patted her hand. "I'll take care of her. Not to worry."

"Girl — in 't root cellar."

"We have her. She's all right," Emma assured her.

The woman grunted as the two men loaded the stretcher into the ambulance and took off for Harlow.

Emma looked at the dog and shook her

head. Poor thing. They would tend to her later. For now she took an old blanket off the sofa and covered the body. Her eyes met those of the policeman.

"Are you ready, ma'am?" he asked.

"Yes, by all means. Let's go."

Emma watched the officer carry Isabel to Lindsey's car then saw it speed away in the distance. She climbed into the police car and they headed down the road toward the village.

"I believe this must be it," Emma said, recalling Lindsey's directions. They stopped in front of a small cottage with a thatched roof. Roses grew in abundance across the neatly tended front of the house.

A woman stood at the door as they alighted from the car.

"Mrs. Burrows?" Emma called.

"Yes, and who are you?" Her eyes scanned the two with some suspicion.

"I'm Emma Winberry, Tracie's friend. Is she all right?"

"Oh." The woman relaxed and greeted Emma with a smile. "She'll be so happy to see you."

"The constable wants to ask her some questions," Emma said.

Mrs. Burrows escorted the two into the

parlor where Tracie lay dozing on the sofa.

"Tracie." Emma knelt down beside the girl and grabbed her in her arms.

She opened her eyes. "Oh Mrs. Win, I'm so glad you're here. Is Isabel all right?"

"Yes, yes. Lindsey is taking her home. The policeman here wants to talk to you." Emma deliberately refrained from mentioning Miss Weatherby or the dog. There would be time for that later.

"Miss, I'm Constable Porter and I want you to tell me everything that happened. Take it slowly and try to remember as much as you can." He pulled up a chair, sat next to Tracie and pulled a notebook and pen from his pocket.

"I'll make some tea," Mrs. Burrows said, leaving the room.

Tracie rubbed her eyes, took a deep breath then winced in pain as she adjusted the ice pack on her ankle. She began with her capture at the abandoned building and recounted the entire nightmarish experience. When she finished, she gladly downed a cup of tea and nibbled on a biscuit.

Emma sat frozen, hardly believing her ears.

The policeman frowned as he looked at the girl. "That's quite a story. Would you be able to identify the two men?"

"Oh yes. In fact I can sketch their faces from memory. I examined them very carefully."

"She's a first-class artist," Emma said, a note of pride in her voice.

Then she turned her attention back to Tracie. "How bad is your ankle, dear?"

"It really hurts and it's all swollen."

Emma carefully removed the ice pack and was startled by the black and blue color sneaking from under the bandage. "I hope it's not broken."

Constable Porter examined it. "You'll need to go to Casualty for an X-ray, Miss. Now I'm going to Bellingham House to interview the other girl." He rose from his chair and put his notebook back in his pocket.

"What about us?" Emma asked.

"I have a car," Mrs. Burrows said. "I'll be glad to take you to Harlow for the X-ray. This is a very brave young lady."

"Then I'll leave you," the policeman said and walked out the door.

At that moment George Burrows came loping into the house, his eyes wide. "Lots of excitement," he said. "Police and all that."

"George," his mother said. "I'm taking Tracie and Mrs. Winberry to Harlow to have her ankle looked at. I trust you can do your

chores and not get into any more mischief."
She gave him a stern look.

"Yes, Mum. Not to worry. When I'm finished, can I go to Jeffrey's and tell him all about this?"

She thought for a moment. "All right. I'll come and collect you when I return."

CHAPTER 39

When they reached the emergency entrance to the hospital, Emma hurried inside and asked for a wheelchair. An attendant came with the chair and helped Tracie out of the car. The girl grimaced but didn't utter a word of complaint. Emma followed her inside while Mrs. Burrows parked the car.

The emergency room looked very much like the ones back home. Emma shuddered at the memory of too many trips to these places, especially the most recent visit to see Susan. She watched Tracie's face, which mirrored her own painful reflections.

Emma quickly explained the situation to the woman at the information desk and mentally thanked her Guardian Angel for reminding her to bring her purse with their passports inside.

"We'll take care of you, young lady," an older nurse said, taking the wheelchair and escorting Tracie and Emma to an examining room. "Can you manage to get onto that table so the doctor can have a look at you?" Her motherly smile comforted them both as Tracie did as she was told. The nurse wrote down the history of the accident, took the vital signs and made notations on a chart.

Before long a weary-looking woman came into the room. "I'm Dr. Harwood," she said. "Let's see what we have here." Carefully she unwrapped the ankle and gently palpated.

"Ow," Tracie said between clenched teeth.

"Sorry. I know that's sore. I don't think it's broken but we'll take an X-ray to be sure." She smiled and walked quickly out of the room.

How many patients does she have to see? Emma wondered. She had noticed the emergency room beginning to fill up as they came in. She was grateful they had come first.

When an attendant arrived to take Tracie to X-ray, Emma went out to speak with Mrs. Burrows then went up to the information desk.

"Can you tell me if an ambulance brought in a Miss Weatherby a short time ago?"

The woman looked at some records. "Are

you a relative?" she asked, frowning at Emma.

"No, just a good friend. I don't believe she has any family."

"Well, I can't give you any information other than that she is here and still in Casualty."

By the look she received, Emma knew she would find out no more. She went back to Mrs. Burrows and told her she would wait in the examining room for Tracie.

"Would you like me to bring you a cup of tea?" Emma asked, noticing a beverage dispensing machine.

"No, thank you," Mrs. Burrows said. "What comes from those machines bears no resemblance to a proper cup of tea. I'll just sit and read this magazine. With a traveling husband, I don't get much time for such luxuries at home."

Emma asked no questions about the woman's husband. It was none of her business. She again thanked her and returned to wait for Tracie. Within a half-hour Tracie was back. She grimaced in pain as she again climbed onto the examining table.

"Boy, it really swells a lot when the bandage is off," she said, looking down at her eggplant-colored ankle. She gave Emma a half-hearted smile and Emma hugged her in return.

"Tracie, I'm so sorry I got you into all this mess. I promised you a trip to England, not a life threatening experience." Emma shook her head in regret.

"It's not your fault, Mrs. Win. I came to help Isabel and now that she's safely home, we can relax." She lay back, closed her eyes and gritted her teeth.

Emma wasn't too sure about that. She felt this business wasn't over yet.

Soon the doctor returned with a half-smile on her face. "No fracture," she said, pulling up the X-ray image on the computer. "It's a bad sprain that will, unfortunately, take quite some time to heal. What have you been taking for pain?"

"Mrs. Burrows gave me some paracetamol, but it didn't do much," Tracie said.

"No, it wouldn't. I'll give you a prescription for something stronger. Now you *must* keep this leg elevated and wrapped at all times. I can't emphasize that enough. A nurse will be in to show you the proper way to bandage it," she said. "And keep ice on it to control the swelling."

Emma suddenly thought of something. "We're supposed to be returning to the States by the end of the week. Will she be all right to travel?"

The doctor frowned and slowly shook her head. "Only if you can elevate that leg. Are you in first class?"

"I'm afraid not," Emma answered. "I wish."

"Then it would be wise to delay your return for a bit. I'll give you a letter for the airlines so they don't charge you for changing your flight. Now goodbye, and good luck." Without another word she hurried off to the next patient.

Emma had wanted to ask about Miss Weatherby, but had no opportunity. The doctor probably wouldn't have told her anything anyway. Privacy laws were the same here as back home.

Shortly the nurse returned and expertly wound the elastic bandage around Tracie's foot and ankle, instructing Emma in the procedure. She gave her a pair of crutches and watched closely to see that she could navigate safely.

"Brilliant," she said, as Tracie walked across the room. "Here's the prescription and the note for the airlines." She handed Emma two pieces of paper and escorted them out.

"What about payment?" Emma asked.

"Everyone in the U.K. is cared for by the National Health. That includes visitors.

Now, no more accidents young lady." She winked at Tracie.

"I'll certainly try."

Mrs. Burrows brought the car around and they headed back to Roydon.

When they arrived at Bellingham House, Tracie was visibly exhausted. Amelia eagerly helped Emma settle her on the sofa with her right leg elevated on cushions. She was afraid to attempt the steep flight of steps and Emma agreed this was the safest place for now.

"How can I thank you?" Emma asked Mrs. Burrows. "May I at least pay for the petrol?"

"No need. Glad to be of help. We don't get much excitement around here and this will give me something to chat about with the ladies." She smiled and took her leave.

Davey came into the room and hesitantly approached Tracie. He placed an ice pack on her injured ankle and was rewarded with a smile. His eyes reflected both sorrow and relief. He made a few signs and uttered a grunt. Tracie patted his hand and nodded in return.

"Here, dear," Emma said, "take one of these tablets and try to sleep a bit." They had stopped at the chemist's shop on the way and filled the prescription.

"Thanks, Mrs. Win. I'm beat. Please check on Isabel, will you?" Her eyes mirrored her concern.

"I shall. Now you just rest and don't worry about anything."

"Amelia," Emma called. "Where is Lindsey?" She hadn't seen her since they returned.

"She's with Isabel." The woman wrung her hands and shook her head. "The poor thing has a high fever and is talking out of her head, she is."

"Did Lindsey call the doctor?" Emma asked.

"Phones are still out."

"I believe my cell phone is working. I'll go to her right now. Please keep an eye on Tracie."

"I will do that." She picked up a blanket and carefully covered the girl. Tracie made no movement.

Emma watched her chest rising and falling regularly and was satisfied that she was asleep. Good, that's what she needs. Now I'll go to Isabel.

Oh, Guardian Angel, I do so want to go home.

It isn't finished yet, her inner voice said.

But Emma already knew that.

She dragged herself up the stairs. This whole matter was taking a heavy toll on her. From the far end of the corridor, she heard Isabel crying out and Lindsey trying to sooth her. She knocked softly on the door and peered inside. Isabel thrashed on the bed while Lindsey tried to hold her hand. Duchess lay beside her, whining.

Lindsey turned. "Oh Aunt, what am I going to do? I don't even think she knows who I am." Then she seemed to remember the other girl. "Is Tracie all right?"

"Yes, yes. The ankle is sprained, that's all. She's comfortably settled on the sofa. Amelia is looking after her."

"Good. I need to phone up the doctor, but the lines are still down."

Emma pulled her cell phone out of her pocket. "Use this." She placed it in Lindsey's trembling hand.

"Oh, your mobile. I never thought of that." After three attempts, Lindsey managed to make the connection. The doctor said he was very busy but would come as soon as he could. He told her to give Isabel a couple of capsules of paracetamol to take down the fever.

Lindsey's face reflected her exhaustion. "Too many things have happened," she murmured absently. "I don't know how much longer I can go on." She grabbed Emma's hand. "Without you I could never have survived this."

Isabel opened her eyes and stared about the room. "No!" she shouted. "I won't!" She waved her arms about, almost falling off the bed.

"Isabel," Emma said sternly, grabbing her hands. "It's Aunt Emma. Do you know me?"

For a moment Emma was greeted with a vacant stare; then recognition. The girl clutched at her.

"Take me away from here," she begged.

"Calm down," Emma said, sitting beside her and trying to embrace the frightened girl.

"They took her away," Isabel moaned.

"Who?" Emma had no idea what the girl was talking about.

Wild eyes darted from one side of the room to the other. "The evil men. They took Annabelle, my only friend. Now I have no one." She began to wail.

"Listen to me," Emma commanded, taking both her shoulders. "You have Lindsey and me and Tracie. We're here and we won't let anyone hurt you ever again. Do you understand?"

The girl nodded.

"Now take these capsules. The doctor will be here soon to help you."

"Are they poison?" she asked.

"Isabel, they're paracetamol," Lindsey said, holding out the bottle for her to see. "You've taken them many times before. They'll take down your fever."

Reluctantly she swallowed the medication then cocked her head, seemed to be listening to something.

Emma heard a moaning sound.

"Do you hear?" the girl said. "The house is talking to me."

"No, no," Lindsey said, trying to comfort her. "It's the wind in the rafters. We hear it all the time. You know that."

Isabel shook her head. "It's the house telling me to do bad things. No!" she shouted. "I won't." She continued to thrash around and moan, ranting about the house talking to her and her imaginary friend, Annabelle.

Emma wondered if the girl had suffered a breakdown. It was certainly possible with everything she had endured.

Oh my God, she suddenly remembered she hadn't called Nate. "Lindsey, I must call Nate. He'll be concerned about us." If he was trying to call, she knew he would be frantic. I hope there's enough charge left, she thought. She hurried to her room and punched in the numbers. He answered on the first ring.

"Hello." An anxious note to his voice.

"Nate, I'm so sorry I haven't been able to call you sooner."

"Emma, I've been worried sick. What's happening?"

Quickly she told him the sequence of events.

"I'm relieved that the girls are safe but it sounds like Isabel's in a bad way. How serious is Tracie's ankle injury?"

Emma gritted her teeth. "She won't be able to travel for a while. The doctor gave me a statement for the airlines. I'm afraid we'll have to postpone our return for a few days."

"How many days?" he asked.

"I don't know. Let's see how she does by the end of the week. Now you're breaking up. I think my phone is out of juice."

"I have to tell you what I found out about the coin . . ." With those words, the phone went dead.

Oh Lord. Emma went into her room, plugged the phone into the charger and threw herself on the bed as she heard Isabel's cries softening to a murmur. Within minutes, she was asleep.

CHAPTER 40

Emma was awakened by voices from downstairs. She quickly rose from the bed, went into the bathroom and dashed water on her face. What time was it? What day was it? At least she remembered to call Nate and relieve his mind.

She held onto the banister, descended the stairs and was startled to see Detective Inspector Allenby sitting beside Tracie. Her head was bent over a piece of paper as she busily sketched something. Davey stood beside her, gawking.

Emma didn't want to break her concentration so she stood quietly for a few minutes.

"There," Tracie said, biting on the end of the pencil. "That's a good likeness of the man with the birthmark on his face." She handed the paper to the policeman and began another sketch.

"Hmm," he said. "You are good. I recognize this man all right." At that moment he noticed Emma and greeted her.

"This young lady is extremely skilled. If she ever wants a position with the force, we could use someone with her abilities."

Emma noticed a smile cross Tracie's face as she continued to work. "I believe she's quite committed to her work in the States." Then she frowned. "So, you do know this man?"

"He bears a striking resemblance to someone we've dealt with before. He's been known to cover the birthmark with makeup. Must have gotten careless this time. I'll come by later with photographs of known criminals for her to identify. Now I'd like to see the other girl."

Emma shook her head. "I don't know if that will be possible. She's quite ill and not making much sense. We're waiting for the doctor now."

He frowned and rubbed his chin. "That's regrettable. The more time that passes the less chance we have of apprehending them."

"May I speak with you alone for a moment?" Emma whispered. The inspector followed her into the dining room where Tracie wouldn't hear them.

"I'm very concerned about Miss Weatherby. Is there any way I can learn about her condition?" Emma gave him a pleading look.

"I know she's in critical care, but one of my men is at hospital now questioning her."

"Then she is conscious?"

"Oh yes. Keeps asking about her dog. We haven't told her that the animal is dead."

Emma clasped her hands. "I want to see that it's buried properly in her garden. I'm sure she would want that," she said. "Is that possible?"

"The police don't do that sort of thing. But if you can get someone, I'll give permission to release the animal."

"Thank you so much. I'm sure I can get one of the local boys to help me. It would mean a lot to the poor old woman."

He nodded in agreement. "I'll take care of that straight away and, the sooner you get the job done, the better. Now I really must try to question the other girl, just for a moment." He didn't seem willing to leave without seeing Isabel.

"No! No!" Shouts from upstairs.

Emma shrugged. "Let's give it a try."

She climbed the stairs followed by the detective. More shouts from the bedroom. As they entered they saw Lindsey holding Isabel's arms as she thrashed about the bed. Lindsey turned as the two walked in.

"Oh Aunt, I can't handle her. I'm about done in."

"Go downstairs and have some tea," Emma said. "I'll stay with her for a while."

Lindsey breathed a sigh of relief and left the room.

"Isabel," Emma said in a commanding voice. "You *must* calm down."

The girl opened her eyes and stared at Emma and then at the man beside her.

"This is Detective Inspector Allenby. You remember him," Emma said. "He wants to ask you about the two men."

Isabel cringed. "No!" she shouted.

"Now Miss," the policeman said, "the only way we can apprehend these two is with your cooperation. Can you answer just a few questions?" He sat in a chair next to the bed and looked directly at her.

She gave Emma a questioning glance.

"Go ahead, dear, talk to him. He's here to help you."

Isabel looked around the room, wide-eyed, then nodded.

"Good. Can you tell me what they looked like?"

She ran her hand down the right side of her face. "Mark."

"Excellent. What about the other man?"

Her brows knit together and she squeezed

her eyes shut. "Ugly . . . mean . . . called me an animal . . . locked in a cage . . ." Her voice rose with each word until it became a hysterical howl.

"All right," he said. "That's enough." He turned to Emma and shook his head. "Maybe she'll be calmer when I return with the pictures."

As he left the room, Emma took his place and crooned in a singsong voice to the tortured girl. "It's all right. You're safe. Nothing will hurt you ever again." She gently ran her hands down Isabel's legs. After a while the girl began to relax and finally fell into a fitful sleep.

As Emma tiptoed out of the bedroom, she heard the phone ringing downstairs. Oh good, she thought, they've repaired the lines.

"Mrs. Winberry," Amelia called, "it's for you."

Emma took the phone and walked into a corner of the dining room. "Hello."

"Emma, thank God the phones are fixed."

"Oh Nate, it's awful here. Isabel is in such a state that I fear for her sanity."

She heard a muffled sound from the other end. "Listen," he said, "I must tell you about that coin."

"Oh." Emma had completely forgotten

about it.

"From your description, it sounds like a St. Gauden's double eagle 1933 twenty-dollar gold piece. A limited number were minted from 1907 to 1933 and, later, when the government recalled gold coins, not all of them were turned in. Collectors will pay as much as two million dollars for one in mint condition, so to speak."

"My God!" Emma couldn't believe it.

"So that seems to be what the American is after. The question is, how does he know it's in Bellingham House?"

"I have no idea," Emma said. "Perhaps he doesn't know for sure, only suspects."

"That doesn't wash," Nate said. "There has to be some grounds for suspicion or he wouldn't be so insistent."

"How did you get all this information?" Emma asked.

"Easy. I called a couple of coin dealers and identified myself as a writer. Described the coin I planned to use in a story and they told me all about it. It seems that people will tell you anything if you're a writer."

"You are becoming an accomplished liar, Nate Sandler."

He laughed. "It wasn't a total lie. I do write for the investment newsletter. Anyway, I looked up Augustus St. Gaudens on the

Internet. Quite an interesting man. He was a noted sculptor as well as a designer of coins."

"Okay, that answers that question. By the way, Tracie did two remarkable sketches of the abductors. The inspector was impressed and offered her a job."

"I'll bet that made her feel good," Nate said.

"Oh yes, but she told him she had other plans. He's coming back later with photographs of known criminals for her to identify. He did seem to recognize the men from the sketches. I can see her from here sketching Davey's likeness. He's besotted with her." Emma laughed.

"Sparrow, you must be exhausted." Nate's voice had a forlorn tone to it.

"I am. But this isn't finished yet. I hope Tracie and I will be coming home soon. I miss you so."

"And I miss you. The house is empty without your chatter."

She sighed. "Now I have to make arrangements for someone to bury Miss Weatherby's dog. I hope I can see her soon. The policeman said she will recover."

"Glad to hear that. She's a crusty old gal. I liked her."

"Me, too. I'll call soon — promise. Love you."

"Love you, too."

When Emma put down the phone, she saw Tracie hand the sketch to Davey. He sighed, put his hand over his heart and walked away.

"You've made him very happy," she said, walking into the room.

"He's sweet. But now I'm tired. Think I'll take a nap. Do you suppose we can go home soon?" she looked hopefully at Emma.

"I have a feeling it won't be long." Emma sighed and settled in a chair next to the sofa.

The doorbell startled Emma out of a doze. Tracie still lay on the sofa. They both looked up. The shouting had begun again from the upstairs bedroom. Amelia spoke softly to someone then led him up the steps.

"That must be the doctor at last," Emma said with relief. Then she looked at Tracie. "There's something I have to tell you."

"Miss Weatherby is dead," Tracie said, a note of grief in her voice.

"No, no. She's going to be all right, but the dog . . ." She left the sentence unfinished.

Tracie remained silent for a while, then

wiped away a tear. "Poor old girl. She probably died defending her mistress."

Emma nodded. "I expect so. I asked the police to leave the body for us to bury, but I can't wait any longer." She pulled herself off the chair, suddenly feeling twice her age.

"You can't do it alone," Tracie said. "I wish I could help you. Say, why not call Mrs. Burrows. Her son and his friend will do it, I'm sure."

"Great idea," Emma said, "or as they say in this country, brilliant." She gave Tracie a weak smile as she picked up the phone and called directory inquiries for the number. Within a few minutes everything was arranged.

"I'm to meet the boys at the cottage," Emma said. "If Lindsey asks where I've gone, tell her I needed some fresh air and went for a walk."

"Okay. Now I think I'll draw a picture of the dog. I remember her well enough. We can get a frame for it and give it to Miss Weatherby."

"Good thinking." Emma grabbed a jacket and forced herself out the door.

The brisk air revived her a little as she walked along the lanes. It seemed like so long ago that she and Nate had taken this very route to visit Miss Weatherby the first time. Was it only a few weeks ago? So much had happened since then.

When Emma arrived at the cottage, she found the boys waiting outside, spades in hand. The crime scene tape had been removed from the door.

"Hello boys, are you ready?"

"Yes, ma'am," they said in unison.

Cautiously she entered the now deserted house, the smell of decay already permeating the parlor. The dog lay where she had left her still covered with the blanket. She pulled it back and took one last look at the animal, patted the graying head, then recovered her body.

"Roll her up in this and take her out in the garden," Emma instructed.

The boys did as they were told without any indication that they found the task distasteful. Emma noticed the urine stains on the floor where the body had lain. She would clean it up while they were digging the grave.

In the back garden they found the perfect spot beside a pink rose bush in full bloom. "This is the place," Emma said as she paced out the length. "Go to it, boys, while I clean up inside."

Effortlessly they began to dig the soft earth, one at either end.

Inside, Emma opened all the windows then went into the kitchen and found the necessary cleaning materials. By the time she finished, the room smelled fresh — all traces of death removed, but the loneliness remained.

Outside the boys had just completed their job. Reverently they lowered the body down and quickly covered it with soil.

"Well done," Emma said, suddenly overcome with weariness. Perhaps later she would put some sort of marker on the grave, but all she wanted to do now was to stretch out and forget this nasty business.

Not yet, her inner voice said. *It's not finished.*

Emma blew out a breath, annoyed with her Guardian Angel for burdening her with more worry.

She pulled a five-pound note from her pocket and handed it to the boys.

"No, ma'am," George Burrows said, shaking his head. "Can't take no payment for this."

The other boy agreed.

"Well then go to the bakery and buy some biscuits or cakes to take home to your mothers."

They looked at one another and nodded in agreement, took the money and their spades and hurried off.

Before she left, Emma closed all the windows and secured the cottage as best she could. Then she began the long trek back.

At Bellingham House Amelia greeted Emma with a cup of tea and a tray of biscuits.

"Thank you," Emma said. "I'm about played out." She sank into a chair and smiled at Tracie who also held a cup of tea in hand.

"All done," Tracie said as she held up her sketchpad with the completed picture of Miss Weatherby's dog.

"She'll love it," Emma said. Then she turned to Amelia. "What did the doctor say?"

"Isabel is suffering from shock. He gave her some medicine that put her right to sleep."

"Good. And what about Lindsey?"

The woman shook her head. "Worn like an old rug, she is. Lying down herself."

"I think that's what we all need now — rest."

But, that wasn't to be.

Emma went upstairs and stretched out on the bed and had just fallen asleep when the sound of the doorbell awakened her. "I'm not getting up," she muttered. Voices from downstairs . . . who? The male voice sounded familiar.

"Lindsey," Amelia called, "Detective Inspector Allenby is here to see you."

Emma rubbed the sleep from her eyes and swung her legs over the side of the bed. She was surprised to see that dusk had settled outside. She must have slept, but didn't feel a bit rested.

Lindsey poked her head in the door. "Aunt, can you come down?"

"Give me a minute." She let out a breath, collected her thoughts, went to the bathroom and dashed cold water on her face, then followed Lindsey down the stairs.

They found the policeman sitting next to Tracie showing her sheets of photographs.

"This one and this one." She pointed to two men.

Emma looked over her shoulder. They closely resembled the sketches Tracie had done.

The policeman nodded. "Those are the ones all right. They've been in jail for petty crimes, but nothing as sophisticated as abduction." Then he handed the sheets to Lindsey. "Do you recognize anyone?"

Immediately she identified the man with

the birthmark. "He's the one who followed me and I saw him looking in the window. I'm sure of it."

"Well done," he said. "Two positive identifications."

"Will it be necessary for Isabel to identify them also?" Emma asked. "She's been given medication by the doctor."

"That won't be necessary now," he said. "Perhaps later." Then he saw Lindsey was still staring at the photographs. "Do you recognize someone else, Miss Bellingham?"

Lindsey sat, examining them for a long time. Then she pointed to one. "Who is this man?"

"Why do you ask?"

"He looks very much like the detective who came after the break-in. In fact, I'm certain it's the same man." She looked at him, her mouth open, her eyes wide.

"That's very interesting. I've been trying to identify that policeman since you mentioned him. I can find no report by anyone on that date. Are you sure he showed you his warrant card?"

Lindsey appeared confused. "I think he did. He flashed something so quickly that I didn't look closely at it."

"Hmm." He rubbed his chin and thought for a moment. "And you said he searched through every room in the house."

"Yes, he was extremely thorough, even went out into the garden."

He was "casing the joint," Emma thought.

"This man could very well be the leader of the other two. He has a record for more serious crimes than the others, is extremely clever and has eluded apprehension on several occasions. We consider him a very dangerous man."

Lindsey continued to study the photograph. "What's his name?"

"He's used many aliases, but his real name is Gerald Larkin," the Inspector answered.

"No, it can't be." Lindsey's eyes grew wide as she looked from the policeman to Emma and back to the photograph.

"Do you know him, Miss Bellingham?"

"Yes, I do. Oh he's all grown up now but I do see the resemblance. Now that I think about it more clearly he never made eye contact with me. In fact, he kept his head turned away most of the time. I was too upset over the break-in to notice it before."

She took a deep breath, then continued. "Gerald Larkin grew up in this village. He was a bad boy right from the start, always causing trouble. He and some of the other boys would taunt Isabel every chance they got. They called her hateful names, made her cry. Mum tried her best to keep Isabel away from them.

"My grandfather caught young Larkin one too many times breaking the glass panes in the orangery and destroying Grandfather's plants. They were his pride and joy."

She stopped for a moment to collect her thoughts. "Because of Grandfather and some of the other residents whose property he also destroyed, Gerald was arrested and spent time in a juvenile home. I'll never forget the look on his face. I was cringing behind Mum's skirts. He said he would get even — someday."

She looked at Detective Allenby. "Could he have harbored all that hatred for so many years?"

The policeman shook his head. "I'm afraid he's escalated to much more serious crimes. I've seen resentment over something minor grow all out of proportion until people do unspeakable things. Does his family still live around here?"

"No, they moved away shortly after he was arrested. No one has seen them since. I forgot all about that family."

"Well, apparently young Larkin didn't forget. He learned some hard-core lessons in a number of years in lock-up. But don't worry, Miss Bellingham, we'll catch him, sooner or later."

"What do we do now?" Lindsey asked.

Emma grabbed her shoulders and held her tight.

"We'll alert the airports and train stations to watch for these three men. In the meantime, keep your alarm activated at all times. I will post a police car outside your home for the next few days." Allenby got up from his chair, thanked Tracie for her keen observations and assured Lindsey that he would do everything possible to apprehend the criminals.

After the inspector left, Amelia called everyone in to dinner. It was a somber affair. Lindsey stared at her plate; Tracie picked at her food; Emma wished with all her heart that she were back home with Nate. Isabel remained in her room sleeping.

"Did Isabel eat anything?" Lindsey asked.

"She took a little broth, but that was all, poor lamb." Amelia sighed deeply. "I'll take her some tea and biscuits later."

"Thank you." Lindsey turned to Emma. "I don't know what to do for her. She's so withdrawn."

Emma thought for a moment. "Perhaps Dr. Lunetti can help. If she gets involved with her music again, she may be able to climb out of the shell she's built around herself."

"Perhaps." Lindsey toyed with her pudding, a rhubarb crumble, getting the spoon halfway to her mouth, then dropping it back into her plate. "I'll call him in the morning."

As Mrs. Perkins began cleaning up, the doorbell rang.

"I can't see anyone," Lindsey said as Amelia went to answer it.

She returned in a moment, her face wreathed in a frown. "It's Mr. Wilkins."

"He's the last person I wish to talk to," Lindsey said through gritted teeth.

Avery Wilkins stood in the doorway of the dining room. "I have something important to tell you. Please hear me out."

Emma was surprised at his appearance: his clothes disheveled, face unshaven. He seemed to have shrunk in stature.

Lindsey stood up, fists clenched, her eyes wide, her face red. "I think we've said all there is to say."

He held his hands out in supplication. "There's something more, something I haven't told you — please."

"Perhaps you had better hear what he has to say," Emma said, standing beside her.

"First let me say that I've taken steps to return the money I invested from the trust fund. I did it for you, please believe that."

"Spare me the excuses," Lindsey said, her voice cold. "You embezzled that money for your own use."

He shook his head. "Believe what you like, but it *is* being returned."

Lindsey stood, her back straight, her hands fisted at her sides. The woman had begun to grow out of her dependence and exhibited self-assurance. Emma was proud of her new resolve.

"There's another matter," Avery continued. "It concerns the American."

"I thought we had seen the last of him," Lindsey said. "I told him and I'll tell him again, this house is not for sale."

"Let me tell you the real reason he wants to buy it."

Aha, Emma thought, I knew he never intended to turn it into a museum. Her curiosity was piqued.

"Hear me out," Avery continued. "The American's father was an eccentric and an avid coin collector. He had acquired a twenty-dollar gold coin designed by a famous artist as part of his collection.

"When the American government recalled all the gold coins, some collectors refused to part with theirs. The American's father was one of them. He smuggled it out of the

United States and was on his way to Brussels to sell it for a large sum of money. He stopped here in this very house, Lindsey, to visit your grandfather. Apparently they were old friends. He hid the coin somewhere then suffered a fatal heart attack before he could tell anyone where it was." He stopped for a moment and rubbed his hands over his face. Then he continued.

"Your grandfather found a letter in his personal belongings that he never posted. It was addressed to someone in Brussels telling that person he had 'the item.' So, you see, that seems to verify the legend that something of value is hidden in this house."

Lindsey and Emma exchanged glances, but neither said a word.

Avery continued. "Apparently the American is convinced the coin is here. That's why he wants the house." He sat back, let out a breath and looked expectantly at Lindsey.

"And what do you expect Lindsey to do about this?" Emma asked, feeling compelled to put the matter to rest.

He frowned at Emma, apparently resenting her intrusion, and turned his attention back to Lindsey.

"Why are you telling me this now?" she asked. "What are *you* getting out of it?"

"I'm ashamed to say I succumbed to

greed. He offered me a large sum of money if I could convince you to sell. But, if *we* can find the coin, I can take it to Brussels and sell it for much more. Then we can split the profit."

Lindsey glared at him. "Do you take me for a complete fool? If we did manage to locate this coin, what would prevent you from selling it and keeping all the money for yourself? There is no coin. We've searched for years and found nothing." She walked to the doorway. "I intend to verify the transfer of the funds back into my account. If everything has been replaced, I won't prosecute you. But I never want to see you again, Avery. Now, get out of my house."

Emma stood and grabbed her arm as she faltered.

"I think you had better leave now, Mr. Wilkins," she said. "We've all had a harrowing experience and you've never once asked about Isabel." She gave him a look of disdain.

"I presume she's all right," he said lamely.

Neither woman said another word.

Avery lowered his head and shuffled out the door.

"Bravo, Lindsey," Emma whispered, giving her a hug.

"With everything that's happened, I had forgotten all about the coin. Where is it?"

"We'll deal with it tomorrow," Emma said. "Now let's get some rest."

Emma made sure the alarm was activated, helped Tracie navigate the stairs and get settled, then, without even undressing, flopped on her bed and slept a sound dreamless sleep.

CHAPTER 41

Early the following morning Lindsey called Dr. Lunetti and told him what had happened. He promised to come as soon as he could. Then she turned to Emma.

"What shall we do about that coin?"

"I've been thinking," Emma said. "It belongs in the bank where no one but you can get a hold of it. It certainly isn't safe anywhere in this house."

Take it out of the priest's hole, her inner voice said. *Secure it to Lindsey's person.*

There must be some reason for my Guardian Angel to tell me such a thing. I'd better follow instructions.

"Let's retrieve it from the priest's hole," she said, "then decide where it will be safe until you can get to the bank."

Tracie had dressed and hobbled downstairs for breakfast. Now she was lying on the sofa in the parlor reading a book.

Emma and Lindsey went into the bedroom and Emma took the wrapped coin from its hiding place. When she showed it to Lindsey, the woman gasped.

"It's a magnificent piece of work."

"Yes," Emma agreed. "I feel that it belongs in a museum. Of course, it is worth a tremendous amount of money to a collector. It's your call, Lindsey."

She put her hand to her chest and drew back. "I couldn't do that."

"I didn't think so." Emma knew she had too much integrity to do anything illegal.

"I'll probably turn it over to the British Museum and let them decide whether or not they want to return it to the United States. The responsibility will be theirs, not mine."

Emma gave her a hug. "Wise decision. You're a true Winberry." She was rewarded with a huge smile and a hug back.

"The only good thing that has happened in all this mess has been meeting you, a real relation." Lindsey wiped tears from her eyes and looked away. "I won't be able to get into London for a while. I don't feel comfortable leaving Isabel while those criminals are still wandering about."

"No, absolutely not," Emma agreed. Then a thought occurred to her. "Do you always wear this vest?" She fingered a knitted sleeveless sweater that Lindsey wore over her clothing.

"Yes, my mum made this jumper for me." She caressed the heavy cable stitch that ran down the sides. "See, she even knitted a pocket on the inside for carrying money."

"Perfect," Emma said. "You can sew the coin in that inside pocket. No one would dream of looking for it there."

"Brilliant," Lindsey said. "You're so very clever. I'll get a needle and thread straight away."

Emma followed her into her bedroom and, within minutes, the coin was secured in the hidden pocket. They smiled at each other. Emma felt a real kinship with this woman and was glad she had been able to help, just a little.

Sometime later, Dr. Lunetti arrived. "My *Bambina Rossa,* where is she?" He raised his hands in the air in a theatrical gesture.

"Oh, I hope you will be able to help her. She's so withdrawn," Lindsey said. "Refuses to do anything. She's barely eating enough to keep a bird alive. We thought you might be able to rekindle her interest in music. She keeps saying those men took her voice away from her."

"I talk to her," he said with determination. "She always listen to me. Let me go up alone, please."

Lindsey and Emma stood at the foot of the stairs, listening. They heard the muted voices, then the sound of scales being played on the piano in Isabel's room. More voices followed by a weak attempt at vocalizing. Over and over Isabel started, then faltered.

Lindsey shook her head. "That doesn't even sound like her voice."

Soon Dr. Lunetti descended the stairs, shaking his head. "The voice is too weak. She says she can't sing anymore. I come back tomorrow and we try again. But she did say she would look at the book I gave her about great sopranos of the past. That's good, no?"

Emma nodded and escorted him to the door. "Thank you, Dr. Lunetti."

After the music teacher left, they sat around the parlor trying to think of some way to help Isabel. Amelia came into the room. "I'll take some tea and biscuits to Isabel if you like," she addressed Lindsey.

"Let me go," Emma said. "I'll try to connect with her."

"If you think it may help," Lindsey agreed.

"I can only try." With that Emma went into the kitchen and prepared a tray, then carried it precariously up the stairs. These steps are a hazard, she thought. If I can't do anything with Isabel, I think Tracie and I should consider leaving.

It isn't over yet, her inner voice said.

Stop reminding me, Guardian Angel. All I've done so far is get Tracie into trouble.

With determination she put the tray down on a small table in the hallway and called softly, "Isabel, it's Aunt Emma."

"Come in," a weak voice answered.

When she opened the door, Emma was shocked at her appearance: her pinched face, sunken eyes; the hair on her body smelled rank and feral. The unopened book the music teacher had brought lay on the floor.

Picking up the tray, Emma walked into the room. An aura of sadness permeated everything. The shades were drawn, showing only an outline of the slight figure lying on the bed.

"I brought tea and biscuits."

"I can't eat anything."

"Yes, you can. I want you to try."

"I'm not hungry," she said like a petulant child.

"Will you do it for me, please?"

A tear slid down the crease in her cheek. "For you, I'll try."

"That's my girl." Emma sat on the side of

the bed and placed the cup against Isabel's dry, cracked lips. She took a swallow, then another.

"That's enough," she whispered.

"Have a biscuit," Emma urged. "They're chocolate, your favorite."

Isabel picked one up and began to nibble on it. With a great deal of coaxing and patience, Emma managed to get two biscuits and a cup of tea down her.

"Now, how about taking a shower and coming downstairs for a while," Emma suggested.

Isabel looked around, suspicion in her eyes. "Oh no, they're coming back you know."

"Who's coming back?"

"Those men. They took Annabelle away and they stole my voice. Now they want to destroy me because I'm a freak."

Emma's heart ached at those words. She took the girl in her arms and held her tight. "We won't let anyone hurt you, ever again. The alarm is on and a police car is sitting outside. No one can get in. Do you understand?"

She pushed Emma away. "They'll find a way. They're devils, that's what they are."

Duchess sat at the bedside, whining.

"Duchess is here for you, my dear," Emma

cajoled. "She'll protect you."

"She couldn't help me the last time. No one has any power over devils."

Oh Guardian Angel, this girl is beyond my help. She needs a professional.

"Can you try and play the piano and practice a few scales?" Emma persisted. "Dr. Lunetti will be back tomorrow. And you didn't even look at the lovely book he brought you when he was here."

She shook her head. "No use. No use." Then her body jerked around. "Did you hear that?"

Emma listened, but heard nothing. She thought it best to humor her. "It's only the wind in the rafters."

A cunning smile crossed the heart-shaped face. "It's the devil calling. He wants me." She covered her head with the duvet and began to cry.

Emma was totally helpless. At that moment Lindsey came into the room.

"It's time for your medicine, Isabel."

The girl peeked out at Lindsey, swallowed the liquid, and ducked back into her refuge.

The two women quietly left the room. "She's completely losing contact with reality," Emma said. "She needs professional help."

"The doctor is coming back tomorrow.

I'll ask him what he can do."

Lindsey descended the stairs carrying the tray and Emma went into her room to call Nate.

"Hello." He answered on the first ring.

"Oh Nate, I miss you so," Emma blurted out, barely able to keep her emotions under control. She told him all that was happening.

"My brother just left and I've finished everything pressing for now."

"Were you able to help him solve his problems?" she asked.

"I think we got everything straightened out. He knows nothing about investing, so I gave him some pointers. And, as far as the marriage is concerned, they're going for counseling."

"That's good," Emma said without much enthusiasm.

"I'm getting a flight out as soon as I can. I want to be with you, and as soon as Tracie can travel, I'm bringing you both home."

Emma swallowed the lump in her throat. Those words were music to her ears. "Yes, please come. I don't know what more I can do here."

"Perhaps for once, you have to accept the fact that you can't fix everything and everybody," he said, but his voice mirrored her concern.

"You're right. I just want to come home."

"I should be there in a few days. I'll let you know."

CHAPTER 42

That night all Emma could think about was Nate. He was coming to take them home. That thought brought her happiness and relief but still she felt a certain amount of guilt. She knew the situation here was far from resolved.

When morning dawned, Emma had managed to sleep with no dreams that she could recall. *Oh Guardian Angel, I almost feel rested.* A nice shower should set me right. When she had dressed and was ready to go downstairs, she peeked into Isabel's room. The girl lay curled in a ball with the duvet covering her head, just as she had the day before. Only the slight rise and fall of the fabric told Emma she was alive.

She shook her head and sighed then knocked on Tracie's door. "Are you up?"

"Come in, Mrs. Win. I'm having trouble with this bandage."

Emma looked at Tracie's ankle and was

pleased to see that the swelling and bruising were almost gone. "Soon you'll be up to par," she said, "and we can go home."

Tracie looked at her with an expression of sadness. "I really do want to leave, but everything is so topsy-turvy here. Will Isabel ever be normal again?"

"Tracie," Emma sat down on a chair and took the girl's hand in hers. "Isabel has never been what we consider normal. Her life has consisted of this house and the people who live here. Now that that life has been threatened, she's shut herself up in a cocoon where she feels somewhat safe. She really needs a psychiatrist or she may never come out of it."

After Emma adjusted the bandage, Tracie slid off the bed, grabbed her crutches and stood up. "It's all so tragic." She pursed her lips and, with determination, put her injured foot on the floor. "Look, I can put a little weight on it without pain." She turned to Emma and smiled.

"Go easy, dear. You don't want to reinjure the ankle."

"I will. A little at a time, like the doctor said."

Slowly they descended the stairs and went into the dining room where Amelia was just laying the table for breakfast.

"Good morning, Ma'am," she said. "And how are you today, Miss?"

"Much better," Tracie said, taking a deep breath. "And very hungry."

"That's always a good sign," Emma said, pulling out a chair for Tracie.

"Lindsey is going to attempt to bring Isabel downstairs this morning."

"I certainly hope she succeeds," Emma said. "It would be a positive sign."

A few minutes later Lindsey entered the room. Her haggard face and puffy eyes attested to the fact that she hadn't slept much.

"Isabel refuses to come down but she has agreed to take a tray in her room."

"That's some progress," Emma said. I have to tell her that we'll be leaving as soon as Nate gets here, she thought.

"I can put a little weight on my ankle and the swelling is down," Tracie said as she slathered jam on a piece of toast.

Lindsey managed a weak smile. "I'm happy to hear that." Then her eyes met Emma's. "That means you two will be leaving soon, doesn't it?"

"I'm afraid so." Now that she had opened the conversation, Emma continued. "I spoke with Nate last night. He's coming out in a few days to take us home."

"Of course." Lindsey turned away for a

moment.

Emma knew she was on the verge of tears but there was nothing more she could do.

They ate breakfast in relative silence, only Tracie exhibiting the hearty appetite of the young.

A few minutes later, Amelia came into the room with a spring in her step, a smile on her plain face. "Isabel is indeed eating toast and drinking tea. She says she'll shower and dress after breakfast, but she refuses to come downstairs."

Lindsey let out a breath. "At least that's somewhat encouraging. I'd better go up and help her. She's so very weak."

After breakfast Emma and Tracie went out in the garden for a breath of fresh air.

"It is beautiful here," Tracie said. "All those rose bushes are blooming and the air smells like perfume."

"Yes, it does. Now you had better sit down in this lawn chair and put your foot up. I notice your ankle is beginning to swell a little."

"Okay, but I wish I had my sketch pad and pencil."

"I'll get them for you." As Emma went back into the house, she noticed Detective Inspector Allenby's car pull up. She sent Davey out with Tracie's artist's pad and went to speak with the policeman.

"Any news?" she asked.

"Yes, both good and questionable."

Oh dear, Emma thought, what does he mean by that? She led him into the parlor then called to Lindsey.

"Can you come down for a minute?"

Lindsey poked her head out of the bathroom.

"Inspector Allenby is here."

"Right, I'm just getting Isabel out of the shower. Be down in ten minutes."

"Come and have a cup of tea," Emma said. "Miss Bellingham will be down shortly."

When they were seated, each with a cup of tea, Emma told him of Isabel's withdrawal. "I hope the news you have will put her fears to rest." She gave him a questioning look but he said nothing to satisfy her curiosity.

By the time Lindsey came down Emma was out of small talk and the detective was growing visibly impatient.

"I'm sorry," she said, breathless. "But she is somewhat difficult to handle. Any news?"

"We've apprehended the two thugs who took the girls."

"Oh, thank God for that." Lindsey breathed a sigh of relief then looked at the

Inspector's face. "What about the third man?"

"I'm afraid he's fled the jurisdiction. We think he's gone to the continent."

Lindsey crumpled into a chair and covered her face with her hands. Emma grasped her shoulders and tried to be supportive.

"That doesn't mean he'll return, does it?" she asked.

"I really doubt it. All the airlines and train stations have his identification and description. If he does attempt to return to England, he'll be picked up straight away. So, you see, I don't think you have anything further to worry about." He hesitated a moment. "Now that the immediate threat has passed, I will have to remove the patrol car from your property."

"I see." This was all Lindsey could say. She was visibly upset.

"Then I'll be leaving," he said, walking toward the door.

Emma followed him. "Will the girls have to identify the two men?"

"No need. They've willingly confessed and will spend a long time in prison."

"Thank you." She closed the door behind him then turned to see Isabel standing at the top of the stairs, her eyes wild.

"I heard what he said," she screamed.

"The devil is coming!" She ran into her room and slammed the door.

An hour later Dr. Lunetti came, eager to see the girl. "Is she better?" he asked.

"I'm afraid not," Lindsey answered. "She won't see anyone. Why don't I call you when she has recovered? There's no use your making the trip out here for nothing."

"Si, my Bambina Rossa." Dejectedly he walked back to his car muttering something in Italian.

Later that morning, the family doctor arrived harried and somewhat disheveled. Emma was surprised that the man made house calls. Thank God for that.

Lindsey told him of Isabel's behavior and her talk of the devil. She seemed more frightened every time she verbalized it.

"Let me go up alone," he said.

Emma and Lindsey retreated into the parlor and sat — waiting. The day that had begun with sunshine and a warm breeze was now overcast, portending rain and cooler temperatures.

Oh Guardian Angel, how can I leave them? Emma prayed. *There's still so much unfinished.*

It will be resolved, her inner voice said. *The way it must be.*

Emma felt a chill. She didn't like that message at all. It bode more trouble.

The women looked up as the doctor came down and into the room. He sighed and sat next to Lindsey. "She is so far withdrawn into a world of her own making that I can't reach her. I'm sorry Lindsey, but she belongs in hospital."

"How can we take someone like Isabel to hospital? Everyone will call her a freak." Lindsey's voice faltered at the last words.

"The hospital in Harlow has a psychiatric wing separate from the rest of the patients. No one would see her but the staff. She would have one-on-one sessions with a psychiatrist. I can do nothing for her."

Lindsey looked into his kindly face. "And without such treatment?"

He shook his head and frowned. "She'll retreat deeper and deeper into her fantasy world until no one will ever be able to reach her."

Emma took Lindsey's hand. "My dear, I don't think you have any choice. This appears to be her only chance."

Lindsey thought for a while. "All right. She certainly won't agree, so how do we get her there?"

"I'll write out a prescription for a heavy sedative. Give it to her in the morning and, when she's in a deep sleep, call me. I'll send an ambulance to get her."

"No," Lindsey said, defiance in her voice. "I don't want strangers touching her. I'll take her to Harlow myself."

"But how will you get her down those stairs?" He looked toward the steep flight of stairs.

"We'll manage. She doesn't weigh much and Davey can help. He's a strong boy."

The doctor shrugged. "If that's your decision. Here is a prescription. I'll alert them that you will be coming. Go to the side entrance. There is less foot traffic there. I'll tell the staff to watch for you."

He handed her the piece of paper, gave her a commiserating look, nodded to Emma and left.

"Oh Aunt Emma, I hate to do this. She'll be terrified, think she's been kidnapped again." Lindsey rubbed her face with one hand and gripped the arm of the chair with the other.

"There doesn't seem to be any other way," Emma said.

"I'm afraid that once she's in there, she'll never come out."

Just then Tracie hobbled into the room followed by Davey. She had been outside in the garden sketching. Her face glowed with health, so different from the poor girl upstairs.

"Look at these neat pictures, Mrs. Win." She stopped when she saw the looks on their faces.

"What's wrong?"

"We're taking Isabel to the hospital tomorrow," Emma said. "She needs intensive treatment."

"But she will get well?"

Lindsey said nothing. Emma forced a smile. "We certainly hope so." But the look on her face was not convincing.

CHAPTER 43

Later that night the wind howled through the rafters of the old house. Isabel heard it calling to her. *The devil has come back, the house is evil, it must be destroyed.* As if in a trance, she pulled back the duvet and swung her hairy legs over the side of the bed.

She was surprised to see that Annabelle had returned and was urging her to walk across the room. "Oh my dear friend, you're back. Have you come to help me destroy the devil?" A cunning smile crossed her face.

Isabel stopped at the doorway, turned and looked around for a torch. What had she done with it? She always kept it at her bedside. The devil must have taken it, but she would outsmart him. She spied a candle, picked it up along with a box of matches and continued out the bedroom door.

The house kept calling to her . . . *come . . . come . . .* the whistling wind seemed to say *evil . . . evil . . .* as Isabel reached the attic door and looked up. It was so high. Carefully she put the candle on the floor and took the ladder from the corner. It was so heavy. Annabelle held one side and helped her move it into place. Her friend knew what to do. She wouldn't fail her. Isabel smiled. Annabelle wouldn't leave her ever again. She would tell her what to do, would guide her all the way.

She was careful not to make any noise. If Lindsey and Aunt Emma woke, they would surely stop her. With the ladder placed securely under the trap door, Isabel picked up the candle and matches and slowly began to climb up, one rung at a time. She was so weak that she barely made it to the top, but she knew that Annabelle was behind her, encouraging and protecting her.

The heavy wooden door lay just above her, preventing her from reaching her goal. She pushed and shoved, but it wouldn't move.

"Annabelle, hold the candle so I can push with both hands." Annabelle didn't move. Frustrated, Isabel gripped the candle between her teeth and put the matches in a corner of the last rung of the ladder. With all the strength she could muster, she put the palms of both her hands against the door and pushed. A creak. She pushed again. It moved just a fraction. She stopped for a moment, breathing hard, then filled her lungs with air and lunged at the heavy wood. At that moment a clap of thunder masked the sound of the door swinging back and hitting against the attic floor.

Isabel stopped and listened. Had anyone heard? Silence, all except the howling of the wind . . . *evil* . . . *evil,* and the house calling . . . *come* . . . *come* . . .

She grabbed the matches and climbed into the attic.

Emma started. Something woke her. A noise? She sat up and listened but all she heard was the wind whistling through the rafters. How glad she would be to leave this cursed place and get back to her life.

She felt something was wrong, but what? A sudden clap of thunder made the old house shudder. Emma crawled under the duvet and pulled it over her ears. She knew there would be little sleep tonight.

Isabel opened the box of matches and scratched one against the coarse grain of the box. It burst into flame. Carefully she lit the candle and watched the colors as they swayed back and forth, back and forth, in a graceful dance responding to the cadence of the wind. It blew harder here in the drafty attic.

Isabel felt cold. She put the candle down on an old table and looked around for something to cover herself. Then she spotted the hobbyhorse. Smiling she climbed onto it and rocked as she had when she was a child, momentarily forgetting the chill. As she rocked she watched shadows cast by the light of the swaying flame. They danced in a hypnotic fashion, leaping up, then falling back, like an eerie ballet.

Suddenly the candle sputtered and went out. Who had blown out her candle? It was the devil. He didn't like light, didn't want anyone to be happy. He controlled this house, made it evil. He had brought the men here to hurt her and his leader was still out there. He would come back — the house would call him. He would take her away again. She could not let that happen, must destroy the house. She groped around until she found the box of matches and, again, struck one. A pile of old papers lay in one corner. Carefully she held the match against the edge of the yellowed paper. Then she dropped it as the pages quickly blazed. She grabbed old rags and pieces of broken furniture and threw them on top. At first she thought she had smothered the fire, but soon wisps of smoke curled around the rags, then a bright flame burst out. The flames grew as Isabel stared, mesmerized by their wild dance. They licked the dry rafters and spread, eagerly consuming everything in their wake.

I must get out now, Isabel told herself, but she remained immobile, unable to move. Suddenly she felt the burning heat as the flames came closer, but she wasn't afraid. She would simply climb down the ladder to safety.

But where was the ladder? Within minutes the attic had filled with smoke. Isabel began to cough. The window. Where was it? She couldn't find it. She crawled into a far corner, covered her face with her hands and sat back, confused and disoriented.

"Annabelle, where are you? What shall I do?" No answer came from her friend.

Emma woke with a start. What was that shrill sound? She jumped out of bed, looked around and sniffed. Smoke! The smoke detector was screaming! She plunged her feet into her slippers, grabbed her bag and slung it over her neck and shoulder, then pressed her hands against the door. It wasn't hot, but she saw a white film snaking underneath. She snatched a scarf from a chair and wrapped it around her nose and mouth, cautiously opened the door and drew back as the hallway rapidly filled with smoke. She heard Duchess barking a warning from somewhere downstairs.

"Fire!" she shouted. "Tracie, Lindsey, Isabel — fire!"

Lindsey ran out of her room and began coughing.

"Get Tracie downstairs and call Amelia and Davey," Emma called. "I'll bring Isabel."

Lindsey disappeared into Tracie's room and Emma hurried down the hallway to Isabel's. It was relatively clear, but the girl was gone. Maybe she was downstairs already, Emma thought.

She ran back into the hallway and noticed the ladder going up into the attic. Smoke billowed from the open door.

"Isabel!" Emma shouted. "Are you up there?"

She heard something. A voice. Yes, Isabel was attempting to sing in the attic.

Emma grabbed the sides of the ladder and, with caution, began climbing the first few rungs. Although the scarf covered the lower half of her face, the smoke stung her eyes. She tried to take shallow breaths but she coughed with each inhalation.

"Isabel," she called again, to no avail.

Suddenly flames crawled out of the attic door and began licking at the top rungs of the ladder. Emma felt the heat. It became worse as she attempted to climb higher. She turned her face away, smelled her hair beginning to smolder.

Oh Guardian Angel, what shall I do?

"Isabel," she called one last time, but there was no answer. Even the singing had stopped.

Go back. You can't help her.

The heat was now unbearable. Emma slid down the last rungs of the ladder through the thickening smoke and sank to the floor. She remembered reading that more air remained near the floor. Quickly she began crawling, but was she going the right way? Her burning eyes made it impossible to see anything.

Terror gripped her, releasing more adrenaline into her bloodstream. She coughed and crawled as fast as she could. Was someone calling her? Wasn't sure. Was that a siren? Ahead her hand felt empty space. The stairway! She turned her body and backed down, in total darkness, her eyes shut tight against the blinding smoke.

As spots danced before her eyes, Emma felt strong arms grab her and drag her outside. She gasped as someone clamped an oxygen mask over her face. She gulped in the life-saving gas.

"Aunt Emma."

"Mrs. Win."

Anxious voices around her. She opened her eyes to see Tracie and Lindsey hovering over her. "I'm — all — right," she gasped. Amelia and Davey stood apart, looking horror-struck at the burning house. Duchess whined and shivered, running aimlessly around.

"Where's Isabel?" Lindsey asked, her voice panicked.

"Couldn't — reach — her."

Isabel heard the window explode with a loud crash. Flames and smoke escaped through the opening. She knew she would never be able to reach it. She could no longer breathe; her mind was cloudy. She closed her eyes and simply let go.

Then something strange happened. She was outside looking in. She watched as flames engulfed the creature that had housed her all her life, but Isabel felt nothing. She was free and floating through the air with Annabelle beside her. Little by little she drifted away from the burning house, flames now shooting through the roof. She looked away and followed a bright light that beckoned to her.

The first fire engine had attached hoses to the water truck and firemen quickly entered the inferno, forcing the flames back with a high-pressure hose.

After pulling Emma out, the firemen themselves were forced out by the intensity of the blaze. The attic floor had burned through and dropped debris onto the floor below. It quickly spread across the hallway and into the bedrooms.

Another crew attached hoses to the nearest underground hydrant and back to the fire engine. They attacked the exterior of the building with as much force as the engine could supply.

The officer in charge came up to Lindsey. "I'm sorry, ma'am, but the fire is too advanced for my men to safely enter the house again. All we can do is keep pouring water on the outside."

"But my cousin, Isabel, is still in there."

He slowly shook his head. "At this point, no one could survive the intensity of this fire. I'm sorry."

Lindsey covered her face with her hands, sobbed, and dropped to her knees as Duchess stood beside her, whimpering and shaking. Emma watched in horror as the roof collapsed and the entire house blazed like a giant torch against the night sky.

Then she saw what looked like a spark shoot away from the house and off into the distance. A half-smile crossed Emma's face. She knew who it was and uttered a prayer.

CHAPTER 44

Emma lay in the Casualty Department of the hospital, oxygen flowing through two plastic prongs in her nostrils. It made her nose dry and, from time to time, she coughed. Her throat felt raspy. She noticed her bandaged hands and squeezed her eyes shut as the memory of the nightmare surfaced.

Oh Guardian Angel, what a terrible way for Isabel to die.

She felt nothing, her inner voice said. *Her spirit had already left that ill-fated body. She is free.*

Emma sighed. Yes, free, and so is Lindsey.

The curtain to the cubicle where she lay parted open, and her myopic eyes squinted at the figure entering. "Nate!"

In a moment he was there, really there, holding her tight.

"Oh my darling Sparrow."

She felt his tears combining with her own

as neither one spoke for a long time, just held one another.

After a while Emma looked into his dear face, the few remaining hairs on his head uncombed, dark circles around his eyes, his face unshaven.

He sat in a chair and gave her a stern look. "Emma, this has got to stop. This is the second time I've found you in a hospital, narrowly escaping death. If you wish to kill me before my time, please use poison. It will be much faster." His lips twitched in a suppressed smile.

She grabbed his hand with a wince and kissed it over and over again. He caressed her face. "I don't do it on purpose, dear, really I don't." She let out a deep sigh followed by a violent cough. "Water," she whispered.

Nate held the cup with the bent straw to her lips as she swallowed.

"Good." She smiled at him. "I'm fine."

He ran his hand over her hair, grinning. "I don't much care for this new hairstyle you've adopted."

"I'm lucky the fire only singed it. I'll get a proper cut when we get home." *Home,* that word sounded like heaven.

At that point a woman wearing a white coat entered the room. "Mrs. Winberry, I'm

Dr. Percy." She nodded to Nate. "I have the results of your chest X-ray and your blood tests. Everything came back normal. You didn't breath in enough smoke to do any serious damage to your lungs. Let me have a listen and a look at your throat."

Nate turned away as she examined Emma.

"Lungs are clear but your throat is a little inflamed, which is to be expected. I'll give you some lozenges to ease that and the cough should subside in a few days. The burns on your hands are superficial. We'll give you a tube of salve and they should heal quickly. You can be discharged as soon as I complete the paperwork. And you don't need this anymore." She pulled the prongs from Emma's nostrils and turned off the oxygen flow.

"Thank you so much, Doctor."

Emma turned to Nate, her brow furrowed. "I have no clothes."

He smiled. "We can't have you parading around in hospital garb, now can we? That very efficient woman, Mrs. Burrows, has taken Tracie shopping. I gave them my credit card. I'm sure they'll pick out something appropriate. It's a good thing you had the presence of mind to grab your purse. Otherwise our trip home would be delayed without your passports."

"My Guardian Angel reminded me." Emma leaned her head back and closed her eyes. "Where is Lindsey?"

"The nice thing about small towns is that when tragedy strikes, the folks help one another. Mrs. Rayfield has put her up in the bed and breakfast. Her renovations have been finished."

"And Mrs. Perkins and Davey?"

"I believe Lindsey said something about friends in Yorkshire. That's where they're headed."

Emma bit her lip and thought for a moment. "Nate, before we leave, I must see Miss Weatherby. I have to tell her where we buried her dog."

"Yes, Tracie suggested that." He held up a bag she hadn't noticed before. "Cream cakes."

Emma swallowed the lump in her throat, unable to speak. He had thought of everything.

"Close your eyes," Nate said, "and rest for a while. I'll sit in this chair and relax."

She watched as he unwound and soon heard the comforting sound of his snores.

A short while later, a smiling Tracie and Mrs. Burrows came up to Emma laden with bags, the logos of the stores gracing their fronts. "Hi, Mrs. Win, how are you?" Tracie asked, her eyes full of concern.

"On the mend," Emma answered, over-joyed by the sight of the girl. "Mrs. Bur-rows, how can I thank you enough for tak-ing care of Tracie?"

"She's a darling and no trouble at all. I've never had a daughter of my own and her company is grand. We've had some good talks, haven't we, dear?"

A blush spread up Tracie's neck and cheeks as she lowered her eyes.

"She is a joy," Emma agreed.

"Look what we bought you," Tracie said, sitting down next to the bed. She began opening bags displaying socks, underwear, two pair of slacks, two tops and a light jacket. "I hope these shoes are the right size," Tracie said, proudly displaying a pair of bright green sandals. "Aren't they cool?"

Emma's eyes opened wide and she burst out laughing as she noticed a similar pair in pink on the girl's feet. "They're perfect."

"Oh, and Mr. Nate, here's your credit card." She gave him a guilty look. "I'm afraid we spent a lot of money."

"That's all right. I'll make the two of you work it off." He grinned as he put the card back into his wallet.

Mrs. Burrows gave him a questioning look.

Emma noticed. "He was joking."

The woman nodded and gave him a smile. "My husband doesn't know how to joke," she said. "It would be a nice break once in a while."

"I'll check at the desk to see if the papers are completed while you get dressed," Nate said. "I'll also find out where Miss Weatherby's room is."

"Okay, let me at those clothes." Emma reached for a bag. With a little help from Mrs. Burrows, she was dressed in record time and everything fit reasonably well. She laughed again as she put on the sandals. They were a little large and she knew that once she got home, they would go right to the resale shop.

Emma saw Tracie fiddling with something at a corner table.

"What have you there?" she asked.

"I sketched another picture of Miss Weatherby's dog. The first was lost . . ." She couldn't finish the sentence. "I'm putting it in a frame that we bought." She held up the finished product.

"It's brilliant," Mrs. Burrows said, clasping her hands.

"She'll love it," Emma said. "Now let's get out of here."

Mrs. Burrows carried the picture so that

Tracie could navigate safely with her crutches. She was weight-bearing a little but still needed the support.

They caught up with Nate who held the discharge papers in one hand and the cream cakes in the other. "Miss Weatherby's room is this way," he said.

Emma knocked on the door and peeked inside. The old woman sat up in bed, her face a mask of healing bruises, her right arm and leg in casts. She turned her head, frowned, then smiled at the sight of them.

"Well, ye' finally come t' see me."

Her eyes lit up as Nate handed her the bag. Tracie hobbled over to the bed and sat in a chair next to her.

"What 'appened to ye', child?"

In halting sentences she told of her fall and the boys rescuing her.

"Good lads," Miss Weatherby said. Then her eyes found Emma's. "Me dog?" she whispered.

Without embellishment, Emma told her where she and the boys had buried the animal.

The old woman closed her eyes for a moment; a tear sneaked down the craggy cheek. "She were tryin' to pertec' me. Them buggers 'it her on t' 'ead. There was no call t' do that. Used me shotgun, but missed."

She lay her head against the pillow and sighed deeply. "We all 'ave our time."

Then she frowned at Emma. "Ye' ain't told me yet about Isabel."

Emma knew there was no way to tell her but straight out. Miss Weatherby was that kind of woman. She took a deep breath, then began.

"Isabel was very disturbed. Her mind kept telling her that the house was evil, controlled by the devil. She really believed it had to be destroyed." Emma hesitated for a moment. "I don't know how she was able to open that heavy attic door, but she did and started a fire. I really believe she intended to escape but was blinded by the smoke. I tried to reach her, but . . ." Emma looked down at her hands, remembering the heat, the smoke, the flames.

"The firefighter said that she would have been overcome by the smoke long before the flames reached her."

"Mrs. Win was a real hero," Tracie said.

Emma shook her head and said, barely above a whisper, "A hero rescues someone. I failed."

"You tried," Tracie persisted. "And you didn't even think about yourself and you got your hair all singed and your hands burned."

"It were 'er time," Miss Weatherby said. "Poor lil thing 'ad no life. Now she's free."

"Yes," Emma said. "I actually saw something sail away. I'm sure it was Isabel." She wiped away a tear that had sneaked out of the corner of her eye. There was silence for a moment, then Tracie held out the sketch of the dog. The old woman swiped at her eyes. "Looks just like 'er. Yer good, girl. Maybe ye' could send me a letter from time t' time."

"Oh I will. I promise."

They said tearful good-byes and left.

"She's a strong old gal," Nate said, "a survivor."

"I was thinking," Emma said as they climbed into Mrs. Burrows's car. "Perhaps Lindsey would consider giving Duchess to Miss Weatherby. I believe they would help each other heal."

CHAPTER 45

Lindsey picked them up at Mrs. Burrows's house. Her pale face appeared drained of every bit of energy. She wore mismatched clothing that people had obviously donated, but Emma noticed the vest covered her top.

They thanked Mrs. Burrows profusely for all her help. Nate offered her money, which she flatly refused.

"In this village we help our neighbors," she said.

With hugs and more thanks, they drove away.

"When does your plane leave?" Lindsey asked mechanically.

"This evening," Nate answered.

"I'll drive you to the airport."

"We can get a car service," Emma protested.

"No, you're the only family I have left and I insist. Besides, I have business to conduct at the bank."

Emma nodded, knowing full well what that business was.

"Do you have any idea what you will do now?" Emma asked.

Lindsey looked off into the distance. "Haven't got my head around that yet."

"No, of course not." It was too soon, Emma thought. She needed time to grieve and rethink her life, but she was pretty sure Lindsey would call Derrick Saunders very soon.

At the airport, Emma and Lindsey held each other, neither one able to express her feelings in words. Finally, Emma looked at her. "You've grown strong, even though you may not realize it. I've watched you. When you're settled, consider coming to visit us. Your cousins will be delighted to meet you."

A smile crossed Lindsey's drawn face. "I promise."

They hugged again and left.

At the terminal, Nate spoke to the woman behind the British Airways counter. She nodded, looked at their passports, punched something into the computer and directed them to the gate.

When they boarded the plane, the flight attendant directed them to seats in business class.

"Wait," Emma said. "This isn't right."

"Yes it is," Nate answered. "Tracie, you sit on the end so you can lean back and raise the footrest easier."

"But . . . but . . ." Emma stammered.

"Not another word." He pushed her gently toward the window seat and settled himself between the two. He looked from one to the other and grinned. "Let's just say I have some influential friends."

EPILOGUE

Some time later

Emma took a batch of muffins out of the oven as she heard the phone ring. "Coming," she called to no one in particular. She picked it up with a cheery "Hello."

"Aunt Emma, it's Lindsey."

Emma's eyes lit up with pleasure. "Oh my dear, how wonderful to hear your voice. How are you doing?"

"I'm adjusting quite well. As soon as I recovered from the shock, I knew that my life had taken a drastic turn." She hesitated for a moment.

"We buried Isabel next to my mum in the village cemetery." Emma heard a soft sob. "I'll miss her, but I'm certain that she's in a better place where no one will ever make fun of her again. And, as you suggested, I gave Duchess to Miss Weatherby when she returned home from hospital. They're getting along just grand."

Emma heard a sigh from the other end. "And what about you? Where are you living?"

"I'm in Devon. Derrick and I have resumed our relationship and plan to marry in the near future. I even have a job in an office. I'm part of the world again, never realized how isolated I'd become."

"Yes," Emma said, "you were a prisoner. I'm delighted to hear about the positive changes in your life."

"You'll be glad to hear that the authorities apprehended Gerald Larkin. He was trying to board the Eurostar in Paris to return to London. He had a new identity, but an alert customs officer recognized him. He's now in prison, safely locked away for a good long time."

"That puts that worry to rest," Emma said.

"The house was a total loss," Lindsey continued. "So I donated the property to the village with the stipulation that they turn it into a public park. Now that Avery Wilkins has returned the money he stole, there is plenty in my trust fund to provide for anything I need."

"Wonderful," Emma said. "And, what about the coin?"

She heard Lindsey laugh.

"I gave it to the British Museum. They'll decide what to do with it. And, I made sure to tell Avery that I had found it and what I had done."

"Good for you. How did he react?"

"He sputtered and fumed and told me I was a fool. I disconnected the call in the middle of his tirade."

"Well, it seems as though everything has been settled. Now, when are you coming to visit us?"

"I thought, perhaps, Christmas, if that's all right."

"That's perfect. Will Derrick be with you?"

"I don't believe so. That's a busy time for him. But we do hope you will be able to come to the wedding."

"Wouldn't miss it. Now give me your phone number and new address."

After she finished the call, Emma sat in the atrium looking out over the lake, and over at Nate sitting in a chair reading the newspaper.

"I take it that Lindsey's life has settled down," he said.

"Yes, and she and Derrick will be getting married in the near future."

"Good. She needs a life of her own."

"And I spoke with Tracie earlier. She's writing up her adventure for a school project in the coming semester. I believe that Maria has forgiven me for bringing her back on crutches, but we told her it was a minor accident."

He grinned. "Maybe now we can just enjoy the rest of the summer."

"Absolutely," Emma agreed. "No more adventures for me."

She sat back and pondered.

Oh Guardian Angel, life certainly takes us on some unexpected journeys.

Only if you're willing to go.

AUTHOR'S NOTE

The genetic condition, hypertrichosis, to the extent that I have described it in this story, is extremely rare. It usually involves hair growing on the face as well as the rest of the body. I have taken the literary license to eliminate the hair from my character's face. I'm sure my readers will understand.

ABOUT THE AUTHOR

Helen Osterman lives in a suburb of Chicago. She has five children and nine grandchildren.

She received a Bachelor of Nursing degree from Mercy Hospital–St. Xavier College and later earned a Master's degree from Northern Illinois University. Throughout her forty-five-year nursing career, she wrote articles for both nursing and medical journals.

The Elusive Relation is the third in the Emma Winberry cozy mystery series published by Five Star. *The Accidental Sleuth* was published in 2007 and *The Stranger in the Opera House,* in 2009.

Helen also wrote a paranormal/historical book, *Notes in a Mirror,* in 2009. *Song of the Rails,* a love story, was published in 2011.

Helen is also an accomplished artist. Four of her paintings of historic Maxwell Street

in Chicago are part of the permanent collection of the Chicago History Museum.